Praise for Linda Grant's
When I Lived in Modern Times

"Informed, intelligent . . . Tel Aviv inspires Grant's most vital,
original writing."
—*The New York Times Book Review*

"Witty and intelligent . . . Ms. Grant's fast-paced novel succeeds
on many levels. It re-creates the historical era accurately with
sophisticated prose and lively jests about the human condition."
—*The Dallas Morning News*

"An unsentimental, iconoclastic coming-of-age story of
both a country—Israel—and a young immigrant, Grant's
novel both introduces an unusually appealing heroine and
provides an unforgettable glimpse of a time and place rarely
observed from an unsparing point of view."
—*Publishers Weekly* (starred review)

"Grant's prose is simple and moving, clearly expressing the
intensity of a young girl's quest for herself, and of a young
nation seeking to establish its boundaries."
—*Booklist*

"Written with uncluttered economy, high in quietly astute
observation, and underpinned by a rigorously searching
investigation of its themes, this is a novel that both
stimulates the mind and satisfies the heart."
—*Scotland on Sunday*

"Full of sharp humor, complex ironies, and an acute eye for
cultural clashes, this is a superb coming-of-age novel."
—*Independent on Sunday*

LINDA GRANT is the author of three previous books, including *The
Cast Iron Shore* (winner of the David Higham Prize for best first
novel) and *Remind Me Who I Am, Again,* her acclaimed account
of her mother's dementia. She lives in London. Visit her website at
www.lindagrant.co.uk.

Also by Linda Grant

FICTION

The Cast Iron Shore

NONFICTION

Sexing the Millennium
Remind Me Who I Am, Again

When I Lived in Modern Times

Linda Grant

A PLUME BOOK

PLUME
Published by the Penguin Group
Penguin Putnam Inc., 375 Hudson Street, New York, New York 10014, U.S.A.
Penguin Books Ltd, 80 Strand, London WC2R 0RL England
Penguin Books Australia Ltd, Ringwood, Victoria, Australia
Penguin Books Canada Ltd, 10 Alcorn Avenue, Toronto, Ontario, Canada M4V 3B2
Penguin Books (N.Z.) Ltd, 182–190 Wairau Road, Auckland 10, New Zealand

Penguin Books Ltd, Registered Offices: Harmondsworth, Middlesex, England

Published by Plume, a member of Penguin Putnam Inc.
Previously published in a Dutton edition. Originally published in
Great Britain by Granta Books.

Ⓟ REGISTERED TRADEMARK—MARCA REGISTRADA

The Library of Congress has catalogued the Dutton edition as follows:

Grant, Linda.
When I lived in modern times / Linda Grant.
p. cm.
ISBN 0-525-94594-6 (hc.)
ISBN 0-452-28292-6 (pbk.)
1. Jewish women—Fiction. 2. Tel Aviv (Israel)—Fiction.
3. Palestine—History—1917–1948—Fiction. I. Title.

PR6057.R316 W47 2001
823'.914—dc21   00-059623

Original hardcover design by Julian Hamer

For Michele and John

ACKNOWLEDGMENTS

I am greatly indebted to A. J. Sherman for his invaluable research on this period. Some of the dialogue given to my colonial characters has come directly from letters, memoirs and diaries from which he quotes in his book *Mandate Days: British Lives in Palestine 1918–1948* (Thames & Hudson Ltd, 1997).

For the portrait of the early years of the kibbutz, I drew on a vivid series of articles by Assaf Inbari published in the Israeli newspaper *Ha-Aretz,* on the establishment of Kibbutz Afikim.

Very late in the day in terms of the writing of this novel, Joachim Schlor's *Tel Aviv: From Dream to City* (Reaktion Books, 1999) was published. If you want to know more about the history of the city, this is the book.

My deepest thanks to: in Israel, Yasaf Nachmayas, Lotte Geiger, Jonathan Spyer and Dr. Michael Levin; and in London, to Judah Passow; my editor, Frances Coady; and my agent, Derek Johns.

They are a people, and they lack the props of a people. They are a disembodied ghost . . . We ask today: "What are the Poles? What are the French? What are the Swiss?" When that is asked, everyone points to a country, to certain institutions, to parliamentary institutions, and the man in the street will know exactly what it is. He has a passport. If you ask what a Jew is—well, he is a man who has to offer a long explanation for his existence, and any person who has to offer an explanation as to what he is, is always suspect . . .

Evidence from Chaim Weizmann
to the United Nations Special Committee
on Palestine, July 8, 1947

When I Lived
in
Modern Times

W HEN I look back I see myself at twenty. I was at an age when anything seemed possible, at the beginning of times when anything *was* possible. I was standing on the deck dreaming; across the Mediterranean we sailed, from one end to the other, past Crete and Cyprus to where the East begins. *Mare nostrum.* Our sea. But I was not in search of antiquity. I was looking for a place without artifice or sentiment, where life was stripped back to its basics, where things were fundamental and serious and above all modern.

This is my story. Scratch a Jew and you've got a story. If you don't like elaborate picaresques full of unlikely events and tortuous explanations, steer clear of the Jews. If you want things to be straightforward, find someone else to listen to. You might even get to say something yourself. How do we begin a sentence?

"Listen . . ."

A sailor pointed out to me a little ship on the horizon, one whose role as a ship was supposed to be finished, which had reached the end of its life but had fallen into the hands of those who wanted it to sail one last time. "Do you know what that is?" he asked me.

I knew but I didn't tell him.

"It isn't going to land," he said. "The authorities will catch them."

"Are you in sympathy with those people?"

"Yes, I'm sympathetic. Who wouldn't be? But they can't go where they want to go. It's just not on. They'll have to find somewhere else."

"Where?"

"No idea. That's not our problem, is it?"

"So you don't think the Zionist state is inevitable?"

"Oh, they'll manage somewhere or other. They always have done in the past."

This time it's different, I thought, but I kept my mouth shut. Like the people on the horizon, I was determined that I was going home, though in my case it was not out of necessity but conviction.

Then I saw it, the coast of Palestine. The harbor of Haifa assumed its shape, the cypress and olive and pine-clad slopes of Mount Carmel ascended from the port. I didn't know then that they were cypresses and olives and pines. I didn't recognize a single thing. I had no idea at all what I was looking at. I had come from a city where a few unnamed trees grew out of asphalt pavements, ignored, unseen. I could identify dandelions and daisies and florists' roses but that was all, that was the extent of my excursions into the kingdom of the natural world. And what kind of English girl doesn't look at a tree and know what type it is, by its bark or its leaves? How could I be English, despite what was written on my papers?

On deck, beside me, some passengers were crossing themselves and murmuring, "The Holy Land," and I copied them but we were each of us seeing something entirely different.

I know that people regarded me in those days as many things: a bare-faced liar; an enigma; or a kind of Displaced Person like the ones in the camps. But what I felt like was a chrysalis, neither bug nor butterfly, something in between, closed, secretive, and inside some great transformation under way as the world itself—in that strangest of eras just after the war was over—was metamorphosing into something else, which was neither the war nor a return to what had gone before.

It was April 1946. The Mediterranean was packed with traffic. Victory hung like a veil in the air, disguising where we might be headed next. Fifty years later it's so easy, with hindsight, to understand what was happening but you were *part* of it then. History was no theme park. It was what you lived. You were affected, whether you liked it or not.

We didn't know that a bitter winter was coming, the coldest in living memory in the closing months of 1946 and the new year of 1947. America would be frozen. Northern Europe would freeze. You could watch on the Pathé newsreel women scavenging for coal in the streets of the East End of London. I had already seen in the pages of *Life* magazine what was left of Berlin—a combination of grandeur and devastation, fragments of what looked like an old, dead civilization, the wreckage that was left in the degradation of defeat. I had seen people selling crumbs of what had once been part of a civilized life. A starving woman held out a single red, high-heeled shoe. A man tried to exchange a small bell for a piece of bread. A boy offered a soldier of the Red Army his sister's doll.

All across the northern hemisphere would be the same bitter winter. The cold that killed them in Germany would kill us everywhere. But winter was months away and I was on deck in balmy spring weather, holding the green-painted rail of the ship, watching the coast of Palestine assemble itself out of the fragrant morning air and assume a definite shape and dimension.

In the Book of Lamentations I had once read these words: *Our inheritance is turned to strangers, our houses to aliens. Our skin was black like an oven because of the terrible famine. The ways of Zion do mourn, because none come to the solemn feast: all her gates are desolate: her priests sigh, her virgins are afflicted, and she is in bitterness.*

But all that was about to change. We were going to force an alteration in our own future. We were going to drive the strangers out, bury the blackened dead, destroy the immigration posts and forget our bitterness. There would be no more books of lamenting. Nothing like that was going to happen to us again. We had *guns* now, and underground armies, guerrilla fighters, hand grenades, nail bombs, a comprehensive knowledge of dynamite and TNT. We had spies in the enemies' ranks and we knew what to do with collaborators.

I was a daughter of the new Zion and I felt the ship shudder as the gangplank crashed on to the dock. I put on my hat and white cotton gloves and, preparing my face, waited to go ashore at the beginning of the decline and fall of the British Empire.

WHO *was* Evelyn? Who took a train through France and boarded a ship at Marseilles?

Just a work-in-progress, not even that; a preliminary sketch for a person. I was only twenty and what does twenty know?

Listen, to start with I never met my father, so fifty percent of me was blank. My mother said he was an American, from San Francisco. She had a picture of the two of them standing in Trafalgar Square in 1923, taken by a street photographer. I can't see his face properly because the brim of his hat casts a shadow. His name was Arthur Bergson and he returned to America promising that he would be back four months later, to marry her. She never saw him again and I suppose he never knew that he had a daughter somewhere in the world.

She grew up in Whitechapel in the East End of London. Her parents came from Latvia on the Baltic coast and they spoke no English. She was the youngest of seven, a wild, disobedient girl, the only one of all her brothers and sisters to be born in England.

I used to sit on her knee at bedtime while she reminisced about her own childhood, her brown eyes seeing things I had never seen, which did not seem right when we had nothing but each other and for each other we were everything. "You know, we lived in a big dirty house," she told me, "or at least it seemed big to me, and we all slept in feather beds and my mother and father would sit up all night playing cards, talking together in Yiddish about the old country and the town they had come from and a man who had done a crooked deal over the sale of a cow or a *cheder* teacher who had beaten my father or the wind blowing through their wooden houses.

"We kept a barrel with herrings in it at the end of the yard, Evelyn, and there were chickens in a little wooden pen and my mother would go out in her slippers on Friday mornings and with her big red hands she would take one of the hens and wring its neck and I would be in the house with my hands over my ears because I couldn't bear to hear the other hens squawking. My brother Hymie would laugh at me and run around the room imitating a hen—he was a horrible boy Hymie, spiteful, but he came home from the war with a wound in his head that wouldn't heal and then he died of the flu, my sister Gittel, too. She was sixteen and lying in bed and on the fifth day her lungs were full of blood. My mother would come in from the hens and with a cleaver she would cut the bird's head off and the kitchen smelled of dark blood. It was horrible, Evelyn, horrible. Everything was horrible to me. Everything.

"The lavatory was at the end of the yard too and in the winter the water in the pan froze. We used the Yiddish papers, cut in pieces, to wipe ourselves with, and when I sat there in the dark listening to the hens scratching I used to dream of another life, a pretty life where things smelled nice and there was no unpleasantness."

I sat on her lap with my hair curled in twists of paper and she undid one to see if there was a proper corkscrew yet.

"They called the pennies and shillings and sixpences kopecks and this made me angry. They were here in London but they behaved as if they had never left Latvia. They used to curse the tsar and they danced in the yard when they heard he had been murdered—and all his children with him.

"When I was fourteen they sent me to Cable Street to get a job in a factory that made ribbon but I didn't want to go. I walked down our street and when I got to the end I took a tram all the way to the West End and went to a picture house and saw a film with Mary Pickford and from that time on I tried to make myself look like her and wanted the other girls to call me Mary. Mary! My God, was ever there such a name for a Jewish girl?

"Well, my father thrashed me when I got home and he made me go back to the ribbon factory the next day but he couldn't stop me going to the picture houses. I met your father on the Edgware Road one day, when I was seventeen, and when I heard his American accent, of course I agreed at once to go with him for a cup of tea, especially when I found out that he was from California, the home of the film stars. You know I thought then that England was a halfway house, only part of the way toward the New World, and with Arthur I was going to finish the journey that my mother and father had started but not completed because of my father's stupidity, because he did not understand the writing on the ticket, and brought us passage here instead of to America."

This was the story of my mother and of the life she had spent without me. I heard these tales until they were almost worn through and transparent. Then she would rush forward to my birth in a home for wayward women of the Jewish faith. They don't like to talk about the fact that such institutions existed, but they did, supplying the contents of the cots at the Norwood orphanage. She said it had a number of wealthy benefactors, some of whom took a keen personal interest in the future welfare of the girls that passed through, and my mother came to the attention of one of them, who set her up in a hairdresser's shop on Regent Street around the time that bobbed hair and the Marcel wave were all the rage. His name was Joe Hertz. Uncle Joe, to me. In the register her name was Miriam Chernovsky but she

put the past behind her and became Marguerite. The surname
she chose for both of us was Sert, because, she said, it was brief
and it did not seem to come from anywhere.

"Tell me about my father," I would beg her. But all she would
say was this: "Oh, he was a good-looking man. He wore his hat
with the brim down, shading his face, and he smoked cork-
tipped cigarettes." And that was all. I had a Jewish father with
the shortest story in the world.

But I had Uncle Joe and what a story *he* had! He came as a
young man from Warsaw and his family took winter cures at
Austrian spa towns and his own father had traveled across the
continent in his business, which was jewelry. Uncle Joe could
still taste in his mouth the chocolate that his father brought
back from Paris and the cheeses wrapped in a gauze which returned with him from Antwerp. He remembered him talking of
the years at the century's end when he would journey through
Russia to deliver sapphires to Riga. Of the endless forest and its
parched, fragrant stillness, the crunch of dry snow beneath the
wheels of his carriage, of coming upon a town—a small metropolis of Jewish loggers and sawmill workers, crude men in
long beards, their *tzitzes* hanging from beneath their waistcoats,
shirtsleeves rolled up as they manhandled birch planks, shouting and cursing in Yiddish to each other, their words freezing in
the icy air, then dissolving into white clouds of vapor. Where
were they now? Followed their language, become mist.

So I found out early that England was not the whole world. I
learned that I belonged in part to anther country, another continent even, where things were done differently and that what I
thought was real was not inevitable or incapable of changing
into something else, as the Russia of the tsar's time was not the
same Russia as now.

My mother dedicated her life to being a mistress and learned the
arts of a minor courtesan: how to dress and paint her face and

which perfume to use. I would watch her in the mornings sitting in front of the mirror in her curlers, cold-creaming her face, or plucking her eyebrows with sharp tweezers into two surprised black parentheses, powdering the bald place above her lids where the hair had been. She knew the erotic attractions of her body and how to attract her man with it. She cultivated an exquisite femininity, understanding exactly how to entice with hats and fragments of veil and a painted-on beauty spot. She understood the mysterious power of allure and I was fascinated and appalled by the secret arts she practiced.

My mother and I shared all our secrets. We were inseparable. We went to the pictures and out to the ABC for tea and toasted teacakes. Once a year we took the train to Brighton and stayed for a week in a small hotel, enjoying the musical shows at the end of the pier. We both loved Max Miller. "Very smutty," my mother said. "But you can't help laughing."

Uncle Joe ran a number of concerns including a cigar shop on Jermyn Street and kept a *real* wife in a house in Hampstead Garden Suburb. We were family number two and we lived in a flat on three floors, each with two little rooms on it, above a grocer's in Soho. I spent my childhood and youth with the Italians and the Belgians and the man who sold knives and chef's hats. They felt sorry for us at Christmas and bought us yeasted cakes like domes, made with butter and scented with lemon, or tarts of flushed, scarlet strawberries on a mound of custard, or marzipan sweetmeats in the shape of fruits.

Was he like a father to me, Uncle Joe? Well, we sized one another up and he saw me as the child he had to keep in with if he wanted the mother, and I saw him as someone to manipulate for my own ends, for God knows my mother was incapable of manipulating anyone. I always knew that we were the second string, that there were other daughters, four, as it happened, pampered and spoiled and showered with even more luxuries, which they took for granted and which I *calculated* to receive.

They were the family he showed off, the public family, the ones whom he went to the synagogue with, the ones whom his business associates met. And when he died *they* were the ones whose hands people would shake at the funeral and say what was said on such occasions. "Long life."

We were the shadow family, we didn't quite exist. Sometimes, walking along the street, I felt that I couldn't be seen, that you could pass your hand through me. And I wanted to be seen. Inside I was shouting, look at me, pay *me* some attention.

But I have to concede that Joe was loyal to my mother. They whispered together in Yiddish, their private language. I suppose he loved her. If she asked for something (and she didn't ask very often) he always gave in, got his checkbook out. He paid the fees for a private school where I got an education that prepared me for a future far above the station in life I might otherwise have expected. He did it because he was a Jew and believed in the best, the best that money could buy. He was convinced that learning was never wasted, once you had it. It was something no one could take from you.

"A great man once said"—Uncle Joe was a devout admirer of great men—"if you learn a poem by heart and they put you in prison, still you've got the poem." I was set to work to learn to recite by rote chunks of Wordsworth and Tennyson and Browning. Always the narrative works. "What is a poem," asked Uncle Joe, "that cannot also tell a story?"

So yes, he was a good man, a *mensch,* but that didn't stop me worrying that my mother was not getting any younger, despite her dexterity with cosmetics, and—old before my time, with a precocious, courtesan's wisdom that I shouldn't have had—I thought that sooner or later his sexual and financial favors might be withdrawn and we would be stranded, back where we started, with nothing.

Meanwhile, I was looking around to figure out who exactly I was. In the end, all I had to know myself was a fragment of something and I was trying to find out what was the main whole it had broken off from.

It turned out that the fragment was part of a story, I was part of a grand narrative that had started before I was ever born. Who was I? I was a Jew. How did I know? Because of the tales they told me, of Poland and Latvia, and also the times we lived in when anti-Semitism was a wolf roaming the world.

And because we lived in Soho.

Maybe in some other place my mother and I would have been forced to dissolve our identities. Maybe we would have tried not to attract unwanted attention, an unmarried mother and her child, but in Soho it didn't matter. No one asked questions. Within those few streets off Shaftesbury Avenue and Charing Cross Road it was acceptable to be different, it was *normal*. We were all ethnics, from somewhere else. Everyone had their own churches and social clubs, little colonies in which we preserved the customs of the place we had come from, as my mother and I had the synagogue on Dean Street we attended three times a year, for the most important high days and holidays. We bent our heads over our prayer books among a congregation of market traders and shopkeepers, actors and theatrical impresarios.

I grew up in a world of night streets, of stage-door johnnies ardent or wan with hopelessness holding bunches of flowers; of little ballet dancers from Sadler's Wells like brown wrens when out of their costumes and in their gabardine macs, warming their thin hands over cups of tea; of wrecked men from the first war blowing into harmonicas along the Strand; of the amber and scarlet flame of the braziers that roasted chestnuts on street corners; of the lit-up windows of Fortnum and Mason—once with a fairy coach pulled by silver-painted plaster horses and Cinderella inside it; of the electric advertisements at Piccadilly Circus and bronze Eros with his bow and arrow.

This was my home, but I always knew I was a Jewish child growing up in a Christian country. That I woke up, every Sunday morning, to the sound of church bells ringing across the whole of Christian England and when I heard them I was not summoned to God. After the bells, silence. The shops shut, the traders on Berwick Street market not loading their stalls or sweeping up cabbage leaves, the theaters dark, the pubs closed. If you got on a bus and went to the suburbs there was nothing but the monotonous smell of roast dinners squeezing out through the cracks under the closed front doors. On Sundays life halted. England became a morgue. Outside there were a few walking corpses on the streets. I never understood why England did this, stopping the very flow of blood in its veins on Sundays and allowing it to flow again on Monday mornings. To rest? Why rest? You rested at night, in your bed!

I was a Jewish child in a country where, unlike America, there was no contribution I could make to the forging of the national identity. It was fixed already, centuries ago.

I was eight years old, and already I was an exotic. The English fed their dogs better food than they ate themselves. They fascinated me. *They* were exotic.

I was a round-faced, stubborn, dark-haired girl whose lips were too red and whose eyes were too black. I would grow up into a watchful young woman who stared at herself in the mirror and thought her neck was a fraction too short and whose hair had to be bullied into curls with strong chemicals. I was naturally argumentative but my mother warned me early on that this was not considered an attractive quality in the female sex and so I learned, from her, to curb my tongue and to do what I could to cultivate prettiness and a feminine style.

Joe always said, when customers balked at paying top prices for his finest cigars: "Sir, there's only one thing worse than having nothing, and that's looking as if you've got nothing. Sit down at a table in a restaurant and light up one of these cigars and you can order a glass of water and they'll think it's a rich man's fancy. Light up a Woodbine and you'll be out on your ear."

Show them you're on top of the world, even if you're not. What do you have to lose?

"Buy cheap pay dear" was another of Joe's maxims. And, "Only the rich can afford cheap shoes."

And all these lessons were something else that made me a Jew.

I DON'T know what he bought his other daughters, but from the time I could read Uncle Joe would arrive at the flat with brown paper parcels of books: the novels of Charles Dickens and Anthony Trollope which, unwrapped and read, stood in a row between matching china bookends in the shape of horses with white faces and brown manes, until the line grew too long for the dressing table and a three-shelf bookcase was delivered from Selfridges. When I was thirteen, he presented me with a volume containing reproductions of various old masters like Leonardo da Vinci and Raphael, which drove me to the National Gallery to see the originals for myself. In its chilly rooms on quiet Sunday afternoons surrounded by the unfamiliar landscapes of Tuscany and Florence I came across a crowd of recognizable faces—kings and dukes and popes and cardinals and young men with large brown eyes and pale-faced madonnas with their lusty muscular babies, all looking very much like my Soho neighbors. For the boy who served behind the counter at Lina's must have been a descendant of the Medici and the priest bending over the infant Jesus was the exact spit of my friend Gabriella's surly, black-browed father who laid mosaic floors in the houses of the wealthy, the trade he had brought from Italy and which his father and grandfather had carried out before him in the churches of the Veneto.

So in the National Gallery I felt more at home than in England and I decided to become an artist and asked for a sketchbook and received one, along with a flat tin box of Caran d'Ache pencils and began to render what I saw of life in colored crayons.

"You killed our Lord," a teacher hissed in my ear, grabbing my wrist as twenty of us thundered out of class and down the stairs toward our break. It was not the kind of anti-Semitism that made you frightened, just the type that ensured you knew you did not belong and it was in your best interests to try to conform.

In Scripture, they showed us pictures of the Holy Land. All we saw were churches and the Via Dolorosa and the Sea of Galilee where Jesus walked on the water. A teacher who had been there described Bethlehem to us. She regarded Palestine as a British affair, thought the place was hers and not mine. The King James Version of the Bible, she said, was a *triumph* of English literature.

"Did you go to Tel Aviv?" I asked, putting up my hand.

She frowned. "There is nothing of any interest there." Palestine, to her, was in a two-thousand-year-old time warp. She saw nothing later than, say, the Crusaders.

"I have heard that the British in Palestine . . ." I continued.

"No politics, if you please, Evelyn."

But I had been brought up on politics. On our mantelpiece in the flat in Soho Uncle Joe had placed a blue and white collecting tin for the Jewish National Fund, in which we put our halfpennies, pennies, threepenny bits and sometimes even a shilling. Every birthday Uncle Joe pushed through the slot, to commemorate another year of my life, a whole half a crown.

"So part of little Evelyn," he said, "will make things grow in the earth of the Jewish home." In the office at the back of his cigar shop hung framed posters of noble, muscle-bound figures tilling the soil of Palestine. A new one arrived every year. I imagined of myself as a flower or a tree in the hands of a Jewish farmer. It was quite a thought.

On a wet Sunday afternoon in 1938, when London smelled of damp tobacco and sodden gardens and unwashed flesh, my mother and I got the tube to a cinema in Hendon and saw a film called *The Land of Promise*. We saw the Western Wall and pioneers dancing on the deck of an immigrant ship. We saw the laying of the electrical grid, drilling for water, farming on a kibbutz. We saw Jewish newspapers, a Jewish bank, a Jewish medical center in Jerusalem, and we heard Haydn's *Creation* performed in the Mount Scopus amphitheater. In a fiery speech at the end spoken by a trade-union leader, we were told that the Zionist homeland was Utopia Today.

My mother and I were awestruck. A Jewish land! Everything Jewish! How could it be? We saw Uncle Joe in the audience with his other family, the four girls yawning with boredom. But Uncle Joe was the first to rise to his feet when the curtain closed and applaud and cheer. "Next year in Jerusalem," he shouted.

Once he showed me in a newspaper an advertisement seeking recruits for the Palestine Police.

If your health and intelligence are good, if you're single and want a *man's* job—one of the most vital jobs in the British Empire—if you like the glamour of serving a crack force in a country of sand dunes and olive groves, historic towns and modern settlements—if you prefer this type of life on good pay *that you can save* . . . here's how you can get into the Palestine Police Force.

There was a drawing of a man in shorts and knee-length socks directing traffic. A car was coming in one direction, a donkey in the other. Below this, another picture depicted Arabs riding on camels.

"Where's the Jews, Evelyn?" Uncle Joe asked.

"Nowhere, Uncle Joe," I replied.

"Then this picture is a lie, for Palestine is *full* of Jews."

Of course he was a Zionist. Who wasn't back then?

Sometimes my mother and I went to Speakers' Corner in Hyde Park, and I would try to distinguish between those who talked sense and those who were merely crackpots—religious maniacs, vegetarians. We knew that Jews were being beaten on the streets of Vienna and Berlin. "Down with the appeasers," I shouted, at twelve. My mother shivered in her coat.

"What is to happen to us?" she whispered, on the bus home.

"Don't worry, Mummy," I told her. "I'll protect us," for I was fierce and my fists were bunched together in fury, inside my mittens. I looked at her beloved face and thought, "Neither of us will ever die."

When the war started my mother and I held each other tightly as we lived through the convulsive shaking of a city tormented by air raids, passing houses turned into sticks, seeing the ruins of the white Georgian terraces near Regent's Park which when I was a child had seemed to me like high, white cliffs, hard and permanent and unscalable.

"Why can't things be nice?" my mother asked me. "Why does someone have to spoil everything? Why can't we all just live, and be happy?"

I thought this was simple-minded but I only said, "Because there are unjust people in the world and they have to be fought."

"If only we had gone to America," she replied. "There's no war there."

The bombs got on her nerves. She was a wreck. Last thing at night she sipped milky drinks but they did not help. She lost weight and the plump cheeks receded in her oval face, giving her a vaporous femininity. She lost herself in movie magazines and kept up to date with what the stars were doing for the war effort. "If only we were in America," she said. "They'll never bomb America. We're too close, too close."

"Don't cry, Mummy."

"Yes. I should buck up." And she dried her tears and repainted her lips and powdered her nose.

But at night when I lay in bed, I thought of a German invasion and of the swastika flying above Buckingham Palace and the Houses of Parliament and ourselves rounded up, marched off to somewhere I didn't want to start imagining.

London was a huge, drab metropolis. The color of men's uniforms imposed a khaki sameness on the world. There was too much navy blue in women's suits and dresses. Before the war, I remembered, there seemed to be more red: more red dresses and shoes, more pillar-box-red coats, more crimson and scarlet and magenta everywhere. Hair had been more visible, too—Veronica Lake peek-a-boo styles falling over the face, instead of tied back in the inevitable net snood to keep it out of your eyes while you worked at your lathe or pounded a typewriter. We were on a war; footing and frivolity was banned. The Italians had been taken away and interned and the Belgians struggled to make their fabulous pastries on the ration.

From a young age I had stood at my mother's side at the salon, handing her pins and clips, listening ungratefully while she taught me everything she knew. I was sent on humble errands: to Steckyn's on Wardour Street to pick up shampoo capes and sleeping nets and snoods. As others hoarded string, we were sharp-eyed for hairpins that had strayed on buses or in the street, collecting them up in our handbags, knowing that the metal they were made of was diverted into the production of airplanes and helmets and ships and bombs and that these few slivers of steel had to be gathered and kept in a safe place, sometimes, when there were shortages, under lock and key.

After school and on Saturday mornings, I learned all the techniques of hairdressing and the habit has stayed in my fingers to this day. Whose hair did I dress? The mothers of the very girls I was at school with and sometimes the girls themselves. They knew me as the hairdresser's daughter and I was excluded from their busy social lives. My true friends were in Soho and what did I feel when Gabriella, at sixteen, watched police officers take her father and older brothers off to be interned as enemy aliens, a fate which she was only spared because she had been born in England? I thought, "We are fighting fascism but who are the anti-Semites?" Gabriella, whose father had taught me how to eat spaghetti with a spoon and fork and always tipped his hat and gave a half-bow when he passed my mother in the street, admiring her chic suit and hat with a little half-veil? Or the schoolgirls whose fathers and brothers were in the RAF or the Navy or with their regiments winning medals and who never invited me to their birthday parties?

I was seventeen and leaving school and what I wanted to be was an art student. I wanted to study at the Slade where the Jew Mark Gertler had learned to paint three decades before, and whose work spoke of a life more savage and less placid than the decorative compositions of Duncan Grant or the spare, bleak landscapes of Paul Nash with their tendency toward abstractions. I wanted the art student's life, to get away from the bourgeois conformity of my schoolfriends. I read Bertrand Russell; not the philosophy, of course, but the pamphlets on free love and marriage.

But Uncle Joe said that if I wanted to be an artist he could get me a job in an office. I could be a *commercial* artist, helping in the preparation of advertisements for things like Horlicks or aiding the war effort by designing illustrated pamphlets showing housewives how to stretch the ration or urging them to save string. Gradually, he chipped away at my confidence. Who was I to think I could be anything other than an amateur, a private painter? And if he wasn't prepared to pay, that was the end of the matter. I took the job. I walked to Holborn every morning and made tea and ran errands and watched the men in their shirtsleeves, with bow ties knotted round their necks and I tried to pick up some techniques from them. But God, they were a dull lot, too old to fight or still waiting for their call-up papers.

Eventually they gave me a little job to do. An advert for a women's magazine for "feminine hygiene" in which the facts of biology were rendered so vague that in the end my drawing depicted a woman sitting in an armchair with nothing more than a pained expression on her face. My boss came and took a look. "No good," he said. "You've done laxatives."

I only had to endure the office for a few months. Fate had a greater indignity for me. Something about my mother was unraveling. She was coming apart at the seams. She took more and more days off from the salon and sent me in her place. She sat at home, a nervous wreck, crying.

"Why can't things be nice?" she asked me, over and over again.

Sometimes I thought that when she addressed me, it was as one of her sisters. "Gittel," she said, "make us a nice cup of tea, will you?"

"Evelyn," I said. "I'm Evelyn, not Gittel."

"Yes. Evelyn. Has someone fed the horse?"

"Mother, pull yourself together."

"Yes, I must. Mum will be back soon."

"Stay home," Joe said. "Look after her." So I did. And who could blame me for feeling so low in London, going to the salon for a couple of hours every afternoon when she was sleeping, doing perms and sets and nearly knocking myself out on the stench of peroxide in the back room.

May 1945. The war over. The camps liberated. The voices of the pacifist appeasers not believing what they found there, saying it was war propaganda. Then sitting in a darkened cinema watching the newsreels. Uncle Joe sobbing, his head on my mother's lap. Sixteen cousins gone. Sixteen.

Next day he said, "Never mind the six million. What about the eleven million?" And he put a five-pound note in the JNF tin.

The survivors sat in the displaced persons camps. No one wanted them. Britain said no. America said no. After a while they began to organize. They started up schools and synagogues. They elected their own police force. With the past what it was, they had nothing to do except think about the future.

I N the summer I came home one day from the shops to find my mother sitting on the step, her face full of cold, heavy sweat, and her eyes crazy. She tried to speak to me but I couldn't understand what she was talking about. "Put the poppy back," she said, slurring her words like a drunkard. "On the leg. Puss."

I held her in my arms and stroked her hair while the doctor was sent for. The Frenchman who ran the pub around the corner where my mother occasionally went for a small brandy with Uncle Joe sat down next to us and took her hand. We formed a kind of pietà sitting there, triangular in composition, as if we were a living Leonardo on that doorstep on Old Compton Street amid the traffic and the tarts and the spivs and the black-market types in their flashy suits and the expressionless men on their way to see strippers in upstairs rooms and the muscle boys in their prime coming back from shooting the breeze with a punch-ball at Mike Solomon's gymnasium and the dour Hungarian waiters going to work at the Budapest restaurant in Dean Street and the drunk and disheveled old women in broken shoes and moldy hats with dusty feathers and the bohemians in colored shirts opening the doors of the public houses where they would stay until closing time and then vomit in the streets. It was the world I knew and it was about to be overthrown.

They took my mother away to the Middlesex Hospital where a second stroke, a few hours later, poleaxed her at the age of forty-one. After some weeks they drove her in an ambulance to a nursing home on the south coast where she sat staring at the sea. Nor did my own face or that of Uncle Joe cause the corner of her mouth to move or the tip of a finger to lift. But still, to my surprise he paid for everything. She had the best from him, though he owed her nothing in law. What is that secret intimacy between two people that no one who is not a part of it can ever fathom?

I felt numb with the pain of her abrupt removal from my life. Everything we could have said to each other it was too late to say. I wanted her forgiveness for the times when I came in late and did not go to her room to kiss her; or when I complained and grumbled about having to work at the salon; or when I resented that I had not been born into more regular circumstances; or when I was ashamed that the girls at school called me the hairdresser's daughter.

I went to visit every Sunday. She looked at me, uncomprehendingly. Her hair was turning gray and it was fine, and only combed, not permed, or set, or styled. I held her hand and watched our shadows on the lawn. My mother had turned her face against ugliness, she had fled from the slums to a life that was pretty. She had found a protector. But even he could not save her from reality. It was obvious to me that life was not fair and made victims of people who should never have been oppressed in the spirit and the body, and that the only way to live was to summon one's strength to fight back against whoever it was who was trying to dominate you, not retreat into a world of make-believe.

I left her with a charcoal drawing I had made of the two of us together, in our old home, the flat in Soho. I put it on her lap but she didn't look at it. I walked away and then turned and waved. Her head was lolling. She seemed to have fallen asleep.

"She's exhausted after the excitement of your visit," a nurse said.

By the winter she was a wisp of ectoplasm swirling around in a chair. I kissed her papery skin and held her hand. She smelled of old food and urine. On Christmas Eve she died. Uncle Joe was away. He had taken the first family to a Jewish hotel in Bournemouth. I had to get the synagogue to find the ten Jewish men we needed for the *minyan* without which the interment could not proceed. Ten strangers. They stood there respectfully, like so many suitors. She went into the ground. They filed past and wished me long life. But what kind of a life was it to be?

"Now what?" said Uncle Joe. "You want me to find you another place in an office?"

"I'd like to go to art school."

"How can you make a living out of art? Where's the money in it?"

"I don't care about money."

He choked on his cigar. I thought the smoke would come out of his ears.

"Listen, Evelyn, who I have known since you were a tiny baby in your mother's arms, may her good soul rest in peace. No one can live for five minutes without money. They think they can but then they find out different. Have you got a sweetheart yet?"

"No. No sweetheart."

"You're fancy-free?"

"Yes."

"No ties?"

"No."

"Then why don't you go to Palestine?"

"I don't know, I never thought about it."

"How does the idea strike you?"

Palestine. I had never been further than Sussex.

He gave me books to read and pamphlets.

A week later he came to the flat.

"You read the books?"

"Yes, I've read them. All. Every word."

"What do you think?"

"Palestine belongs to us," I cried. "What do we have to do with this place, England? It's nothing. Only the birth of our own country can avenge the death of the six million. *That's* the resurrection."

"Excellent. I knew you'd see it in the right way. Now we have to find a way to get you in, but trust me, I have some connections."

We went together to the Jewish Agency. They were incredulous. What could I offer? they demanded. Nothing, it turned out. They explained, patiently, that the British were only giving out fifteen hundred entry permits and that hundreds of thousands of DPs were ahead of me in the queue. Were I of potential use to them, they could, of course, obtain one of these permits for me, but I was no use at all, as far as they could see.

The rich are not used to taking no for an answer. "Is there any other way?" Uncle Joe asked, taking his checkbook from an inside pocket of his jacket and unscrewing the cap of his gold-plated Parker fountain pen.

They replied that they would think about it.

A week or two later, he telephoned them. Had they had any ideas? Yes. They suggested that I present myself to the Mandate authorities at the Foreign and Colonial Office and explain that I wished to enter Palestine as a tourist, a pious young Christian wanting to visit the Holy Land. I could take a perfectly legal passage on a perfectly legal ship and cruise pleasantly through the Mediterranean to Haifa. It was something that other people did all the time.

"How about this?" said Uncle Joe. "I will sell the salon. Your mother worked there for twenty years and you're entitled to something. Suppose I buy a ticket and give you a banker's draft to cover your first three months?"

"It's very generous."

"The future belongs to the young people, Evelyn. I'm too old to go but you . . ."

Did he really see me as the future hope of Jewish humanity? Or was he just getting rid of me? Still I don't know.

First, I had to obtain a passport and endure the icy politeness of the officials when, looking at my birth certificate, they observed the space where my father's name should have been. Then I dressed in a hot brown scratchy tweed skirt and a modest cream blouse with a peter-pan collar for my interview at the Foreign Office. I borrowed a gold cross from Gabriella who was working in one of the newly reopened Italian restaurants and hung it round my neck. She had great sympathy with my cause. A lot of people did in those days. She gave me a rosary of brown wooden beads too which I put in my handbag. I went with no lipstick or rouge and my hair, which reached to my shoulders, was screwed into a bun with tight fingers.

I walked down Shaftesbury Avenue where the cleaners were busy on the steps of the theaters, to Piccadilly Circus. Past Lillywhites, where there was an artful arrangement of cricketing paraphernalia in the window, then down Lower Regent Street, into Trafalgar Square and across the Mall. Walked along Horse Guards Parade, where on my right the swans and mallards and Canada geese made their way across the lake in St. James's Park, and I saw one rise from the water and take wing above the bare black twigs, and turning saw it fly over Buckingham Palace with the flag ripping against the wind to tell us that our King and Queen and princesses were at home. A car passed and a somber profile that I recognized from the newsreels looked straight ahead. The might of the British Empire was burnished in the frail sunshine of this morning in February 1946, when London had never looked lovelier. The grandeur and majesty of England bore down on me.

I was trying to make myself feel as I appeared to be: a modest Christian girl hurrying through Whitehall, perhaps to polish the candlesticks on the altar at Westminster Abbey or to commune with the tombs of English poets, four hundred years dead. Or whatever it was people did in churches. The rosary beads lay in the darkness of my handbag, clicking against each other. A man passed me in pinstripe trousers and a morning coat and wing collar and he lifted his bowler hat and said a courteous good morning. I smiled back. Across the city, the East End and the docks were flattened, in ruins, but here nothing had changed.

Inside my head the kings and queens of England were stacked like pancakes in chronological order going back to the Wars of the Roses but no one I was related to had ever set foot on English soil until forty-five years ago. What could an immigrant child be, except an impersonator? I felt like a double agent, a fifth columnist. And I knew that as long as I lived in this country it would always be exactly the same. I walked among them and they thought they knew me, but they understood nothing at all. It was *me* that understood, the spy in their midst.

There was no difficulty at all in obtaining permission to go to Palestine. The situation was not stable, they warned me, but with proper care and by closely following the advice of the officials I met there I should experience no danger.

I was told, enthusiastically, of the sights I wound find: one of the Dome of the Rock and the Church of the Nativity and other Christian and Muslim landmarks that did not interest me. Neither archeology nor ancient history moved me in the slightest. All the madonnas of the Renaissance were, for me, studies in perspective and pigment and skin tone.

"You'll want to visit Galilee," they advised.

"Where Christ walked on the water," I replied. "How wonderful to think that I'll see it with my own eyes." But as I regarded things, I was pretty close to walking on water myself.

Uncle Joe gave me a book of modern art as a going-away present. I looked forward to spending the voyage reading about Picasso, and Matisse, Miró and Chagall.

I TOOK the boat train to Marseilles. Farther along the coast, across the Chaîne de l'Estaque at Port-de-Bouc, others were also casting anchor. They were setting out on a more perilous voyage than mine. They had nowhere to go but forward, no choice but to make an illegal journey or stay where they were and rot.

I sat on deck and thought how the whole story was about coming home. As I sailed the Mediterranean Sea, all over the world people were in mass transit. We were moving like tides across the continents and the seas, troopships full of men stamping their boots in impatience, hats flying into the air at the sight of land. The roads and railways were engorged with human, sweating, shivering, stinking, parched or pissing flesh, traveling not for adventure or for pleasure or to take a rest cure or acquire a tan or out of boredom or to find romance or to cure a broken heart—but because they had a hunger for the good earth of home under their feet.

Then there were those, like me, who understood on some primitive level that the state of flux was the one we were in. The political map was changing. A lot of people were about to acquire brand-new nationalities, if not entirely new identities. And I was one of them, on both counts.

My fellow passengers on board ship were mostly returning officers of the Palestine Police and Mandate civil servants with their wives and families. There were a few biblical tourists, as I was pretending to be. They swallowed whole my impersonation of them.

Every morning a small group of Christians held a prayer service and I joined them, for appearance' sake. I told them that I had undergone a revelation the previous year, when I felt that God had touched my hand. I withdrew my rosary piously. A woman looked at it.

"Are you going over to Rome?" she asked, nervously.

"No. Why?"

"I see you have those beads the RCs use."

But how was I to distinguish between the different sects of Christianity? They were all just mindless Gentiles to me. I threw the rosary overboard, where it floated on the dirty foam for a few minutes before being swept under.

How much longer could I have kept up with this invented personality? Not that long. The person I pretended to be was beginning to get on my nerves. But it didn't matter because I was nearly home.

When I saw the Promised Land I nearly cried out: "This is it! Now history starts!" But that would have betrayed me and I was trying as hard as I could to be circumspect, to play simple card games in the second-class lounge, to flirt with the young police sergeants and the Mandate pen-pushers, to make small talk and never to say a single thing that was intelligent, let alone controversial. It was no effort at all for someone who had stood, day after day, winding the hair of middle-class women on to curlers, speaking of film stars and shortages and the infinite virtues of Mr. Churchill, their hero.

I took my first step on Jewish soil, then another. The port was swarming with red-faced Englishmen, burned by the sun, going about their business. A sergeant looked at my passport and entry permit.

"Sert. Evelyn Sert. It's an odd name."

"My father was from the Outer Hebrides," I said.

"Oh. That explains it."

An invention, but I had only done what my mother had done and her parents before her, when they left the lands the Jews had inhabited for centuries and set sail for a new world and a new life. And all the dissembling had just that very moment ended with me because I had come to the place where no Jew need ever invent himself again or pretend to be someone he wasn't. I had read in the books Uncle Joe had given me that the elemental nature of the Jews, stripped of the accents of a foreign language and its customs, was going to reveal itself for the first time since the Exile. We would cease to be composite characters.

I walked through the town to the office of the Jewish Agency, got lost and found myself in an Arab market. It was strange beyond belief. The air smelled of things I didn't know or understand. Eventually I would be able to recognize the difference between cardamom and cumin, to know that the round, flat things were bread and that the bulbous, purple objects were vegetables with the name aubergine. I had never seen a lime, let alone a prickly pear. Palm trees, removed from the artistic impressions of them in paintings, were smaller and browner than I expected and didn't have coconuts hanging from them, but dates. In the streets were little horses which I took to be donkeys because they resembled the creatures I had been hauled on to the back of as a child and which were led, plodding, along the Brighton shingle. I saw a camel.

In the balmy, delicious air, with a light sweat which would soon become a second skin, I felt my center dissolve. The things I seemed to have always known (like a popular song you can't remember hearing for the first time) were useless: how to judge whether or not to heed an air-raid warning; how to increase one's allowance of chocolate; where to obtain black-market stockings. I was going to find out that what I needed to know was how to distinguish whether something was edible; how to squat while defecating in the toilets; how to avoid dengue fever; and how to work out who was an Arab and who was a Jew when surprisingly they sometimes looked much the same if you saw them walking the streets of the cities in a suit or a summer dress.

All my life my world had been bounded by Soho in the east and Hyde Park in the west. I was a West End girl. At first sight, Palestine looked like an untidy oriental dump and I was alarmed, but it excited and unnerved me in a way that even Soho never had.

At the Jewish Agency, they were indifferent to my arrival. I thought they would congratulate me on my daring and audacious achievement, hoodwinking the British. All they were concerned about was evacuating the huge prison camp which the continent of Europe seemed to them to be.

I said that I had come to build the new Jewish state.

They looked me up and down.

"Have you any military experience?"

"No."

"Were you with any of the women's services during the war? The Wrens or the Wracs?"

"No. I did fire-watching. I had to look after my mother, who was ill."

"Have you any agricultural experience?"

"No."

"You've never studied engineering?"

"Of course not."

"We have women engineers from Russia here. What about architecture?"

"I didn't study that."

"Have you any practical skills at all? Have you ever done anything with your hands?"

"Yes. I'm not totally useless. I was a hairdresser." Then they all began to laugh at me, those hard-bitten Jewish men who had seen it all and were impressed by nothing.

"Listen," they said. "Go to a kibbutz. They always need help. Try it, see if you like it. If you don't you can have a little tour of the country and go home when you're ready."

"I thought Zionists wanted every Jew they could get their hands on."

"In time, yes. Now we have other problems. Wait here. Some- one is coming in from a kibbutz in Galilee this afternoon. Talk to him. He'll take you back with him."

So I sat on a chair in the office and waited.

Telephones rang. The air was dense with smoke. Through the window I caught sight of the sea, where I had just come from. The excitement and infatuation with all that was new and diffi- cult ebbed away. I felt nauseous with anxiety. What had I done? I looked at my shoes.

At lunchtime they brought me a strange meal: bread with onions and a green pepper and a glass of hot sweet tea with lemon in it. I had been in Palestine for several hours and I was tired and thirsty. I wanted a *cup* of tea, made properly in a pot, with milk and two spoons of white sugar. And a biscuit. I felt very alone and far from home. But I had no home. That was the point. That was why I was here.

Finally two people turned up, a man and a girl. She had a hard, sunburned body and her legs were covered with long, black hairs. When she lifted her hand in greeting I could see even more coarse, dark hair in her armpits. I was revolted. Hairy Hebrew girl.

The man addressed me in English. He said his name was Meier. "What languages do you speak?" he asked me and I hardly understood his voice at first.

"English. And a little French."

"Hebrew?"

"No."

"Russian?"

"No. Why?"

"The founders of this kibbutz came from Moscow, Odessa, Kiev and Kharkov twenty-two years ago. English is not the language we use here. We know it because we have to deal with the British authorities from time to time. Can you work hard?"

"I don't know."

"There won't be any place for you in Eretz Israel if you cannot."

The girl, who had not spoken, said something to me in a language I didn't recognize. "She doesn't speak English," Meier said.

"Where is she from?"

"Here."

"Here?"

"Yes. This is where she was born. The young people don't bother to learn English because the British will be going soon. But we can teach you Hebrew. Soon it will be the language you think in."

In my heart of hearts I had thought I was coming to a land full of bona fide aliens like myself. When they spoke of Palestine as a land without people for a people without land I had imagined it as a deserted place, an empty quarter crossed by Arab nomads until the Jews arrived, escaping Hitler.

I climbed onto the back of a flatbed truck, gripping the edge with one hand and clinging to my new leather suitcase purchased from Selfridges by Uncle Joe with the other. The city of Haifa receded and now we were driving north across stony ground, through what they later said were olive groves, to nothing I understood, though they kept on saying I was home now.

Earth. Smells. Hills. Dust. I was speechless.

I T was on the shore of the Sea of Galilee, a ramshackle encampment, guarded by look-outs. They grew bananas and other crops.

"It's hot," I said to Meier, as he showed me where I would sleep.

"No," he replied. "This is still spring. The real heat will be later."

My clothes were taken away and I was issued with a wardrobe pared down to a utilitarian simplicity: two pairs of shorts and two sleeveless shirts, a pair of boots and a pair of sandals and a cotton hat without a proper shape. We looked anonymous, all of us, like so many overalled factory hands. Gender was dissolved, annihilated.

I was to share a dormitory with five other young women in a single-story structure, part of a group of eight in a quadrangle with the male and female shower and toilet blocks at one end.

I stood under the water as Evelyn, and scrubbing at the dust and grime on my skin from the journey. I felt that she had been left behind in the office of the Jewish Agency, that confused, conflicted girl who was a mistress of disguises and of duplicity. I was washing away what remained of her. Water streamed down my head and on to my eyes. My hair was stuck to my face and I was returned to the beginning of time, to where things started, not where they ended. I was no longer Evelyn, I was Eve and that as it turned out was what they called me, one syllable being more serviceable than two.

The girls on the kibbutz were matter-of-fact types, friendly but not warm, who took the view that either I would fit in, or I would not. It was up to me. They were indifferent either way having seen other new immigrants come who had rhapsodized in the cafés of faraway Vienna and Berlin about the uniquely Jewish experiment in the formation of new social relations but had slunk off back to Tel Aviv and Haifa when they found cow shit on the soles of their leather shoes and their hair sticky with bull semen.

I was shouted into life at four o'clock the following morning and dressed and washed in darkness. Breakfast was laid out on the tables in the communal dining hall, creaking under its tin roof, its concrete walls audibly cracking. Our meal consisted of bread, which smelled strange, and green peppers and onions and slabs of white and yellow cheese and black tea. There were jugs of milk but it was warm from the cow and had clumps of cream floating on the surface. I did not touch it. I was used to cold milk in bottles. Sometimes, when I cut off the top of my boiled egg I found the bloody cooked corpse of an embryonic chicken inside. It was plain food and usually wholesome but a dreary diet without any of the sensual pleasure of the Belgian cakes I remembered from Soho and the spaghetti in a rich, red meat sauce or the Swiss tarts made with cream and bacon or . . . (the memory of the foods from home was a constant torment during my brief time on the kibbutz).

As it got light, I followed the other girls as they walked toward some trucks. We climbed onto the back and I tried not to fall off as we were jostled along a track and the sky grew more lucid and small fingers of cloud hung on the horizon. After about half an hour we stopped in the middle of a plantation of very small palm trees which grew bananas, they said. Now, I had imagined palms as waving in the breeze on a desert island, curving toward the sand above the crashing waves, because in one of my classrooms at school hung a bad illustration cut out from a magazine. It was supposed to show both the journeys of Robert Louis Stevenson to faraway Tahiti and the pleasures of the tropics where some of my teachers had actually lived and worked as missionaries to what they described as the savage peoples of the Far East. But these palms had nothing to do with storybooks or flights of fancy or the imaginary journeys of day-dreaming English schoolgirls in outgrown cotton dresses on sleepy summer afternoons, but had been scientifically modified in an institute to make them closer to the ground and easier to pick the fruit from. Nature was in retreat under Jewish hands.

I was given a small sickle and followed the others up and down the rows of trees and, bending over, sheared through the brown leaves that flaked from the trunk. It was monotonous and made my back ache. After a while, the sun rose above the Golan hills and warmed, then later scorched my head and face and arms. The brown leaves were like sharp Saracen swords that cut my hands.

At first, I was a few trees behind the others, then half a row, then a whole row, then two or thee rows behind, like the fat laggard girls who always came last in school races and whom nobody wanted or spoke to.

Soon, I was lying on the ground, vomiting my breakfast. The sun was behind my eyes and when I opened them things were black. All I wanted was to leave the light, to crawl under the earth. The other girls and boys passed me, unconcerned. I walked on my knees, like a dwarf and I said that I had to go back but they told me they would not be returning for some hours.

"Take me back," I implored. "Can't you see I'm ill? But they weren't interested in me. I climbed onto the metal bed of the truck. It was like a sheet of flame, after an hour in the sun.

"Stupid," they said, and gestured underneath it. So I lay there, until eleven o'clock when the sun was approaching its zenith and now it was deemed too hot to work.

I slept all day and in the evening I got up and sat in a wooden chair and watched fireflies and moths crash into the lamp that lit the way into out sleeping places. I heard them in the dining hall, eating and singing. They had brought me my free ration of cigarettes and I smoked a couple of them, raw gaspers they were, a brand I didn't know. The moon was over the Golan hills and the air smelled of things that were immeasurably mysterious to me.

The next day I went back to the fields and things were no better. The sunlight was tormenting me. When it shone on my head, even when I was wearing the cotton hat, I began to vomit and was prone to blacking out. I had escaped from the brown days in London when the skies were coffee-colored, days that oppressed my spirit, to a land where the sun would not let you be. There was nowhere to hide from the sun, from its relentless light and clarity. There were no corners where things could be left alone and ignored. The sun found its way into everything.

My work rate did not improve. I lasted only half an hour longer before being sick and I lay under the truck and then returned and slept. But in the evening I joined them for dinner in the dining room. The meal wasn't much. They only served meat at midday and here, again, were the inevitable tomatoes and peppers and onions and bread, with lumps of white, tasteless cheese. Some of the girls had bars of chocolate but I didn't know where they got them from. We sat at long tables, all together. It reminded me of school.

They did not try to welcome me. They passed me dishes of things if I pointed. As Meier had said, many spoke no English.

They never went to the cities, to Haifa or Tel Aviv or Jerusalem, never came across the military presence of the British. They stayed here and everything they had was enough for them.

Meier came and asked me how I was getting on.

I was lonely and frightened but I could not admit it to him.

"Very well," I said.

But he had heard different.

"It's the sun. I seem to react badly to it." Escaping the light was all I wanted.

"I can give you a different job."

They woke me even earlier the next morning. I went with the old people to prepare the breakfast. I did not wash the dust from the tomatoes or put the knives and spoons and cups on the tables. I was lower even than that. They gave me a hose and I sluiced the floors, sending tidal waves of water beneath the feet of the old ladies, the women who had come to the kibbutz before the war, to join their sons and daughters (once held to have had crackpot ideas but now regarded as almost god-like in their prescience) where it was safe. The old people's Hebrew was garbled and they lapsed into Yiddish at any opportunity, another language I didn't understand. I ate my food standing up. While the dining hall was full I was sent to the lavatories with my hose to clean them out.

They smelled exactly of what you would expect—of three hundred men and women who had just washed and pissed. I did not expect that they would send me into the men's block.

"I can't go in there," I said, but they laughed at that. I had never seen a urinal before. I didn't know its purpose. I held my breath as I aimed my hose at the wall.

In the women's block I thrust a jet of water down the hole in the ground with its marks for where the feet were placed.

I returned to the kitchens when the people were leaving to go to work in the fields and I cleared the tables and washed the floors and then the tables were laid again for the midday meal. And the sun came up over the Golan hills.

Work and rest, work and rest. In the afternoon I saw that some people went to lie by the shores of the lake and read and swim which was a skill I had never acquired. They took all their clothes off without concern and so I did too. Their bodies were nothing like mine, they were brown and hard and the women were without curves or voluptuousness. I was thin, but flabby. My skin was very white. They looked at me and I felt that they were disgusted.

Across the lake, where Jesus Christ had supposedly walked on the water, was a town called Tiberias and behind us, on the other side of the hills, was Syria, a land of many enemies. So I mapped the boundaries of my new country.

It was appalling. I wasn't cut out for this. I made my mind up that I would be off and I went to tell Meier. "Sit down," he said. "Listen, let me tell you a story."

The one he told me was, it turned out, the best I had ever heard in my life. It was about the founding of the kibbutz: of the mobile band of young laborers in the service of the Zionist enterprise who came at the age of eighteen in 1922 from the Soviet Union to have their skin roasted and their flesh pricked by thorns under a Jewish sun, because behind their eyes and in their heads was an Idea: the dream of Bolshevism on Jewish soil. Of how for years they roamed the country, setting up camp in olive groves, planting pine trees on Mount Carmel, cutting roads through limestone rock. Of the months they spent draining the Yarkon River, lifting sand from its bed which they loaded on to pack animals to be sent to the construction sites of the new city of Tel Aviv, the first Jewish metropolis since the destruction of the Temple. Of pitching their tents beside a malarial swamp and wading in and draining it. Of the bad time, when life was so hard there was mass emigration from Palestine, a fatal tide of people ebbing back to Europe later to be eliminated from the earth. Of an earth tremor that killed two hundred people. Of the women who died of tuberculosis and the men who died of things that no one had heard of.

But he talked also of their practice of free love, of their abolition of private property so that a letter from home was read out to everyone and how there were no family photographs but the pictures they had were owned by everyone and were kept together in their collective album. Of the children born to them who had no mothers or fathers but who belonged to them all. Of their rejection of religion and their celebration of certain festivals like Passover and May Day with a torch-lit pageant, the men forming a human pyramid, the women dancing with red scarves around their hips. Of the debates about promiscuity, which some thought was a characteristic of a decadent, parasitic ruling class, and about the smoking of cigarettes which some believed showed a lack of willpower among a group whose principal characteristic was the very strength of its will.

Of how they put on plays and held concerts—at first with instruments as simple as paper-covered combs that they hummed into and clacking spoons. Of a dance they called the hora, linking arms and stamping their feet.

Of how some of them determined that it was time to stop being a traveling band and found their own home. Of the bitter discussion that followed, with others arguing that this was a betrayal of their original ideals in making their way to Palestine. Their position was rejected and they left. How the remaining sixty journeyed north and found a site with a ruined cowshed, which could form their immediate habitation. Of waking each morning to the slapping of the water on the banks of the lake, the men and women sleeping together because there were no divisions left between the cow stalls, walking along a dirt road to the fields they were planting, which turned to a mudslide during the rainy season, the endless meals of lentils and the intestinal and digestive disorders they developed as a consequence, of the cold and damp . . . on and on and on he talked but repeatedly he came back to the intense, deep happiness those original founders felt, to be there in the Zionist homeland while on their radio all they heard from Europe was bad news.

And still they stuck to their socialist principles as they built a permanent community. They took their clothes from a common storeroom, which drew heavily on British Army surplus garments. No one owned a clock or a wristwatch. Marriages took place when the girl was ready to give birth and the ceremony only lasted five minutes. A few times the bride was in labor, or too heavily pregnant to stand even for that long, so a substitute represented her. Marriage, he said, was not the highlight of a woman's life, but having children was, for with each infant the kibbutz acquired another member.

They read agricultural journals to determine which crops were suited to their land, which still remained an enigma to them. They built a water tower and administration offices and two-story housing units and communal washrooms and tried to figure out a way of bringing power from a nearby hydroelectric plant.

One night, after there were riots in Tel Aviv and Jerusalem, a group of Arabs from a neighboring village attacked them. Someone was killed by a sniper. The Arabs were getting organized so the kibbutz put up a perimeter fence and watchtower and now every member had to do guard duty. Out of these home-guard defense units came the Haganah, David Ben-Gurion's righteous underground against the cruelty of British immigration policy. They felt they were fighting a war on three fronts: against the British, against the Arabs and against their original enemy, the mysterious, inhospitable soil that thwarted their attempts to grow things in it.

This was existence for them. Hardship. Endurance. In danger of one's life at every turn. Remote from the cities and remoter still from the centers of European civilization, from art and culture and refinement and fashion and hairdressing. Only a ruthless simplicity and an elemental engagement with survival, on top of which they built their hopes for the future: for themselves, but also for the Jewish race the world over, the age-old image of which was being dismantled on the spot, destroyed so that something entirely new could be created. The new Jew, but more than that—the new human being. A renewed human race out of the ashes of a catastrophically close-run thing with total extinction.

And now Meier was asking *me* if I wanted to share in their vision of a radiant tomorrow, when Palestine would show the world what a Jewish land could be, where the class system had been abolished and there were no kings or tsars or feudal barons. If I wanted to enlist in the enterprise of the new humanity they were building from the ground up, the Jew that Meier was himself, untainted by the contamination of Europe and its neuroses and abandoning the dark superstitions of religion, borrowing what he needed from the model of Soviet society, but leaving behind the central authority of its power structures, for here they were creating true people's socialism in action.

Who, in my situation, would not be seduced by the romance of what he had told me? Who could not fall in love with that age-old dream of equality and the collective life? Not me. I'll tell you who I was then: I was a girl without a past: my mother had dwelt in a twilight land between the tenses; my grandparents were unknown to me and where they had come from, apart from the name of the place (Latvia! two syllables, that's all), was also unknown; all of English history just a storybook. And so how could I not tell him—with all my heart and soul—that yes, a new Jew, indeed a new kind of human being, was *exactly* what I had always wanted to be?

And all this time I was noticing Meier. He was tough and thickset and he had little hair. The top of his head was brown, like his body. He wore old khaki shorts and a white singlet and leather sandals on his bare feet. The nails were like horn. Though he was just old enough to be my father I was sexually excited when I looked at him. He seemed powered, to me, by some internal electricity.

A GIRL called Leah taught me how to float, then swim in the waters of the lake. Gradually my body became more like hers. In the afternoon, I lay in the shallows while my skin gradually absorbed the sun. The sun was part of me, now. It lit up everything.

I was picking up more and more Hebrew. By the lake, one afternoon, a boy came and spoke to me. He asked if I wanted to go for a walk. We set off along the road and he told me how he had been born on this kibbutz, had known nothing else. His name was Gadi and this was chosen for him by the Names Committee. It meant Adam in Hebrew, which surprised me because I thought that Adam *was* Hebrew.

He had heard a saxophone on the radio and wanted more than anything else to play one himself, though he wasn't sure what it might look like. The kibbutz council agreed that if any member ever came across a saxophone and secured it for the general good of the whole community Gadi would have first priority in learning to make music from it. But no one had the slightest idea if there was such a thing in the whole of Palestine. Not, they thought, even in the palm-court orchestra that played in the ballrooms of the King David Hotel in Jerusalem. If a saxophone was to be found, it was bound to be in the possession of an American who was unlikely to want to part with it for anything other than a hefty price.

And this was Gadi's sorrow, at twenty, to have heard a sound that resonated somewhere inside him and for it to live only in his head, growing less clear, more invented, as the memory of it receded. "I'm a big dreamer," he said in English. He read weeks-old copies of the *Palestine Post* for practice. He wanted to see America for himself, one day. The British didn't interest him. "It's all up with those chaps," he said, "they're about to be bowled out and sent back to the pavilion."

I burst out laughing. "What a turn of phrase."

He looked at me, offended. He had overheard a British officer in a café in Tiberias use it during the war. "They were speaking of the Germans. It is not correct?"

By a banana plantation, in a cloud of flies, he kissed me. His lips were like rubber and there was too much tongue in my mouth.

"We'll do it here?" he asked me, indicating the ground.

What sex actually came down to was this: Gadi and I wrestled on the dry, dusty earth for a while and he unbuttoned first his shorts then my own, parted my legs and put something in me that was hard and quick, then wet and still. I looked at the sky and thought of my mother in her imitation silk nightgowns under her satin counterpane and inhaled the scent she puffed into her hair at dusk when the shops were shutting and Uncle Joe, stiffening inside his trousers in anticipation, was walking through the West End, down Shaftesbury Avenue, past the theaters and the rowdy gangs of soldiers and the statue of Eros.

We stood up and I noticed that a little of my blood was spilled upon the ground of Palestine and had fertilized the earth of the Jewish national home. And that was it.

"First time for you," Gadi said. "Good. There will be many more."

And we walked back to the dining hall while he talked of

Benny Goodman who played the clarinet in a style called swing and was a Jew.

"We have concerts here," Gadi said. "But all is Tchaikovsky and Beethoven and Mozart. Have you ever seen a dance called the lindy-hop?"

"Yes. I've done it."

"Show me sometime."

In the dining hall we joined his friends at a table. They talked about an Arab raid the previous month and they were remembering the time when they were children and an educated Arab from Damascus tried to join the kibbutz because he had read of the socialist ideals of the movement and had packed his bags at once and moved to Palestine.

"What happened to him?"

"He didn't fit in. We didn't trust him."

"Why not?"

"He was too *smooth*, always wanting to iron his clothes and brush his hair and looking in the mirror. Anyway, the kibbutz is a Jewish idea, for Jews. How could we know what his real intentions were?"

"What happened to him?"

"He went to Jerusalem."

"What does he do there?"

"He writes letters of complaint to us, pleading his case, asking to be admitted. It comes up time and time again at the meeting. Why can't he leave us alone?"

"What do you think will become of him?"

"I've no idea. He has legally changed his name to a Hebrew one. I suppose if he is really sincere, he might be useful as a spy."

Then Gadi left early to do his guard duty and I sat for a while longer, thinking of this man who belonged nowhere and was really no one, a sad case.

No one on the kibbutz could understand why the Arabs had turned against us for none of us really thought about the Arabs at all. They moved about as invisible men and women, they sank into the landscape like the hills and the water and the banana palms. They were a picturesque backdrop to our own industrious business. Where we acted, they just *were*. Meier told me that he was shocked by their backwardness when he first arrived from the Soviet Union where they had been electrifying the country and building factories and collectivizing farming.

"How to bring socialist ideas to these people? I used to ask myself this, but obviously it's a hopeless case," he said. "We forced the peasants in Russia into the twentieth century but we have no power to force the Arabs and they are a thousand times more primitive than the Russian peasantry. All their alliances are based not on the proper opposition between left and right but blood ties and age-old feuds, pride, shame. They have no unions or clubs or real political parties, no contemporary ideologies even in their most debased form. The masses are apathetic until roused to hysteria and then they collapse again into lethargy. They're the stuff of mobs not political organizations."

"What's to become of them?"

"If the British go and we rule benignly, then some of our ideas will rub off on them, they will be roused from their tribal loyalties to a modern consciousness. That, or they should leave. Surely they can find some kind of niche for themselves in these vast Arab lands that surround us? What cannot be tolerated is that they continue to attack us. And why? What have we done to them? We only took what we thought they didn't want. We offered them money for their land and they sold it to us, that is their absentee landlords did. We gave them a very good price, we didn't cheat them. It was them, not us who had let it all go to rack and ruin. I don't know how long they'd been here—centuries, I think—but look what *we* did in just twenty years. And why? Because of what we believe in, which is the future.

"What is a complete mystery to me is why the British take their side. Both of these peoples want us to leave. But go where? Back to the Soviet Union? They hate us there too. Why do you think we left? Listen, we're not like the British, we don't need an empire. Our people in the DP camps just need a place to go to and after what the world has done to us don't you think it owes us a country?"

We had these talks in the evenings, sitting under the dark shadow of the Golan hills, while the fireflies and moths wheeled around the light and the nights were still cool. We drank black tea and now I had received my little pocket money—the same for every member—I found the kibbutz shop and bought chocolate and I shared it with Meier. I wanted him to kiss me with his dry, parched lips but he had a wife and three children: a wife who, like him, had come from the Soviet Union and they shared a common past.

They had been members of a Zionist youth movement together, the Hashomer Hatzair, and they tried to remember with the same intensity the day when, at thirteen years of age, they had rushed into the streets when the Bolsheviks came to power and how their parents sat at home, their fathers praying, their mothers crying, and they knew that they must cut off the past as a woodsman eliminates the diseased branches of a tree with his axe.

I sat as near to Meier as I could. Sometimes our legs touched for a moment, like an electric shock. He turned his palms upward. Dirt was engraved in the grooves of his skin. I wanted to lick his hands. Where the physical and the intellectual come together there is always a chemistry and Meier was making sparks fly out of the dry air as he began a discourse about matters that had absorbed him for a decade or more, the old Jewish question of the nature of time and our place in it.

"But what was the present becomes the past and it is receding," he said, smoking cigarette after cigarette, the same ones which burned my throat and filled my lungs with corrosive smoke until eventually they turned to asbestos and like Meier I did not notice the pain anymore. "We find it harder and harder to regain the rapture we once felt. There are memories I have of my childhood and youth in Russia, from before the time of the revolution, which I keep safe in a strongroom of my mind, because I fear that if I think about them too much I will wear them out. I have memories of our earliest years in Palestine which have eroded and become not the thing itself, but only a memory of a memory. Sometimes, all I recapture is the mood I was in the last time I went into that portion of the past, or the place where I was, and what comes is the sound of the waves on the lake, or the road into the hills, or a café in Tiberias, where I was sitting with a glass of tea and a pastry when we go to buy the goods that soldiers sell us which they pilfer from the stores, the honest British Tommy."

And then he spoke of other memories which had been forgotten for so long that they emerged into the light like something he had read about in a book once, the creatures of the deepest ocean which the pressure of hauling them up to the surface distorts so badly that the fish bears no resemblance to what normally lived its whole life in the darkness.

"You see! We are a country that isn't even born yet, but we already have a past we are cut off from. Those of us who came from the Soviet Union can't return. What awaits us? Will the Central Committee have a band and a banner out to welcome us? Of course not, they'll murder us. And our children, who were not even born there? What rights will they have? So you see this has to be my country. Without it, I'm just a DP. I can't go home, like you can, when you have had enough."

"Believe me!" I cried. "I'll never go home." I was in the throes of a great, unrealized passion. I had been a glacial creature up to now, a lump of shapely flesh. Despite rather than because of the rudimentary tussle with Gadi which had technically ruptured my hymen, I was discovering a sensuality, a sexual self. I saw in Meier the figure who had always been missing from my life: the father and the stranger who had taken possession of my mother, as his successor would inevitably take possession of me.

He smiled. His teeth were quite bad. "You are a fine girl," he said, and despite the teeth I shuddered with pleasure. "But what concerns me, too, is how hard it is to remember who we were when we were in the Soviet Union. We live here, on this kibbutz, in the present and future tenses. I feel like a man without a history. A Jew without history! It's nonsense. It can't be. But that's what I feel like, it's the truth. I look at the kibbutz and I am *astonished* at what we have achieved. I compare us to the Arabs who haven't got a future, at least not unless they accept that they must cast in their lot with us and learn from us how to live a modern life and learn our language and our ways. We set out to build a new kind of Jew and we are succeeding beyond our wildest dreams and we should be happy for that, but sometimes I'm not so sure."

"I heard," I said, "that a boy came from Damascus who wanted to join the kibbutz but you wouldn't let him."

"Join the kibbutz? No. It's absurd. The kibbutz is for *Jews*, it's a Jewish idea, to show what Jews can do when left to our own devices. Anyway, how could we know that we could trust him? Who knows what his real motives were? Do *you* know? I don't."

"Couldn't you take him at his word and see how he got on?" I asked. Besides, the Syrian was educated, a university student, and it seemed to me that I was proud of the Jewish experiment in socialism and felt it should be showed off and even shared with anyone who cared to join and obey the rules *we* had set out.

"Listen," Meier said. "Be realistic. At worst he's a spy, at best a collaborator. Anyway, he's not the problem."

"What is the problem?"

"I don't know, it's thorny. Everything I see is a vindication of what we came here to do and yet I still wonder, what will become of us all? To be modern, we have to deny our past, that there *is* a past, and I don't know if you can tamper with time, like we are doing, without consequences. Do you understand anything I'm saying, Eve?"

"Yes," I said, but I did not. I understood nothing at all. If Meier wanted to talk, then by all means I would listen, or pretend to, but frankly all this was too philosophical for me and not just because I was in love at that moment with action. The only thing I was interested in Meier doing with his mouth was applying it to my breasts, not talking obscure nonsense.

He had Russian editions of the books he loved—Gogol and Dostoevsky—and he wanted me to read their English translations. What he needs, I thought, is the invigoration of a new generation. He's haunted by the old nightmares. I can drive those cobwebs away.

ONE evening the people of a bad dream were made flesh. They did not seem like people to me, but visitors from Hades, the mark of Hades on their wrists. They were the nearly drowned, literally. They had been picked up from a leaky ship that had sunk at the end of the previous year and they were the only survivors. They had been held for months in the detention camp at Atlit and promised in no uncertain terms that they would be deported back to where they had come from, which was a DP camp in Poland. Somehow, a hole had appeared in the perimeter fence at night and the next day, when the soldiers looked for them, they weren't there.

They had been smuggled to the kibbutz but the arrangement was not working. To start with, having spent many years in one camp or another, their sole aim in life was each to have his own room and his own everything else, and this in a miniature society set up to outlaw private property.

They despised the language classes. Each had learned a modicum of Hebrew in preparation for his bar mitzvah in Lodz or Vilna or wherever and then cast it aside as he got on with the business of living. They spoke Yiddish and Polish or Russian and whatever German they had picked up in the camps. After all they had been through it seemed an outrageous demand that they should be required to learn a tongue which had been discarded as a mark of antiquity, the gabbling mutter of the old men who prayed as they were led to the gas chamber instead of keeping their wits about them and looking carefully at the situation to see what tiny advantage could be snatched from it.

Then there was the business of rules. In the camps they had survived because they were good at playing the system and circumventing it to suit their own ends. The sense that rules were to be gotten around by some means or other was instinctive with them. They shirked their work duties, slept in, refused to share anything and were constantly arguing for a larger amount of pocket money to buy chocolate with, of which they were inordinately fond. Thefts began to occur. Small piles of hoarded items like shoes began to be found under their beds.

They spat when they heard what my nationality was. They had picked up some English from their captors. They were young men, graduates of a very different school of life from the one that I had attended.

"The British are anti-Semites," they said.

"That's not true," I told them, "not all, anyway."

"The Labour Party is anti-Semitic."

"No, it's not. They're socialists."

"Like the *National* Socialists."

Inside they were ash, burned out from within. They were receptacles for hatred and there was nothing I could say to them. Their families lay beneath the earth of Auschwitz or were incinerated into nothing. Or they drifted on the bottom of the Mediterranean Sea, fishes eating their flesh with tiny teeth or buried beneath a shoal of sand and shells. Meier said they reminded him of a whole tribe of Jonahs. They had been swallowed by the whale and survived its dark belly and miraculously they had been washed up on dry land. Still they stank of that vast, obscene darkness filled with half-digested flesh in which it was not natural for anything to live.

One day they all disappeared, transferred on a night when there was no moon to another kibbutz and I thought I should not see any of them again.

AFTER a while fragments of sentences started to appear in my mind in Hebrew. The names of the plants and the animals and the different kibbutz buildings were Hebrew now. I had forgotten their different equivalents and many of them I had never known at all. When I spoke in Hebrew I was not Evelyn Sert but Eve from the kibbutz and Evelyn lived inside me, my private self.

It was Evelyn who remembered, in English, an archipelago of wet brown leaves on the pavement on Tottenham Court Road one autumn morning, emerging from the lift at Goodge Street tube station, looking across the street at the windows of Heal's and at the backs of couples staring at sofas and cupboards. Or the Christmas lights decorating the façade of Selfridges before the war. Or the flames of the bonfire they lit on Primrose Hill on Guy Fawkes Day when we burned in effigy the Catholic traitor, the terrorist of his times. Or the smell of beeswax polish on the wooden floor of the assembly hall of my school. Or the small waves dashing their heads off on the gray shingle on the beach at Brighton on summer weekends, when my mother and I walked along the pier to see a music-hall turn. Or the smell of tram oil along Kingsway.

And all these memories were in the English language and

what I saw when I opened my eyes was in Hebrew, so how could I know what I was any more, when I felt just as much a composite character as I had at school where the blond girls with blond eyelashes felt like members of another race?

Something was starting in the country. When we gathered around the radio, on the news we heard that the Irgun underground had attacked the police station at Ramat Gan, escaping with British weapons but leaving behind one of their own wounded, whose name was Dov Gruner. The Lehi penetrated an encampment of the 6th Airborne Division in Tel Aviv and killed seven paratroopers in the car park. The day after, British troops went on the rampage in Netanya and Be'er Tuvya. A nighttime curfew was imposed on the cafés and restaurants of Tel Aviv. All this happened in the course of one week.

They talked about the political situation all the time, but it did not really affect our lives. We lived in a self-enclosed world with its own internal order. Some evenings, out of a need to escape, I would walk a little way along the road and then turn back again. I felt despondent when I realized how far I would have to walk to reach the nearest settlement that was not just another kibbutz.

Occasionally I looked at the babies in the communal kindergarten. There was a kind of controlled anarchy in there, like a Marx Brothers picture. They crawled about without any discernible regulation and made various colorful messes. I wished my own life were so free from regulation.

I had come to a place where life was stripped back to the basics, where survival was, if not the only point, the underlying system from which everything else flowed. Once there had been an original community of wanderers who had come together from the Soviet Union and had acted always through a sense of joy. But where was the joy now? It was no longer the dream of a collective life which seemed to urge them on, but the efficient maintenance of the collective life's conditions in order that crops were grown and buildings erected. And the happiness which saturated their early labors had seeped away with their sweat into the dry soil.

As I hosed down the urinals I longed for the city's friction, for its disorder and everything else that made things interesting. And *still* there was no sign of Meier wanting to have sex with me, a desire which had started to occupy almost all of my attention.

A group was putting together proposals to paint a mural on the side of the administration block, depicting the founding years of the settlement. There was no official rejection of art as an inappropriate activity for a kibbutznik, just an understanding that it came very low on the list of priorities for building the utopian life. There was one artist, but he was so embarrassed about being seen going out with an easel strapped to his back and a box of colors, that he preferred to paint indoors, depicting over and over again the same rectangle of scenery that lay more or less unchanging apart from the minor differences made by the seasons, outside his window. I had had no great urge to paint since I had been on the kibbutz. How could I paint the heat? I had no idea.

A mural, however, was considered to have a utilitarian function. It would act as a visual record, particularly useful for new arrivals who did not speak the language, and would motivate them to continue the same back-breaking labor as the original pioneers without which there would have been no housing units or kitchen or dining room or showers—those luxuries the latecomers like me seemed to take for granted. I was approached and asked if I would like to contribute, and with a paintbrush in my hand I was Evelyn again, even while sketching out scenes in which I showed Meier digging the foundations of our houses or addressing a meeting of the council.

"Do you like Meier?" Leah asked me.

"Of course not," I lied. "He's ancient."

"He likes young girls."

"What do you mean?"

"He has a young girl sometimes. His wife doesn't approve but she has to put up with it. It was discussed in a meeting last year but he defended himself. He says is it a bourgeois romantic illusion to believe that one person can fulfill everything for another person."

"What happens with these girls he has?"

"Just a little sex, a little talking. But the sex always comes before the talking."

"He talks to me."

"Well, if he hasn't wanted sex with you yet, he isn't going to. Maybe you're too old."

"I'm only twenty."

"Fira was seventeen when she had her time with him."

"Why does he do it?"

"He likes to remember what it was like to be young. He wants to be a young pioneer all over again, and not a man of forty-five with a wife who is also forty-five."

"How do you know all this?"

"Everyone knows. And anyway, it's perfectly clear if you understand psychology. I want to leave here soon and go to Jerusalem and study at the university."

"This isn't enough for you?"

"No."

"It's supposed to be utopia."

"Did Meier tell you that?"

"He said that was what they were building."

"He's such a romantic. He's an old-country type. It will be better here when people like Meier stand aside and let the next generation take over. Our parents are the most ideological people who have walked the earth. It's senseless. Pragmatism is the future."

"I've just arrived. I don't see what I could contribute."

"To be frank, I don't know either. I wonder what you're doing here in the first place. What's the point of someone like you on a kibbutz? When you dreamed of studying art in London and couldn't, was it your aim instead to spend the rest of your life washing floors and disinfecting urinals? You think it's hot now? Just wait. I sound unkind but I'm speaking the truth. You don't fit here and you never will. It's just a romantic dream you have."

"Where would I go?"

"To one of the cities. To Jerusalem or Tel Aviv."

"And what would I do there?"

"I don't know. Get a job. There are always things to do."

"What about you?"

"Absolutely I will leave. Maybe I'll come back, but only when I'm ready. I'm going to read Freud and Jung and Adler."

"Aren't they just more old-country types, like Meier?"

"It depends on the use you make of their ideas."

"How would you use them?"

"To understand how your enemy is thinking. To get inside their minds. In the long run, when we have our own country, we'll need everything a country has—an army, for example, and an intelligence service."

"Spies?"

"Yes. You would make a good spy, by the way, if you could do away with your sentimentality."

"What do you mean? What do you know about me?"

"You are a girl who feels herself divided and you don't like it. You want to be a whole person, to mend what you think are fractures in your personality and you seek to do it in this romantic dream of the radiant tomorrow. Why bother? Do you really want to be the new Jew that Meier and the others want to create, which is some fantasy from a poster about collectivization in the Soviet Union in the 1920s? We used to have a poster like that on the wall when I was growing up."

"My uncle had them too."

"Then you know what I mean. Men with big muscles and women with bodies not much different. Not a type of woman Meier is himself attracted to, of course. If we do have a new Jew he will be exactly what we want him to be and he will be dedicated to more than growing a bunch of bananas."

"How are you going to do that? Make the new Jew the way you want?"

"We have a library here. Have you been to it? At first it had one book. A Russian encyclopedia. You didn't just fall asleep when you opened it, the book itself was half asleep. Now we can vote for which books we wish to include and we order them. It takes months for them to arrive but they come in the end. I am the only person who is interested in psychology so if I am sparing, and don't request a book too often, I am unopposed. As a result, we have two books by an American called John B. Watson. From him I have learned that we can discard introspection. All behavior is determined. Behind every response lies a stimulus. You just have to find the stimulus. And by manipulating the stimulus you can alter the response so it's possible to do away with all neurosis such as sexual deviance which can be cured. It's interesting, isn't it?"

"Do you think it's possible," I said, "for there to be a new kind of woman?"

"What do you mean?"

"I don't know."

"Well, with the new science, anything is possible. We can be what we want."

Something occurred to me. "What if you like your neurosis? If you want to be a homosexual?"

"That isn't logical. Who would choose to be unhappy?" And it was true. The homosexuals who hung around in Soho did not seem to be happy though it was possible that this was because they always had the police breathing down their necks.

Talking to Leah was like looking through a sheet of glass.

Everything was crystal clear and I was exhilarated. She *was* the new kind of woman herself, the kind who thought with her brains, not her womb; who took no notice of hairstyles but wanted more than a life of rural servitude; who sized people up and recognized them for what they were; who knew what she wanted and how to get it; who did not live through men.

"But despite everything you say," I told her, "I still want to be a Jew in a Jewish land."

"What do you think a Jew is? Am I a Jew, for example?"

"Of course."

"How? I have no religion, just the same as you. The British call us Jews to distinguish us from the Arabs but when the British are gone, then who will we be? It is always other people who define what a Jew is. Whenever someone asks, what's a Jew, they're posing a slippery question. In Germany before the war there were Jews with blond hair and blue eyes. Who was saying they were Jews? Non-Jews. Did *they* think they were Jews? Maybe not. Maybe they would have been happy to forget about the whole thing. When we have our own state people will enter here as Jews but then we will remodel them and they will be turned into something else. They will be citizens of a country and that is an entirely different matter. Everyone knows what a citizen is. It's someone who holds or is entitled to a passport. And when that happens, all our troubles will be over."

Leah was right. I didn't belong there and I was bored. Apparently it was possible for utopia to induce ennui, which the books Uncle Joe gave me to read had never mentioned. Perhaps if I had been there at the inception of the kibbutz, in the days when women still shimmied with red scarves tied around their hips and the men had formed human pyramids and everyone had danced for the sheer delight of being alive, I could have subsumed my identity into its common purpose. In two weeks, I had six lovers to try to make Meier jealous, make him notice me, but that didn't work.

I lay on the ground as they pumped away on top of me, wondering why I was aroused when I thought of Meier on my own, but felt like a lump of meat when a young and thrusting sexual organ was actually inside me. I went through all that dreary boredom for him, the fumbling hands, the jerky spasms, the wetness sliding down into my shorts an hour later. My reward was for him to say, "You are very popular, I hear. Good. You're young. Enjoy yourself."

And that, I realized, seemed to be that. There was no future here for my search for the liberation of the spirit and there was no future in being attracted to Meier. And because I was only twenty and had not yet had my heart broken, I simply stopped being attracted. How easy it is to recover when you are young.

When I did, my thoughts turned away from the kibbutz and I began to wonder what lay beyond its fields and what the town was like on the other side of the lake.

I did not tell Meier I was leaving. I packed my Selfridge suitcase and arranged a lift with Gadi who was going to Haifa with a shopping list of items he wanted to try to buy from a certain British corporal who had set up a black-market shop in a hut on the Jaffa Road and usually had blankets, primus stoves, petrol, picks and shovels and fire extinguishers available, pilfered from stores.

Driving out of the kibbutz and skirting the perimeter of the lake towards Tiberias, the world I had known for the past six weeks dissolved into vapor, like Brigadoon. I regarded it if not as a false start, at least as an overture. It had not been a complete waste of time. I now had some command of Hebrew and was sexually experienced. I had a tan, which went well with my dark hair. Oddly, my breasts seemed to have grown a little, and my brassiere strained uncomfortably. I could feel the weight of them in my hands. I abandoned to the common storeroom the shorts and the shirts, glad to acquire femininity again.

In the hour before I finally left communal life, I put on a green dress, the color of the leaves on the trees in an English spring, and with a mouthful of pins began to address my attention to my hair.

S TANDING on the Jaffa Road in Haifa, waiting for Gadi to finish his negotiations over a spare tire for the truck before taking me to the bus station, I watched a motorbike pull up and a young man get off, hobbling slightly. He had a pencil mustache on his upper lip, wore khaki trousers and a khaki shirt under a leather jacket. Khaki was the uniform of the country, everyone wore it. His hair was glossy like patent leather. It sizzled in the sun and gave off a slight smell of palm oil. Gadi looked at the bike as if its chromium pipes might turn into a saxophone if he stared hard enough. The corporal looked at it too.

"Norton, isn't it? The Model 17H. I had the 16 myself before the war. Where did you get it?"

"All legit," the young man said. "It's a re-spray but the army sold off a job lot officially to civilians in Jerusalem a couple of months ago. Not that I'm a civilian. Some rank as you, as it goes. I'm waiting for my demob papers."

"It's tried and trusted, that bike," the corporal replied. "Nothing new, nothing unproven but it'll take a lot of abuse, from riders *and* mechanics." He was short and fair. Blond stubble rose up behind his neck and above his ears. When he moved, he carried with him a waft of fresh sweat.

"Do you know where I could find a saxophone?" Gadi interrupted.

"No idea, mate," the motorbike owner said.

"I saw one being played before the war," said the corporal. "In a club in the West End. Fantastic sound, that. You a jazz fan? I might be able to get you some records, at a price, if you're this way next week."

"Shit," screamed the motorbike man.

"What's the matter?"

"Ingrowing toenail. Hurts like hell if I push my foot too far down my toecap."

"You need to see a medic," the corporal suggested.

"I know."

"Try one of the Jewish docs. They're a clever lot, the Jews. No offense, mate. Miss." He dropped a couple of fingers on Gadi's shoulder for a moment, as if to show that he had no objection to touching another race.

"Is that what you reckon?" said the motorbike man.

"Oh yes, clever. If you need a patch-up, go to a Yid as your first port of call."

"I'll try that."

"Been out here long?"

"Four years."

"Four years too long, I'll bet."

"Yes, I lost my lot in '41. Joined up with the 8th. Didn't have a bad war, as it goes. All in one piece, at any rate."

"Bet you can't wait to get home."

"Too right. There's a pub in Bristol, they pull a pint there with a head on it like *clouds*. You could look at it for hours. Barmaid's nice, too. If you know what I mean by nice."

"Ladies present, mate. Now what are you after?"

"Petrol."

"Help yourself." He handed him an oil can and pointed to a drum beside the hut.

The bargaining with Gadi resumed. I stood in the dust and the heat, the smell of dry vegetation in my nostrils. Sand blew across the road. I looked around to see where the hut cast its shade. Gadi's English began to run into difficulties.

"Think I can help out with a spot of translation," the motorbike man said, raising his hand as if he were in school. I noticed dark gold hairs on his forearm, a couple of fingernails rimmed with dirt and a Timex watch with a steel bracelet strap around his wrist.

"Never bothered picking it up, myself," said the corporal. "I mean English is the language of the British Empire. They might as well learn our lingo if we're in charge." And he smiled brightly, all round. "No offense."

As far as I could make out, Gadi and the motorcyclist had begun to discuss the wear on the tire treads. Gadi looked at him.

"Your Hebrew is excellent. Where did you learn it so well?"

"In Eretz Israel," the motorbike man replied.

"I understand," Gadi said, but I did not.

Then he said in English, "Very good. Thank you for your help."

"Where to now?" the motorbike man said when money had exchanged hands and the tire and other items had been loaded onto the truck.

"I return to my kibbutz," Gadi said. "This lady is going to Tel Aviv."

"Want a lift?" He smiled, and his pencil mustache widened. The top teeth were very white and even, but one of the lower ones was crossed against the next.

"No, thank you."

"Yes. It's okay. Go with him," Gadi said.

"Unless you've any objection to riding pillion."

He was just the sort I had wanted to get away from when I came to Palestine. The banal Englishman who loved his pint of beer and his armful of compliant, female stuff. He was a bore.

"No, no objection, but I can take the bus."

"You speak very good English, miss," said the corporal. "Where did you learn it?"

"England," I said.

"He'll look after you," Gadi insisted, and picking up my suitcase walked with it to the motorbike. The corporal produced a piece of thin rope and my luggage was tied to the back.

"Hop on."

I didn't like being told what to do.

"I'll have you in Tel Aviv in a flash."

"All right," I said reluctantly, and lifted my leg over the back wheel.

"Tuck your skirt between your knees so you don't get oil on it."

I did what he said.

"Hold on tight. You can put your arms round my waist if you like."

"It will be more comfortable than you think," Gadi told me.

"Good-bye, Gadi."

"Good-bye, Eve. I liked knowing you." He came toward me, perhaps to plant another rubbery kiss on my mouth but I waved and then put my hands on my lap.

We took off suddenly, with a jerk, and I was pushed back by the force of our departure.

"Best to hang on to me, like I said."

I saw his point.

We took a road that ran along the shore. The sea and the beach were on our right and Mount Carmel on the left. Sand seemed to be everywhere. Between long stretches of orange trees and other greenery, the place became sandy in complexion, like the uniforms. The wind was running through my hair like a dry comb. My skin felt tight. Sand grazed my scalp. I was precarious, terrified and elated. I had never known before the lure of speed, of not caring if you hit a ditch and broke your bones.

After forty minutes or so we turned of toward Netanya. We drove toward the seashore and stopped outside a café. On the street, the air smelled of hot palm trees and their leaves rustled dryly above me. He went inside and he indicated a display of Viennese pastries. "Have a cup of tea. Have a cake. I've got to deliver something, won't be a mo." He walked off, empty-handed.

I ordered coffee and a tart with an almond on it, in basic Hebrew but was understood by a small, middle-aged man impeccably got up in waiter's attire, with a starched napkin over his arm. Outside, a street or two away, I could hear the waves boil onto the shore.

The coffee came with cream. I held a sip in my mouth. It felt heavy on my tongue after the watery stuff diluted with chicory that we drank on the kibbutz.

The motorbike man returned and sat down opposite me.

"I'll have the same," he said, pointing to what I had. "But double helpings of cream."

I didn't know his name. We hadn't been introduced.

"My name is Evelyn Sert," I told him.

"And mine is Levi Aharoni. But since your Hebrew isn't so good, and we're going to be talking in English, you can call me Johnny."

"But you're a British soldier."

"Not anymore. Demobbed last month."

I stared at him, but I could not assemble out of the components in front of me the face of a Jew. "You're a *British soldier.*"

"As you keep saying, I was. A Tommy. I am also Levi Aharoni, born in Jerusalem, 6 February 1923. Joined the British Army to fight fascism, 12 November 1940. In fact I'd have joined anyone's army, anyone who would have had me to kick the arses of those scum. Listen, I'll tell you what it was like back then." He leaned forward across the table. Palm oil was in my nose. "Palestine was full of scraps of armies from every nation that the Germans conquered. The Free French were here, the Free Poles, the Greeks, they were all hanging around in the

Negev and Monty put the 8th together out of all those leftovers. This pastry's nice. Fancy another?" I shook my head. I was too astounded to eat. "Think I will." He called the waiter. "More coffee?" he asked, gesturing at my empty cup.

"All right."

"Where was I? Oh, yes. I'd just joined up. I got attached to a British unit. I was at El Alamein in '42. Then over to wipe the Germans out in Tunisia in '43. Finally wound up on the Palermo landings in '44. I was fluent in English when I joined because my dad was a civilian clerk with the Mandate in Jerusalem and wore a tarboosh every day like all the native workers, as they so charmingly called him, until he retired and we moved to Tel Aviv because my mother likes to be by the sea. If I tell you that *his* father worked for the Turks, you'll see what a family of civil servants we are. We've been here forever. We weren't part of any Zionist *aliyah*. I don't know how we got here—maybe we never even left back in biblical times, though I think in fact we came from Spain via Sarajevo a couple of hundred years ago.

"Anyway, I spent five years with British soldiers—every waking moment. I ate with them, I slept in the bunks next to them, I showered with them. We played football, we drank beer, we talked about girls—excuse me, miss, but this is what soldiers do, all over the world, in every army—I did everything the British did and even when I had the chance I didn't join the Jewish Brigade. I liked my situation. I watched them all the time, the British, every minute. I can do any accent you like. You want Scottish? I can do it. Aberdeen? Glasgow? Edinburgh? I've got them all. Maybe I'm a natural mimic, I don't know. But I can do Bristol, Scouse, Geordie. Where you from?"

"London."

"But you know what? I've never set foot in the place. Never been to England. Seen pictures of course—Trafalgar Square, Piccadilly Circus, Buckingham Palace. But if you put me off the boat in Southampton, I'd be sunk. Wouldn't have a clue. Don't know how to find a railway station, or what a ticket costs or what it looks like. Don't know the lines on the underground or what bus goes where."

His voice began to slip into a kind of neutral gear. It was English, I suppose, but it had lost any sense of place or class. If I'd met him at home I'd have been at a loss to know where he was from. I think I would have known he was a foreigner, without being able to tell how I sensed this. He was an Englishman in translation.

"Why did you say I should call you Johnny?"

"That's what *they* always called me. Johnny the Jew. Jewboy at first, but they forgot about that in the end. I was one of them." He laughed.

"Would you like to see England one day?"

"Yes. But only on a passport issued by the Zionist state. Okay. Now you know everything about me, let's hear about you."

In the whole of the world there has only ever been one person with whom I have been completely honest, whom I never felt the need to lie to, to pretend. Always I have edited my life, leaving out whole sections, or changing or embroidering details. Who doesn't? Tell someone your life story and what you have is exactly that, a story. We cannot help this. You're not loading a video tape which will play back the past. You're not taking a section of it out of a filing cabinet. And remember, the Jews have been telling people our story for three thousand years. We've had practice. We know what it's like when the listener's eyes glaze over or narrow with doubt and you skip forward or miss out a portion when it's getting too convoluted. Do you think the Wedding Guest didn't fall asleep through parts of that story the Ancient Mariner told about the ship and the albatross? If you'd heard it from *him*, might it have been a different poem altogether? Shorter, probably, with romance and a happy ending. He was, after all, on his way to a wedding.

Let's face it, we're all compulsive liars in our way. And though Johnny would repeatedly lie to me in the months ahead, I was as honest as any of us knows how to be, with him. I told him the truth about my birth, about Uncle Joe, school, the office.

Johnny rested his chin on his hand and he was looking into my face, scanning it, his eyes moving from place to place: mouth, eyes, ear, chin, forehead, cheeks, nose. He shook his head now and then in sorrow or outrage, at some fresh detail.

"What a story." He was stirring the dregs of his coffee, gazing at me as if I were something more than I was, as if I were one of the drowned men, a survivor from Europe though I was nothing like that and my tale seemed to me quite unremarkable. But he leaned across the table and took my hand and held it in his for a moment. I looked at the hand as it held mine. It was a man's hand. The palm was dry. Under the smell of palm oil another scent was coming through, of gasoline and cheap soap, and it mingled together into the scent of something that no cosmetics company has ever captured in a bottle, what we used to call back then, sex appeal.

"You're a brave one coming here on your own," he said. "You must be a strong girl. Very strong. So what are your plans for Tel Aviv?"

"I don't know. I thought I'd find a room and a job of some kind."

"Finding a room will be tight. There's a big shortage of housing. What work are you after?"

"Again, I don't know. Anything where I could be of use."

"So you want to help out?"

"Yes."

"Make a contribution?"

"Yes."

Our eyes met. Sometimes a flash of complicity is established between two people, and you don't know why. Connections get made below the level of what you can understand. I understand it now. Looking at Johnny was like looking at myself in the mirror. Each of us existed as a reflecting surface.

W E drove through orange groves until we reached the white city, and it *was* white, then. One day I saw a photograph of a small crowd of men and women in old-fashioned dress standing in the middle of a dune, their footprints pocking the sand. Emptiness stretched all around them—nothing, as far as the eye could see, unless you turned to the south and there was Jaffa, where Andromeda was chained to the rock and Jonah set sail for Tarsus on the ill-fated journey that would see him swallowed by the whale.

The ancient city was overcrowded and the group of pioneers standing optimistically in the sand in 1909 were holding a founding ceremony for their new town which they would call Tel Aviv after a German utopian novel of the previous century. On the left, a woman stood apart holding a child in her arms. Perhaps it was crying and interrupting the momentous commemoration. I don't know what they were doing inside the circle. Laying a stone? Or perhaps just *saying* that they were founding a city was enough to make it happen. The bizarre thing was, it had. It was thirty-seven years ago, the picture. Ten years later, the women's skirts would be at their knees. The little baby, crying on the seashore for milk or comfort or because it was afraid of the sound of the waves or of the empty place it had been brought to, wasn't even old enough to be my mother or father now it had grown up. Plenty of people were older than the city.

We drove on. I had seen nothing like this before—how could I have done, as a citizen of an old country? It was an entire town without a past. All the side roads ran in straight lines, down to the sea, with three or four wide, tree-lined boulevards marching across them, from Jaffa in the south to where the city petered out in the north and became an Arab village.

At first, the houses seemed uncertain, vacillating between the old homelands and the new one. I saw a red-tiled roof. I saw green shutters. I saw the domes of the Orient. I saw a frieze of tile camels form a caravan, stepping above gables.

Then I saw apartment buildings of two or three or occasionally four stories, all white, dazzling white, and against them the red flowers of oleander bushes. Flat-roofed white boxes, I saw, though sometimes their corners curved voluptuously like a woman's hips and two buildings facing each other like this, on a corner, reminded me (and, it turned out, everyone else) of a pair of ship's prows sailing out into the dry waters of the street. They were houses like machines, built of concrete and glass, not houses at all, they were ideas. I saw walls erected not for privacy but as barriers against the blinding light; windows small and recessed, each with a balcony and each shaded by the shadow cast by the balcony above it; stairwells lit by portholes, reminding me that we were by the sea. Sometimes, if I turned my gaze up to the rooftop, I saw a kind of pergola of whitewashed, crisscross beams that served the purpose of casting a latticed shade and these pergolas were the single allowance made for a flight of fancy.

Though all of this was rushing past me at high speed and it was only later that the detail resolved itself into something I could examine and identify, I recognized at once that what I was looking at was something I had only seen in photographs—the inspiration of the pre-war German avant-garde which Hitler had destroyed and driven into exile to far-flung shores, like this one. The Bauhaus! The cleansing of the eye—the spirit in motion—that group which was a gun firing itself into the future—the properly trained modern mind which took the chaos of the city and its noisy, simultaneous events and imposed a strict order upon it.

If the *idea* behind the white city had been imported from Dessau, a cold, gray, snowy German place, in the hands of the Jewish émigrés who brought it here it seemed to live and breathe the climate and the atmosphere of the Mediterranean. There were not dozens of Bauhaus buildings, there were thousands. And if I didn't see a single masterpiece, it was because the entire fabric of the place was the International Style. They were not showcases but experiments in modern living like the cooperative housing on Ben Yehuda Street that I found out about later, where the workers had made a kibbutz in the city with kindergarten, communal kitchens, a cooperative shop—a whole parallel socialist economy.

I was in the newest place in the world, a town created for the new century by its political and artistic ideologues: the socialists and Zionists, the atheists and feminists who believed with a passion that it was the *bon ton* to be in the forefront of social progress and in a place where everything was new and everything was possible, including a kind of rebirth of the human spirit.

We were driving along a road lined with smart shops. Shoes and dresses and refrigerators flashed past. We reached the seashore. More white Bauhaus boxes and across from them the sand where deck chairs were lined up on the beach and men and women strolled and children played. When Johnny turned off the engine there was no breeze and I felt a merciless sun on my head.

"We're here," he said.

"Where?" I looked up and there was a bigger white concrete box in front of me.

"The Gat Rimon Hotel. They'll find you a room."

"I hadn't thought of staying in a hotel."

"Where did you think you'd stay?"

"I don't know."

Since I had come to Palestine one thing had happened after another and my well-being seemed to be taken care of. But I had my banker's draft safe and I considered the attractions of good towels and a comfortable bed and white sheets and someone to clean up after me and these bourgeois luxuries seemed extremely attractive after the spartan rigors of kibbutz life.

We walked into the lobby. From the bar I could hear British voices. "They come here to drink," Johnny said. "They've nothing better to do."

After I signed my name in the visitors' book, and demanded a *good* room, one with a sea view, Johnny asked me if I wanted to go out in a while for ice cream.

"Do you like ice cream?" he asked me.

"Everyone likes ice cream," I replied.

"I'll be in the bar," he said. "Come and meet me when you're ready. Wash, freshen up. Take your time."

Out of my window I saw the Mediterranean I had sailed across to reach the land of Palestine. I draw up a chair and sat, smoking a cigarette, thinking of the hotels at which we had stayed in Brighton, my mother and I, gray waves from a grayer sea foaming on a murky pebble beach. We always shared a room, the two of us, and did each other's hair and called out to each other when we walked along the corridor to the bathroom to bring a forgotten towel or soap or shampoo. We kissed each other good night before we went to sleep and she closed her eyes and was in the land of unconsciousness very quickly, perhaps dreaming of Uncle Joe and his hands on her body in the afternoons when

I was at school and she took an hour away from the salon to receive him, always soignée and perfumed.

But I would stay awake a little longer, thinking of pictures I would paint one day and of stories I had read in the newspaper or a comic program on the wireless or a play I had seen at the theater. And so the spool of thought would wind its way into sleep and sometimes I would dream about the lover I would have and always I pictured him as dark and handsome and certainly not an Englishman. Then in the mornings one of us would wake the other and open the curtains to see if the sky was blue or discolored with clouds, or if it rained or was sunny.

Now, in the Gat Rimon Hotel, I was alone to dream my future and there was no one to share my thoughts with. But I was so happy to have my own bed, with its framed picture above it of a biblical Jerusalem with camels and donkeys, my own washbasin and my own mahogany wardrobe in which I could hang my clothes. I missed my mother terribly at this moment, as the ash from my cigarette gathered into a long, gray frangible column and fell unheeded to the floor. But I had come to the place where there was, mercifully, no past and in which it was the duty and destiny of everyone to make the future, each for himself and for his country. My dear mother had belonged in the twilight, in a place where there is no temporal life at all, between the dead and the living, mute and without memory. Which the Christians at my school called Purgatory. Now she was in the past entirely.

Meanwhile, down in the lobby, I had a date with a good-looking man with a pencil mustache and an ingrowing toenail. So after a while I went to the bathroom and washed, did some things to my hair, put on a good dress and sprinkled a drop of perfume on my wrists.

Johnny was standing at the bar with a glass of whiskey in his hand. He appeared to be the life and soul of the party. The room was full of khaki shorts, which stopped at sore, red knees, hats pushed back from the hot foreheads of officers flushed with drink.

"Sorry, chaps, got to push off," Johnny said when he saw me. "Cheerio."

"I owe you a round, Captain Reynolds," a fish-eyed man said.

"Shan't forget," Johnny replied, "but as you can see, I've got urgent business to attend to."

"Yes, I do see."

They stood, watching our departure. "How did you convince them you were a captain?" I asked him.

"Oh," he said, gesturing vaguely back at the hotel. "They're easily misled once they've had a few drinks. I find it hard to stomach the stuff myself, I don't seem to have much tolerance for alcohol at all. More than a couple and I'm legless. Four and the next day I'm in bed with a blinding headache. But then again, that's my advantage over them, holding back gives me the edge. They're drunk and I'm sober."

"So they're that easy to fool?"

"Well that's what I find. They have been so far."

"What do you talk to them about?"

"This and that."

Outside we passed a group of off-duty British privates searching, without much success, for somewhere where lads of their rank could get drunk. They were boisterous and confident, pink, sandy-haired men behaving as if they owned the place when they looked, to my eyes at any rate, like aliens on the Mediterranean, belonging in another world altogether.

"Here mate," one of them said to Johnny. "Know where we could find a pub?"

"No chance," Johnny replied.

He was a short, sweating private with a broken nose. "Does the young lady know anywhere?"

"Sorry, no."

"I just thought she might, what with her being local."

"Can't help you there." The men walked off.

"What did he mean, me being local?"

"I suppose he mistook me for one of them and you for one of us. Which you are, of course."

"He didn't realize I was English?"

"Suppose not." The corporal selling knocked-off gear on the Jaffa Road had thought the same thing. "It's an easy mistake to make. Just look at yourself."

We drove along the shore, farther south, to where the city nearly ended and a dazzling circular building rose up from the sand to the wide sky so that sitting down at a table it seemed as if we were at sea, sailing west to Cyprus, water around us on three sides, and at our backs the white boxy buildings of Tel Aviv. A row of baby's prams was lined up in front and the young mothers sat in the afternoon heat drinking coffee and glasses of milk and eating cake while their children slept or cried. Everyone was having babies as quick as they could squeeze them out; plump little cushions with noses instead of buttons.

"I could just eat you up," a mother said, holding her infant close to her face.

"So many babies!" I said.

"The men are coming back from the Jewish Brigade and you can guess what they want to do. There's the results, right in front of you. And there's some more results of the war's end, over there. Look at them." He pointed to a middle-aged group sitting on the sand in jackets with ties knotted under their chins, perspiring in the heat.

"Who are they?"

"Old men, chaps in their forties who fled to Palestine straight from Europe before the war started and joined up at once. They've got nothing. No wives, nowhere to live, no jobs in their profession. They can barely speak our language. Didn't get any opportunity during the war. They weren't here, they were all over, but not usually here."

They stared out at the deep blue sea, their backs to the land that had saved them.

"They're aimless. They have nothing to do. They live in hostels. Used to be bankers and professors. Now, they're nobodies. With no routine, who the hell are they? *They* don't know. It's worst of all for the Germans. Instead of a heart, they have a clock."

He ordered a dish of ice cream for each of us. Apart from the depressing band on the beach, nothing could have been pleasanter than to sit with my new friend, watching the surf shimmying up the beach like a flapper's dress. I was turning my head back and forth along the wideness of the horizon stretching from north to south, pointing down to Egypt, pointing up to Lebanon.

"What a wonderful place," I said.

"You like it?"

"Yes, very much."

"Really? This is my city, Evelyn, and it's the city of all the Jewish people. We've been waiting a long time for Tel Aviv, many centuries. When I was a child we had a population of fifty thousand people. It was just a big village but a strange one, a village with two theaters, an opera house and a very large library. We were still covering up the sand and already we had a museum. And you know what is the best thing of all, what makes us the opposite of Yerushalayim?"

"What?"

"Nothing is sacred. Cigarette?" He passed the packet to me, smiling. They weren't the local kibbutz gaspers but English ones, Player's.

"Yes, please. I haven't had one of those in ages." He leaned over and lit it with a chromium lighter.

"We've got everything here," he said, proudly. "People say we're provincial but what's missing? The zoo has just taken delivery of two giraffes from the Sudan." I laughed, but I saw he was serious. "Did you enjoy the ice cream?"

"Yes. Very much."

I smiled at him, narrowing my eyes and looking under my lashes, a sexy look I'd picked up from the movies. He had a kind of healthy, glossy animal quality to him, in an open-necked shirt, his legs stretched out and crossed at the ankles and an animation about him, like a jumping jack. I looked at the black, oily hair, the eyes, like mine the color of plain chocolate, the mouth with its tiny flaw when he smiled and showed the crossed lower tooth. I liked a man with a mustache, in those days, very much so, in fact. And I found I liked his simple masculinity. He was a very *natural* man, easy with his body and in his clothes, the type who looks normal when naked, not vulnerable and ashamed.

I wondered who he might be if I had access to him in his own language, if the idioms of the soldiers he had knocked about with for the past few years were gone and I could hear him speak in his original—his own—tongue.

The heat was receding. The mothers were standing up and shaking crumbs from their dresses and wiping ice cream from their fingers and straightening the thin sheets that covered their babies. They walked off, a line of them in colored cotton dresses, pink and powder blue and primrose yellow and green like my own, a box of sugared dragées on slim calves and ankles, making toward Ha Yarkon Street which ran along the shore. We got up and followed them. We skirted a barking dog by the café's kitchen but it didn't frighten me because I wasn't alone. The sun was a red coin in the sky over the sea. The chimney of the power station at the end of the beach caught its light for a moment. The white walls of the houses gave out their own radiance.

JOHNNY took me back and wished me good luck and from this I gathered that he didn't want to make a date to see me again. I was surprised. I thought he liked me. We shook hands. I wanted to ask him everything: how I would find an apartment and a job and how I would make friends and what I could do to contribute to the establishment of the Zionist state. I wished I had asked him these things instead of imagining him undressed.

"Do you often drink here at the bar?" I asked him.

"Not unless I need to," he said.

"Will I see you again?"

"It's a small place, everyone bumps into everyone else eventually." And I watched him drive off along the street in the deteriorating light.

I unpacked my suitcase and hung my clothes on hangers. I rested on the bed for what I thought would be a few minutes, fell into a doze and then into a sound sleep. When I woke, it was ten o'clock, it was stifling hot and I was very hungry for I had had nothing but cake and ice cream since the early morning kibbutz breakfast. I groaned and perspired and scratched a heat rash on my skin. I looked at myself in the mirror. My face was red and shiny with sweat. My hair was a mess. A couple of flies banged into the walls.

The hotel's dining room was closed. They had nothing to offer me. In the bar British officers were still drinking and the fish-eyed man was dead drunk. I resolved to go out and see what food I could find for myself. On the street I could her the sound of gramophones playing scratchy polkas near the seashore and people sat outside cafés turning their damp faces to catch the breeze. Crowds were surging along the pavements, an unceasing flow of humanity. The holy language that Moses spoke was a neon advertisement flashing above their heads, a film poster, a newspaper headline, a signpost to an amusement park or the beach.

Cake seemed to be the principal sustenance of the inhabitants of Tel Aviv and Netanya. The cafés sold many kinds: gateaux with cream, like the Belgians made in Soho; tortes from Vienna made with glazes of apricot jam; cheesecakes from Poland and Russia; and tiny syrupy, flaky things, decorated with small green nuts. All these you could have at any time of the day or night in Tel Aviv and it was said that if the Messiah was ever to return to the Holy Land he would have to go to the cafés to deliver his message to the people.

I sat down next to a table full of Germans. The waiter seemed to think that they occupied too much space, morose and discontented as they were, demanding glasses of water and complaining about the quality of the one cup of coffee which they managed to make last most of the evening, refusing to have the cup cleared away in case they were required to purchase something else. I knew this type from Soho, where they were, to some extent, indulged by kind hearts. In Tel Aviv, however, they were not considered exotic or even strangers. They were the crowd.

They were arguing amongst themselves. Or rather what had begun, as far as I could make out, as an intellectual discussion in which the names of Attlee, Ben-Gurion, Kafka, Macbeth and Carl Jung were mentioned, seemed to have degenerated into a squabble, perhaps over money, for one of them threw his wallet onto the table and held it upside down to demonstrate its utter emptiness. He was a short, thin balding man in a blue worsted suit. His tie was stained and a smell of stale sweat came off him.

I was trying to inquire in my limited Hebrew whether there was anything savory to eat but the waiter spoke English and so we reverted to that. No, he said. I could have cheesecake. It was nourishing. I ordered a slice.

The man with the empty wallet leaned over and asked where I was from.

"I've just come from Galilee."

"No, no. The *country*. Where were you born, madam?"

"London."

His face lit up. He turned to the other men and spoke to them in German. Some smiled, some scowled. "May I join you for a moment?" I could see no polite means of refusing. "I welcome the opportunity to talk to a civilized individual. My friends bore me. Their company is incessant."

He wanted to know about the London theater and named particular actors and actresses whom he admired, mainly from before the war.

"I never was in London," he said, "but the culture is beyond dispute. They say that Tel Aviv is like a symphony. If it is we're still tuning up. I am surrounded by *Ostjuden*."

"Who?"

"Jews from the East. Poland. Russia. That sort of place. Very primitive people really, peasants or just a generation removed. Rural middlemen, or else slum dwellers in the cities." He held out his hands in a gesture I couldn't read because it wasn't English.

"My mother's family came from Latvia," I told him coldly. "So I am *Ostjuden*."

"Really?" He looked me up and down. "Then I'm surprised. You seem quite cultured."

"What was your profession in Germany?"

"I was a lawyer."

"Do you practice law here?"

"No." He sat up straight with his hands clasped in front of him on the table. His fingers had a number of nicks or small cuts on them. "The law I knew about—Weimar law—no longer exists."

"What do you do?"

He smiled, but it did not soften his face, it merely broke it up into irregular sections. "I mend fractured hearts, the shattered hearts of children."

"You're a doctor?"

"Of a sort. But not human flesh and blood. I stand in a back room in a street off the Allenby Road and repair dolls and when my work is done the little girls who come to pick up their toy, their friend, dry their tears for their doll is better. I do not smile quite as readily for they pay me a pittance."

And this was the fate of the educated Germans who came to Palestine. They thought they had found a road to freedom but it was a cul-de-sac. He told me about the other men at the table. "Bloomingfeld, here, a banker in Vienna but in his spare time he practiced a little conjuring for the entertainment of his children. Now he is Bloomingfeld, the King of the Magicians. He is a headline act in the music halls of Haifa. Gutsman has done the best of all of us. In Hamburg he imported furniture from France. Here he is a French polisher and in considerable demand." And so he went round the table cataloguing the little indignities of his friends, and if I learned anything during my time in Palestine it was that it is one thing to survive, quite another to survive intact, and this was the second lesson I was to receive in a class which had begun that evening on the kibbutz when I met the nearly drowned men and was surprised not to find them pleasant or polite or compassionate.

The man from the doll's hospital was named Herr Blum. He wanted to meet me for coffee the next day and talk to me of literature and art and music, but I fobbled him off with an excuse. I was sorry that they should have come undone, but they were creatures of the past and I was facing forward to the future. Also, I was worried that he might start touching me for money, and I had none to spare for him.

The Jews of Palestine called Blum and his friends Yekkes, which was the word for jacket because however hot it was they never stripped to their shirtsleeves. They formed a somber formal presence in the country and were badly out of place in the clear, unforgiving Mediterranean light but later I understood that the word was also a pun, an acronym of *Yehudi Kashe Havanah*—a Jew who has difficulty understanding. And indeed the Yekkes never did understand the country it was their fate to find their refuge in for if, by their names and by the racial calculations of the Nuremberg Laws, they were Jews, in their hearts and their minds they were Germans.

I noticed some gaudily dressed women lurking about and because I had grown up in Soho I knew exactly who and what they were and assumed that they were Arab girls because in the endeavor to build the new Jew from the ground up in our new home we would not, of course, be needing Jewish prostitutes.

"Why does everyone sit outdoors in cafés?" I asked.

"Because it is too hot to remain inside, of course. We sit by the sea trying to catch the breeze."

"It's not what I expected."

"What is not what you expected?"

"Palestine."

"Nothing is what anyone expects. *Especially* Palestine. That's life. Or life as I have found it. Where do you stay?"

"The Gat Rimon Hotel."

He leaned forward and there was a yellow glint in his eyes. "You have the money to pay for it?"

"I have some money, yes."

"Wouldn't you be more comfortable in an apartment?"

"Of course, but I don't have one and don't know how to find one."

"Would you like me to assist you?"

"Is that possible?"

"Certainly, though there will, of course, be an accommodation."

"You mean a fee?"

"Yes. A finder's fee."

"Which will be how much?"

"Twenty pounds."

"Absurd."

"Ten."

"Two."

"Five."

"It still seems exorbitant."

"Look behind you. What do you see? Many apartments. Which of these needs a tenant? Do you know? No, you don't. *I* know. The men are come back from the war. They get wives. They get children. They have to have a place to live. You think you are the only person to need an apartment? No, you are not. *Everyone* does. And I can find you one."

"Do you have a wife?"

"No. No wife. I had one, and children."

"Were they . . . ?"

"No. We divorced in 1936. She went to America with her sister and brother-in-law and my son and daughter. Why has the conversation taken this turn? Why do you ask such impertinent questions, miss?"

"Never mind. Please excuse me. What kind of an apartment is available? Where is it?"

"On Mapu Street, off Ha Yarkon, just behind us. Very nice. Only ten years old. All the modern conveniences."

"When can I view it?"

"Tomorrow morning, if you like."

"What will the rent be?"

"The rents are fixed by the District Committee. They are unalterable. However, you may wish to offer the owner a consideration of some kind. To be paid weekly. And a deposit."

"Why, if the rents are fixed?"

"You ask too many questions. I find you unduly inquisitive which is not attractive in a young girl. If you wish, I will meet you here tomorrow, at ten o'clock and we will visit the prospective apartment. Do you agree?"

"Yes. I agree."

I walked along beneath the dry rustle of palm leaves and the night air smelled of a dozen things I didn't know. I passed uncurtained windows where people sat, their dark heads bent over books. I looked up and saw windows like ribbons above the stairwells, emitting strips of tangerine light. Buildings stood on stilts, slim columns of concrete, and the gardens crept under them. Jewish cats yowled under a Jewish moon.

Y OU are late," Herr Blum said, when I arrived at the café the next morning.

I looked at my watch. "Only five minutes."

"Seven."

"Not all watches are the same," I replied, angrily. "They run slow or stop. It's not as if we have Big Ben to set them to."

"The country must learn to set its watches accurately and in synchronicity with each other. Otherwise we are . . ."

"We are?"

"Lost. Don't fiddle with yourself, miss."

"What was I doing?"

"Your hands are too active, keep them still." I was undoing a black button at the collar of my polka-dot dress because my neck was moist.

We walked a short distance and turned one block inland. The whiteness of the façades was so dazzling I would find that it would hurt my eyes to look upon my own front door in the middle of the day. Blum pushed open the door and we walked up three flights of stairs and he put the key to a lock.

"Now you are home," he said, gesturing with his hand and smiling at me, that smile with no humor or warmth.

I had four rooms and every one was completely square and

painted white and there were no cornices to soften the edges of things. There were no curtains at the windows, but gray metal venetian blinds. The place was sparsely furnished: a couple of wooden tables of different sizes and folding chairs. It was furniture ignorant of the existence of upholstery or the concept of comfort and ease and lounging about. On these chairs you would sit bolt upright, and pay attention to what was around you. They were chairs to command engagement with life.

There was a small kitchen and I was surprised to see that the cupboards seemed to be attached to the wall and to each other, all of a piece. A long counter running across them connected the sink and the cooker and there was a refrigerator. It was achingly up-to-the-minute, the last word in modern design.

"This is called a fitted kitchen," Blum said. "I read an article about it in the paper. It was thought up by German woman who emigrated to the Soviet Union and our architects who came from Germany imported the idea to Palestine. Whatever next, eh?"

"It's amazing," I said, running my hand across the Bakelite handles of the cupboards. I had a vision of myself cooking meals in this kitchen, perhaps even holding dinner parties. But I could not cook, just boiled eggs and cheese on toast.

The bathroom didn't have a bathtub, but a cubicle with a shower. In the bedroom, which was the same size as the sitting room, was a marital bed, and instead of a wardrobe a line of cupboards formed a continuous wall.

"A lot of space for one person," Blum said.

More space than I had ever known.

"And the wireless, which is a *luxury,* is included in the price. No telephone. There's a long waiting list. If you wish to send a message or receive one, you must inquire at the newspaper kiosk. They will accommodate you." I nodded. "So now we go to see the landlord."

We walked back down the stairs, which seemed more unkempt

and dirty than the apartment. The windows were smeared, dust gathered in the corners of the steps and the banisters were stained.

Blum opened the door of a ground-floor apartment and with one pace I left Palestine. A clock was ticking in its walnut case. Dark wood cast a pall of gloom on the white walls. Carved wooden chairs with high backs and maroon velvet upholstery were arranged like soldiers in lines around a table whose legs imitated the feet of lions. On the table was a brass bowl which held two bananas and an orange. Along one wall was a row of walnut glass-fronted bookcases and the spines of the volumes, in German and English, matched the uniform brownness of everything else. A chandelier strung with necklaces of crystal beads and drops hung from the ceiling, almost reaching the table as if it were made for taller rooms than this. Flies droned and even though it was still morning I felt hot and sleepy while beyond the window the sky stuck to its blueness and the sound of a loud gramophone drifted up from the seashore.

"Where is the landlord?" I asked Blum.

"I am the landlord. I am he. Blum."

"But you've tricked me."

"No. I am owner and middleman all in one."

"Don't think you can fool me," I cried, stepping toward him, a sandaled toe near his foot, fit to stamp. "I'm not paying you the finder's fee. And what about the consideration? Why do I have to pay that?"

"*Fräulein,* as the saying goes among my circle. I did not come here from conviction, I came here from Germany. Understand?" I nodded. "Good. Now understand also that I am not a socialist but a capitalist. The only way we were able to acquire Palestine was to buy it from the Arabs, meter by meter, stone by dusty stone with the money we raised from Jewish capitalists all over the world. I arrived in 1936 with my furniture and a sum of money. Not large, not substantial, but enough to ensure my future. I could not find work in my profession. I saw that there was a great influx of refugees all with somewhere needed to live and that I could exist comfortably on their rents. I paid for this building to be constructed. I even said yes to the architect when he wanted to put in that unfortunate kitchen. Just one, I said to him. As an experiment, to indulge an artist. But socialism is everywhere. It cannot be eradicated. The District Committee has brought in a law that protects the tenants by telling me what rent I can charge them. I cannot live on what they pay so I must labor with my hands fixing dolls, and I must tell you that no one in my family for four generations has fallen to a manual trade.

"I am not dexterous. I am clumsy. I am not neat and my eyesight is not the best. Dolls bore me as do puppets and other marionettes which are sometimes sent to me to fix. I don't like their dead, glassy eyes. I am full of neuroses. Birds' legs, for example, frighten me. And their beaks. All in all I am entirely unsuited to my work and I do not prosper in it. That is the answer to your question. Every pound you pay me on top of the absurdly inadequate rent is a few less dolls for me to repair. Yes, we will forget about the finder's fee but you can have this apartment only if you pay to me directly my additional consideration."

"That's immoral."

"Everything is immoral."

"It doesn't have to be."

"No, perhaps not." He smiled, with small pointed yellow teeth behind yellow lips. "But you can dream, if you wish. I have stopped. Each man must look to himself. And you, young lady, give the appearance of a degree of financial comfort. I don't ask how you acquired this. I don't ask what you are doing here. I don't ask anything about you at all. I ask only that you pay me a sum which you can conceivably afford. Besides, you will not be here long, you will be married before the year is out and I will have to find a new tenant. Perhaps you already have a fiancé?"

"No."

"Then we will try to find you one."

I was beaten. Here I had an apartment; beyond these doors I did not. I told him I would return to the hotel to collect my things and cash my banker's draft. He extended his hand to me to shake on the deal. He shook hands very firmly. His nails dug into my palms.

I walked back to the hotel, shuddering slightly when I thought of my own doll, Mathilda, falling into his hands. When I outgrew toys I gave her to Gabriella's little sister who had never had anything so nice and sat her on a shelf and worshipped her from afar, taking her down every three months to change her outfit, according to the seasons.

In the afternoon I returned to the apartment and was handed my keys in exchange for a folded pile of pounds. I climbed the stairs and let myself into my new home and sat on a folding chair and looked around me, enraptured by my wooden chairs and my streamlined kitchen.

Later, as the room grew hotter, I moved to the balcony. Along the street, on the corner, an Arab in a quaint tarboosh had set up a stall selling watermelons, big and red and juicy and cool they looked to me, tantalizingly cool. How odd that a fruit which was red—the color of heat and danger—should be sweet and watery and cold. I was disinclined to make my hot, weary way down the stairs to the street to buy my watermelon. I watched the Arab on the heat of the pavement with his guaranteed coolers and I wanted what he had and I didn't. I supposed he was watching us, the people who built on sand, and thinking that if he waited long enough, patiently, the sand would return to engulf us.

THAT night there was a curfew. Soldiers and police drove through the streets shouting orders through megaphones. I was hungry again, I was always hungry, in Palestine. I couldn't arrange any meals for myself, there was too much disorder. Things were out of control. I sat on the balcony giving myself a headache, smoking too many cigarettes. Across the street and along it, people were doing exactly the same thing: sitting on their balconies in the nighttime heat.

I was trying to think of what to do with my life, how to find work, and I considered my options. I could go to work for the Jewish Agency in some secretarial capacity but I had no secretarial skills. And I spoke only a kind of kibbutz Hebrew, enough to get by on, not to read documents and draft responses to them.

I could become a fighter in one of the Jewish undergrounds but I didn't know how to make contact with such a thing or what I would do if I joined up. I supposed that Johnny did something of this sort for Ben-Gurion's Haganah—going about with a bucket and paste after nightfall sticking up posters demanding free immigration and that the British should evacuate NOW, or organizing demonstrations or forming one of the bands of men and women who met the illegal immigrants on the beach and smuggled them past enemy lines. But in the absence of Johnny I was just an enthusiastic supporter, not an activist.

I could work for the British and spy on them because people kept telling me I would make a good spy but I had entered the country as a Christian tourist of the Holy Land and I did not know how to explain why I wanted to stay on. I was worried that they would start investigating me for security clearances and discover I had made lies like tissue paper that you could poke a finger through and that my time on the kibbutz would be uncovered.

My school would be contacted for references and they would say, "Ah, the Jewish girl, Evelyn Sert . . ." remembering my lack of enthusiasm for lacrosse on foggy mornings beneath leafless trees, rubbing my hands together for warmth, and my attempt to blow smoke rings with my frozen breath. My insolence and my contemptuous whispers when I thought my spinster teachers were stupid, those harmless Englishwomen wittering about gentle Jesus meek and mild and the milk of loving kindness while across the Channel all hell was breaking loose. Cretins. Appeasers, all of them. So not as harmless as they first appeared with their sagging, shapelessly happy faces.

The ashtray was full and my skirt was gray. My skin was crawling in the heat. My lungs felt lined with damp moss. Someone knocked on my door and I walked over to open it. My ankles were swollen. My heart was panting from the short exertion. On the other side was a delegation, a welcoming committee, holding coffee and tea, sugar and bags of oranges and tomatoes, slabs of white cheese and a cake decorated with macaroons. The tomatoes looked very red against the white walls and the oranges, very orange and I noticed that my brain was glad to receive some color in my monochrome modern home.

There was quite a crowd of them and they greeted me in a variety of languages. At the head of the visitation was a large, handsome, artificially blond woman near the age of fifty, with a head dressed in a mass of Edwardian curls, who entered my apartment in a stately manner reminiscent of Queen Mary on official business amongst the lower orders.

"I am Mrs. Kulp, of course," she said.

"How do you do."

"Delighted." She extended two fingers.

"Thank you for the food, I'm very glad of it."

"You're welcome. You have the apartment with the unfortunate kitchen, I see."

"I admire it. I like modern things."

She smiled a smile as artificial as the color of her hair and coming toward me planted a kiss on my cheek with breath that smelled not of Parma violets as I expected but boiled eggs, a sulfurous odor. Her skin was dosed with a perfume I knew very well, Guerlain's Shalimar.

"Shall I make coffee for you?"

"A pleasure." She waved the others away with her arm, speaking in two or three different tongues. "The others you will meet in time. I am the president of the residents' committee."

"How well organized."

"Our landlord is a swindler. A skinflint. We have to be on our guard."

"Of course."

"So you will join?"

"Absolutely."

"There is a fee, a small one, of course."

"What do you do with the money?"

"We put it aside to pay a lawyer to take Blum to court to make him maintain the building."

"Do you think you'll win?"

She waved her hand. "Oh, Blum will be defeated in time. No one can live long with so many enemies."

I made the coffee and cut slices of cake and we sat on the balcony exchanging polite inquiries about each other, trying not to move, not to exert ourselves and produce a blush of sweat on our skin, a gust of bad odor.

"How did you enter Palestine?" she asked me. I told her. "Then you are a clever girl," she replied, and put another forkful of cake into her mouth.

"Now my story may also be of interest to you."

"I'd love to hear it," I said, politely, though nothing could have been further from the truth. Everyone in Palestine had a tale of some kind and they were prepared to tell it to you at the drop of a hat. In a country with its face turned toward the future, our stories sat on our shoulders like a second head, facing the way we had come from. We were the tribe of Janus, if there is such a thing.

She was a Russian whose mother had been an assistant to one of the hairdressers at the court of the Romanovs and this well-placed lady had known *personally* (as her daughter would very frequently tell me) the Polish Jew Max Factor back in the days when he was make-up artist to the Imperial court, before he left for America and invented the cosmetics for the motion-picture industry. Mrs. Kulp was a refugee not so much from anti-Semitism as Bolshevism.

Setting off in 1925 on her own from the newly named Leningrad when she was around the same age as I was now, she had arrived in Hamburg and married the owner of a medium-sized department store which she revolutionized by opening a beauty salon inside it. By the thirties, her husband, more astute than she and predicting that he would shortly be spending more on the replacement of smashed windows than on stock, sold up and moved the family to Palestine where he immediately contracted tuberculosis from drinking infected milk. The disease spread through his lungs, forming cavities, and ate its way into the bronchi where, advancing through the system, it began to erode his blood vessels, causing him to spit crimson matter into his handkerchief. With rest, good food and nursing care he might have built up a resistance against the bacillus and eventually sealed it off.

"But, my husband, Mr. Kulp, did not rest. Not at all. He was determined to re-create what he had had before—a grand pan-jandrum, he called it, selling everything from socks to divan beds, on Allenby Street. The ice box in this very apartment was almost certainly purchased from my husband's store." As she told it, Kulp flogged himself to death trying to import luxury goods to sell to a market of British Mandate officials and the rising Tel Aviv bourgeoisie. His lungs became a mass of cheesy material. The bacilli spread to his kidneys and killed him, six years after he first set foot on Jewish soil.

Mrs. Kulp was left alone to fend for herself. Widowed, with a son who worked now as a trainee manager at the King David Hotel in Jerusalem, she set out to build a second life for herself as the owner of a hairdressing salon in the center of the city. She had an admirer among the crowd of hopeless German émigrés, who she suspected was only interested in her for her money, and she was probably right for if she had feminine charms, they were invisible to me.

Her feet were swollen in her shoes. I saw her grimace with pain. I knew what it meant to stand on your feet all day when you are past your prime of life. I saw my mother stand and she was younger than Mrs. Kulp.

Outside the curfew seemed to be over. The quiet was disturbed by engines revving and the amplification of soldiers' voices in the street. It was late but the heat hadn't lifted, would not lift until dawn and fresh breezes blew in from the sea and cooled my sweat-soaked sheets. Mrs. Kulp's perfume was in my throat and lungs, heavy and putrid. Apart from the boiled egg on the breath and the perfume, there was a chemical stink about her, exuding from her skin—it was the smell of hairdressing preparations but instead of making me want to vomit, it reminded me of my mother and of my past life and I wanted to walk across and rest my head in her ample sateen lap.

"What," she was asking me, "was your profession in England, Miss Sert?"

WHAT kind of hair is difficult to perm?" Mrs. Kulp asked, fanning herself with a copy of the *Palestine Post* that she had returned to her apartment to fetch for this purpose. I noticed she had surreptitiously half-eased off her shoes.

"Two kinds. First, hair that is dyed with compound henna containing copper salts. When it is waved the copper combines with the sulfur present in the hair to produce copper sulfate."

"Correct. Another kind?"

"Hair already bleached with hydrogen peroxide."

"Very good. When would you use a razor cut?"

"When you want a better taper on the points of the hair."

"And you would perform this kind of cut on dry hair?"

"Never. Always wet."

"Which is the most reliable brand of colorant for the hair?"

"Inecto. My mother traveled to Paris before the war and was very impressed by L'Oréal but they were virtually out of production during the Occupation."

"Name two types of popular cut."

"The Liberty cut and the Maria cut."

"True. Do you have the cold wave with you?"

"Yes. Here it is."

"I have never heard of this make. I use Toni."

"Yes. But it's almost impossible to obtain in Britain."

"Some products leave acid burns on the scalp."

"Yes, the inferior brands but we never had any problems with this one."

"Can you obtain any more?"

"I don't think so. I brought this for my personal use."

When, on a spring morning in London—the flat half-empty, and my mother's faded furniture already sent to the saleroom—I was packing my Selfridges suitcase, I spent a long time wondering whether or not I should find a place in it for my hairdressing paraphernalia: the combs and brushes and Sheffield steel scissors, which were as much a part of my cosmetic repertoire as my face powder, rouge and lipstick. I didn't know what kind of a life I was going to make for myself in Palestine but I didn't see why I shouldn't continue to cut and style my own hair. I knew how, and it saved the expense of paying someone else to perform what I could do more than adequately myself. Before the salon was sold I had used my keys to let myself in one night and went to the stockroom and removed as large a bottle as I could carry of what was then the most precious commodity in the world of coiffure—cold wave.

People think that hairdressing is a puerile, superficial art but if you don't know your chemistry you're in trouble, which is why my mother always read the *Hairdresser's Weekly Journal*, not just to keep up with the new trends but also to understand why she had the occasional failure with a certain technique. She would read these articles aloud to me, so I knew, as well as my times tables, that when you perform a perm the alteration in the structure of the hair is brought about by an electron reaction on the oxygen content. The old technique, the hot perm, where each curl was attached by a wire to a giant contraption suspended above the lady's head, involved an alkaline reaction produced by the evaporation of the chemical by heat. The British had undertaken the research for the cold perm but it was the

Americans who developed and popularized it. With the cold wave, it was an acid rather than alkaline reaction created by treating the curler with a chemical solution. You stopped the reaction by applying a neutralizing fluid.

When we went to war it became extremely difficult to get hold of cold wave; despite protests on behalf of the beleaguered women of Britain, starved of beauty, the government refused to make room for it on the convoy ships that brought essential supplies from America and Canada, and the chemicals involved in its production were diverted to the war effort. But there were certain individuals who by some means or other had acquired the formula and could obtain the ingredients on the black market. The brand my mother liked to use was Lustron but it was rationed and she sometimes obtained a supply from a company in Liverpool which manufactured it under the name of Barri. The owner was a Jew, as it happened, who came into my Uncle Joe's cigar store on business visits to London and on my mother's behalf Uncle Joe undertook certain transactions with him.

Before I left for Palestine I had packed the bottle of Barri cold wave, very carefully wrapped in plenty of brown paper. On the kibbutz it had been enough to wash my hair once a week with the shampoo I had also brought but any day now I would need to reperm my hair to restore some wave to it. My guess was that if cold wave was difficult to obtain in London it would be even more scarce in Tel Aviv, however modern the city was.

Perhaps hairdressing was a way out of my temporary inability to decide upon an occupation for myself, I thought, and it turned out that having a bottle of this precious commodity in my possession was the key to employment in a city where many people were jobless.

I was not qualified as a hairdresser. I did not have my indentures but Palestine was a practical country, more interested in what one could do than what certificates one had. From Mrs. Kulp's point of view, I was a young girl straight from London who knew all the up-to-the-minute styles. I could talk nicely to the customers. Did Mrs. Smith want to have her hair done by a middle-aged foreigner with a guttural accent? No. She would want someone she could talk to about the latest fashions, someone who could chat about film stars and the news from home. For they were strangers here. They felt their loneliness. The heat alone dispossessed them.

And Mrs. Kulp understood this exactly. Looking at me, she saw that in the future there would be considerably more sitting down behind her reception desk, marking up her appointments book, reminiscing about old times in the Imperial court of the tsars and holding forth about hairdressing and other forms of personal adornment. She confided that she had a supply from America of Helena Rubinstein cosmetics (another Polish Jew) which she sold to favored clients from behind the counter.

"I will give you a trial," she said. "Start tomorrow morning and see what you can do. If you are suitable, I will pay you for your time. If not, I will not ask for compensation for any damage you might do to my valued customers."

"That's reasonable," I said.

So in just a day I had found a flat and a job. Mrs. Kulp wasn't so bad. Warmth strove to find its way out of her into the world, as if through cracks in broken masonry. She was another survivor, like Blum. He said of her one day, in an unguarded moment, "She has built high walls to conceal the hunger of her heart: a good heart, a Jewish heart. She must have learned how to do this during her time in Germany."

The salon was on Shenkin Street, near the intersection with Allenby Road, the very acme of Palestinian elegance, such as it was. A few postwar Renaults were already cruising its length, driven by youngish men with carefully trimmed mustaches, wearing jazzy ties. It was provincial, but raffish. The shops displayed an excellent selection of ladies' costumes and the previous season's hats; there was no clothes rationing here. The cinemas played to capacity crowds. At night, if there was no curfew, the streets were thronged with people seeking pleasure and prostitutes hurrying down to the seashore to start their evening's work.

The salon smelled of exactly what all salons smell of, all over the world: peroxide and shampoo. White steam rose from the equipment which sterilizes the combs and brushes and fans spun furiously on the ceilings, trying to bring a breath of air to the hot faces of the hairdressers and the customers. They sat beneath their metal helmets, heads bristling with rollers like porcupines or curls held in place by pins, as scaly as anteaters, reading weeks-old copies of magazines from home.

They wanted an illusion, that they had stepped out of the piercing Middle Eastern sun, away from the land of the belligerent dispossessed into a coolish West End afternoon with tea and cakes at Fortnum and Mason to look forward to, before a bus home to prepare for the cocktail hour.

My first customer was Mrs. Paget-Knight. She wanted "something different." She had a thin face, pointed nose and a scrawny neck on which you could already detect the plucked chicken skin of advanced middle age. She wore her hair pinned up in a French pleat so her head resembled the blade of a kitchen knife. Here the rules of hairdressing and the basic art-school principles the commercial artists in the office had taught me came together: the composition had to be broadened, length minimized.

I parted her hair on the right, combed it flat to the head for a few inches, then established a double layer of curls on one side and a single layer on the other, creating an asymmetrical look. From the temples, it was swept up into a lower sheath of softer waves. The backs and sides I left to hang almost to her shoulders.

While I worked, she chattered way. She was going to a tea dance in Jerusalem in the afternoon. Her husband worked for the CID. She couldn't decide on a blue or a pink dress. Did I think that she was too old for pink? Her best friend, Mrs. Simmons, had said so, but was she just being catty? The children were at school, at home in England. She missed them, and worried about them when they wrote in their letters that they had colds or had hurt their knees but her husband said they must be toughened up. They had gone off without their beloved teddy bears. The youngest had cried bitterly and Mr. Paget-Knight had ruffled his curls and told him to be a man.

"How old is he?" I asked.

"Six," she said.

She was delighted when I held the mirror behind her head so she could see her reflection from the back and sides. I asked her if, next time, she might consider a preparation which would "bring out" the chestnut tones in her hair. She blushed but said she would like to make an appointment. She gave me a good tip.

As she was paying, she looked at me and said, "My dear, haven't I seen you somewhere before?"

"I don't think so," I said. I told her that I had just arrived in the country. I had had a whirlwind romance with a policeman on home leave in London, married him and arrived in Palestine just as he was, inconveniently, posted to Tiberias.

"Oh my dear, I'm so sorry. Perhaps my husband can do something. What's his name?"

"Jones," I said. "But please don't put yourself out on my behalf."

"You know you *are* familiar. You look a little like a girl who was on the ship with me when I came back in April after leave. She was a religious tourist. I didn't speak to her but I saw her on deck."

"How curious," I said.

"Well, quite incongruous things do look familiar. When we first arrived here, I thought it quite like parts of Hampshire. After a time, the impression wore off. I don't think it's a patch on Portugal. Too bare for my taste."

*   *   *

After the salon said good-bye to its last customer I bent over the sink and dyed my hair platinum blond. I shaved my eyebrows and penciled in a fine arc. I looked in the mirror and now I was Priscilla Jones. Mrs. Kulp was pleased with me. She was prepared to give me a position, starting the next day. Priscilla, Evelyn, they were just names. If I was to pass myself off as a non-Jew, this was all to the good. "The British like their own," she said. "They'll tell their friends about you. You will be good for business."

On my way home I walked past Mrs. Paget-Knight's house out of curiosity. In the garden, tall blue flowers that I now know to be lupins and small ones called anemones in various stained-glass colors were struggling to hold their own in the fierce heat. The path was scattered with parched rose petals and some kind of life must have gone on behind the pristine starched whiteness of the lace curtains that hung behind her windows. In Jerusalem, Mrs. Paget-Knight was doing the foxtrot and perhaps even the tango. She twirled about to the strains of a Jewish orchestra, her teacup refilled by Jewish waiters and on her side plate, tiny sandwiches cut in the kitchen by Jewish hands.

Then I caught the bus home but when I got there I discovered that my purse had been stolen by a pickpocket, which was surprising as I did not expect to find thievery in utopia or among the members of the new human race.

AFTER a while I discovered that there were two countries called Palestine. The Jewish Zion was a raw, strained immigrant society in which the middle classes struggled to keep their heads above water and the poor took life by the throat and throttled it half to death. From far away, the struggle of the Jews against the might of the British Empire had seemed to us in England, Uncle Joe and me, to be no less than David's battle against the giant Goliath or the resurrected Maccabeans opposing the Romans. Right was *obviously* on our side. But when you got close up you noticed the crooks as well as the heroes.

I hadn't expected that. People think that suffering ennobles, but they're wrong. They were Jews who were sullen or violent or depressed or conniving or lazy or untruthful or greedy. They were a catalogue of the seven deadly sins. One night, one of the many when there was a curfew and we sweated indoors deprived of the cafés and the cooling breeze of the seashore, the residents of the Florentin district were rounded up and taken in for questioning. When they were finally released back to their homes they found that they had been burgled. A bookkeeper in a poultry shop was shot in the head by thieves who took his empty wallet. Mysterious fires broke out in factories and shops. The slums of eastern Europe had been emptied of their gang-

sters and petty criminals. All the Jewish kings of all the Jewish
thieves had built new dominions in Palestine. A young man was
found dead, leaning against a sandy wall near the zoo, his hat
still on his head, a bullet in his chest. He had no identity papers
on him and went to the cemetery as a *galmud*—an unattached—
in an unmarked grave. Then the news reported that he had been
going around collecting money for the Irgun underground. He
was unknown to that organization and when they heard about
it, they shot him.

It was not difficult for a girl brought up in Soho to detect vice
and beggary when she saw it and it was all around me: in Tel
Aviv, the most modern city on earth, I recognized the little
pimps in their imitation silk shirts and loud ties with fake dia-
mond stick pins; I knew the prostitutes whose faces washed and
sponged of their nighttime make-up still revealed the kohl caked
in the fine lines around their eyes; I saw beggars sitting on the
ground, their hands outstretched, one of them wrapped in a
tallis, making out he was the prophet Elijah. I saw sallow faces
and dark ones and stained white robes. In the market I saw a
tailor with a tape measure around his neck and pins in his
mouth measuring up an Arab for the alteration of a pair of
trousers. I heard snatches of song rise for a moment or two
from the mouths of the stallholders in languages I could not
guess the meaning of, and piles of olives and unfamiliar
fruits and bunches of loofahs and bags of sweets and cheap
toys and dusters and facecloths and shoes and bunches of bananas and baskets of silvery onions and piles of flat, golden
bread. And everyone was pushing and jostling and arguing
and screaming at their children and a woman suckled her
baby where she stood.

I bought bread and fruit and meat and tea and coffee and
sugar, sometimes in Hebrew and sometimes by pointing. A
brawl broke out one time between an Arab and a Jew over the
price of something and because I did not want to see blood I

looked up to the thin strip of blue sky like the seam of a stocking above us.

I saw dusty alleys of crumbling houses and trees with leaves like feathers, bearing red flowers, and some kind of vegetation spilled out over walls with more red flowers of a different kind and I couldn't put a name to anything I had seen. In and out of these houses came beings I had never imagined existing: the men with beards on their chins but hairless on their lips, the women whose heads were covered entirely with scarves revealing not a single hair and around whose necks hung rows of beads and metal necklaces as if they were breastplates. Their earlobes were weighed down with more baubles and the place that they had come from was called Yemen which I was later to look up in an atlas of the world and find at the tip of Saudi Arabia. I guess that when the Jews were expelled from Jerusalem in the earliest times of the Diaspora some had turned east instead of west and lived nearly two thousand years cut off from the rest of us, people for whom the Bible lands were all there was or ever had been or, for all they knew, ever would be until the end of time.

I felt as if we were all half here and half somewhere else, deprived of our native languages, stumbling over an ugly ancient tongue. We knew that we were to be remade and reborn and we half did and half didn't want to be. We were caught up in a plan to socially engineer our souls and this was being carried out by men who seemed like the distant gods on Mount Olympus or Valhalla, the deities such as David Ben-Gurion and the others from the Jewish Agency who were smelting the Jewish future in which we would all be poured, like so many alloys in the melting pot of immigrant life, to emerge as molten, liquid, golden Jewish humanity.

The second Palestine was the one I lived in during the daytime, at the salon and sometimes on my day off and that was something else altogether, British Palestine, the rule of the Mandate.

As much as I felt that I belonged heart and soul to Zion, it was the British whose taste and idioms, language and dress, cooking and habits I knew and understood. The British were the only people who did not seem like foreigners to me, although they were the colonial, the oppressive power. They were the enemy and the paradox of my life was that the ways of the enemy were partly mine too. This state of affairs perplexed and troubled me when, with my platinum hair and penciled eyebrows, the soldiers on the street now never thought that I was anything but one of them.

One weekend I went to the beach with Mrs. Gibson, or Susan, as she told me to call her, who was my own age. She was the wife of a CID inspector at the police station on Levinsky Street, where he was more concerned with arson and burglary than terrorism. Palestine bored her stiff. She came into the salon for her weekly shampoo and set and studied all the latest women's magazines sent by her sister in Reigate, struggling to concoct tasty recipes from unfamiliar ingredients, trying new ways of applying eyeshadow and rouge, and running up her own frocks, fashioning the latest styles from Mayfair, on a Singer sewing machine she had shipped out when they arrived the previous year.

"It's hard to make friends," she told me. "I don't meet people and the English ladies here are missionaries and schoolteachers, terribly drab types. Norman and I are C of E, of course, but Norman says that just because we're in the Holy Land, we don't want religion rammed down our throats night and day. What about you, Priscilla?"

"I haven't been to church since I was christened," I said. "My mother didn't find our vicar very inspiring."

"Where did you grow up?"

"Lewisham."

"And your husband?"

"Lewisham, too."

"You must miss him."

"Yes. He's put in for leave."

"That will be nice."

"I know. I'm keeping my fingers crossed."

On the beach they sat on the sand like a school of fat pink fish. The Sheppards, the Boltons, the Mackintoshes, and Susan and her husband Norman, all policemen and their wives, second-raters who had passed the war directing traffic and catching Jewish con men, breaking up knife fights in Jaffa or issuing driving licenses. They insisted on a formality I had forgotten about since arriving in a country where codes of social conduct had been thrown out to make way for a new system of social relations.

We lay about in our bathing costumes absorbing the sun and taking turns to swig from bottles of lemonade. The women were quite nice to me. They thought it was a shame that I was so far from home, a young married without my husband. They promised that they would all patronize no one but Mrs. Kulp's when they had their hair done. "And Priscilla is awfully good!" Susan cried. "I doubt if you'll find better in all of Palestine. She trained on Regent Street, you know. Terribly grand."

Mrs. Bolton looked up and smiled with painted lips, a dark crimson no food or drink seemed to dislodge. She sat quietly reading a book, a detective novel. She was in her mid-thirties, a well-turned figure in a plain blue bathing suit and vermilion-lacquered, square-cut toe and finger nails.

"Any good?" I asked her, looking at the book over her shoulder.

"Dorothy Sayers. I'm quite a fan."

"Oh yes, I think I read one or two when I was at school. It's Lord Peter Wimsey, isn't it, her detective? And that rather clever girl who assists him." I missed books like these which came without a lecture.

"Read much?" Mrs. Bolton asked.

"Quite a bit."

And then we began a conversation about novels, which was pleasant to have with your toes curling in the sand and the smell of the beach in your nose, after you had just been through a long war.

Her husband was telling a joke involving a horse going into a pub. "And the barman says, 'Why the long face?' " We all collapsed laughing. It was stupid, of course, but sometimes silly things are the funniest. Then everyone chimed in with their own. They were puns, all terrible puns. A man goes into a pub and the peanuts on the bar tell him he's wearing a spiffing tie. It's because they're *complimentary,* the barman says. Good God! And yet we laughed harder and harder with each one. Susan's husband began doing dreadful impressions of war leaders. His Mussolini wasn't bad but other people on the beach began to turn around when he did Hitler. But it was so pleasant to relax. We were talking about the radio and the programs like *ITMA* which had kept us going throughout the war because one thing all of us knew was that if it's your darkest hour you hang on to your sense of humor if you possibly can help it.

I cannot think of many Jews of the then Palestine who would have laughed at the puerile humor of Norman's off-color jokes, but I did. They were the same jokes my mother and I heard when we went to see Max Miller at the London Palladium. What they were not were Jewish jokes. There wasn't a mote of darkness in them.

"Proper wartime humor," Susan said.

"You should have seen it *here* during the war," Sheppard replied.

"What was it like?" I asked him.

"A convalescent camp for Allied troops. Clubs all along the sea front, for officers and NCOs. Cafés. Teeming with soldiers, it was, and most of them British. You felt at home."

Norman said, "I'll never feel at home. This place has always been full of extremists. You only have to go halfway to Jerusalem and the landscape changes. Get into the Judean desert and you'll see where they got the raw material to stone people with. The whole country is a dump. There's no music, no night life apart from Third Programme type stuff, all those gloomy cellos."

"Too true," Sheppard added.

"I must say, it's not what I expected," said Mrs. Mackintosh, who had delicate, pale skin and could not understand why someone as blond as me should tan so easily. She sat, fully clothed, under a wide-brimmed hat, embroidering flowers on table napkins stretched over a wooden hoop, and smelling, to me, of lavender water and bread and butter. She had brought packets of seeds with her from England and went about surreptitiously scattering them over portions of waste ground so that Palestine would become a country of lupins and delphiniums and hollyhocks and pansies and marigolds and other familiar flowers of the cottage garden. "My father is a vicar and I grew up on the biblical stories but there's no oriental atmosphere and it's full of absolutely unscrupulous people. I find them gruesomely go-ahead. I've never been anywhere with so little charm."

"I was surprised too," said Susan, applying to her skin a dark brown oil which she had had sent over from London. It was supposed to promote the acceleration of a tan which she associated with a group of people she read about in her magazines who would become known, in a few years' time, as the jet set. "I thought that Arabs would sit on camels eating dates in flowing robes. It's nothing like that at all."

"But there *are* camels," said Mrs. Sheppard.

"Yes," said Norman. "They don't half smell."

"I don't think any of that is the point," said Mackintosh, smiling under a blond mustache, thick and clipped like a pale privet hedge. "What we like or don't is a matter of indifference. We're here to play our imperial role. That was what was instilled in me when I was at school, at any rate. We have a responsibility toward the colored races."

"Are the Jews colored?" I asked.

"They're certainly gaudy enough," his wife said. "Some of the woman on Allenby, they remind me of the overdressed types you see in London, on the Strand."

"Oh, Jews and Arabs, what's the difference between them?" asked Bolton, who had earlier told the joke about the horse. He was in the middle of a tricky investigation which had been going on for months involving a protection racket along Herzl Street and had been commended the previous year for cracking a complex fraud case involving the transfer of funds between various banks. The perpetrators had been convicted and sentenced but he suspected that the Haganah was at the bottom of it. The trouble was, he told us, no one would talk. He kept visiting them in prison, but they just smile at him and asked him if he would care to join them in a game of draughts. He told us about an Irgun terrorist under sentence of death. "Someone brought him a bottle of brandy and after three weeks he'd finished it. According to the Jews, that made him an unreliable alcoholic."

Everyone screamed with laughter. "The Jews," they cried, "the Jews!" Who could understand them?

"Don't mistake me," Bolton replied. "Jews, Arabs, in the end, they're all wogs. I don't care about either lot. I'm just here with a box of rules and my job is to get people to obey them. I don't make the rules. I don't care about them one way or another. I'm not a passionate man. I don't take sides. I've never seen a side worth taking."

Wogs. The word he used.

Yet the policemen and their wives asked polite questions and listened to the answers, without interruption. I understood how to behave with them. If they offered you a sandwich, I knew that it was customary to refuse the first time and then accept only when pressed, while amongst the Jews of Palestine, if you said no, you went hungry. It was relaxing never to have to wonder as I did when I was amongst my own kind, "What is going on? Why do they do things this way? Why do I, who am one of these people, not know how to be a Jew in a Jewish land?" With the English policemen and their wives I could be an Englishwoman. It was a disguise, of course, but wasn't it true that everything the English did was performed according to a code and what people said and what they thought were often two different things?

So there, on the beach, with the sandwiches, I was very comfortable. And yet, they sat next to me, these pleasant individuals swigging lemonade, and they were the enemy of everything I believed in.

"I grant you the Jews have been through hell but they never ask us what *we've* been through," Susan said, turning to me. "You know yourself, Priscilla, what the Blitz was like. But they don't care. It's all them, them, them."

"The Jewish problem," Mackintosh said, "is that they don't understand what is fundamental to our make-up: fair play. They see it as a weakness to be exploited. They have a ruthlessness we don't possess, not anymore, at any rate. You know what I long for? The Golden Age. Queen Elizabeth's time. We were bankrupt, we'd been invaded over and over again but we made something of ourselves. We were the lords of the world, back then. Now we're just doing out duty. But it's got to be done."

"The problem with the Jews," said Mrs. Sheppard, "is that they have a talent for rubbing people up the wrong way."

"I quite like some of the Arabs," said Norman. "They have lovely manners."

"At least they're not socialists," added Sheppard. "If there's one thing that really puts me off about Palestine it's that there are too many Russian Bolshevists. The place is swarming with them."

"What's the difference between here and back home?" asked Norman. "The government's nationalizing everything in sight. We'll be under the red flag before the year's out."

"Too true."

"Do you remember before the war," Susan asked, "when you could get that lovely seed cake at Lyon's Corner House?"

"Yes!" I cried, for indeed, I did remember it, could taste it in my mouth, the sponge melting on your tongue with real butter, the sharp, dusty sensation of seeds. And we began to talk about Alvar Lidell on the wireless, the sound of the big bands and cups of Ovaltine before bedtime, which reminded me of being tucked in by my mother who had closed the curtains against the sodium orange of the streetlights outside. I thought of a snowy late afternoon on Primrose Hill, the setting sun pink on the frozen ground, my hands in mittens and the velvet collar of my coat turned up while my mother struggled in galoshes along the steep, icy path.

"To get back to the Arabs," Mackintosh said, "their difficulty has always been lack of leadership and organization and this is where the Jews beat them hollow. At the end of the day, though, the land belongs to them and the Jews are interlopers, however it might serve our own national interests to have a European presence here. Our job is to keep each bunch from each other's throats. That's policy. But if you have to choose between them personally, I know which lot I prefer, the Arabs every time."

"Andrew has read Mr. Lawrence's book, *The Seven Pillars of Wisdom*," his wife told us.

"Yes. It's fine, very fine. I wish I'd been here in 1917 instead of at prep school when Lawrence marched behind General Allenby and we captured Jerusalem. That would have been a sight."

"As far as I'm concerned, they needn't have bothered," Bolton said, looking around for more beer.

"But don't you see the Arab virtues?" cried Mackintosh. "Their physical courage is beyond doubt, their pride in their traditions, their exquisite courtesy and their hospitality—my God! Just last January gone I had to go up to Jaffa during Ramadan when they aren't allowed to touch a morsel before sunset. Yet they invite you in and they order tea for you and the most elaborate display of cakes, and even though they aren't allowed to let a drop pass their lips they *insist* that you shouldn't go without. And they have a sense of honor which I'm afraid the Jews just don't share."

"Yes," said Mrs. Mackintosh, "they're so touchy. That they denied our Lord is a *fact,* it's in the Bible, but if you remind them of it, why they fly off the handle."

"Load of codswallop," Bolton said, "about the Arabs, I mean. I don't know where Lawrence got his ideas from, but it wasn't this lot. You find them picturesque? I don't. Their fawning makes my flesh crawl. All I can say about them it that they share a great dislike of any kind of work. They're lazy and unenterprising and if they do lose ground to the Jews it will be because of their own lack of effort. You can't accuse the Jews of that even if they're pretty unappealing in every other way, those fat-hipped women in particular."

Susan was bored and wanted to bathe. All of us except Bolton got up and walked toward the water, our feet sinking in the sand. We laughed and threw balls at each other while Mackintosh struck out toward the horizon and Bolton sat on the beach drinking beer, watching us and smiling, and watching the other people on the beach too, for he was a policeman through and through and felt that he was on duty all the time.

MRS. Kulp was becoming less interested in hairdressing and more obsessed by her battle with our landlord. She walked around the exterior of the building and looked for cracks in the concrete. She showed me places where the brilliant surface had begun to discolor and turn brown as if some toxin was eating away at it from the inside. She brushed away encrusted salt. There was no doubt that our brand-new home was in the early stages of deterioration. It was like a young child struck down with a terrible illness and Blum was doing nothing to arrest its decline. His life was spent either mending dolls or sitting in cafés eating cake.

Mrs. Kulp kept threatening to move to an even newer apartment, one of the kind built on columns so that the dust and heat from the street flowed under the house instead of rising up to its windows. Sometimes she spoke of leaving Tel Aviv altogether and transferring her business to Jerusalem where everything was made of stone and things remained cool indoors instead of the concrete city which all the day sucked the heat through its thin white walls until at night you could not breathe and everyone was driven out into the cafés.

"So why don't you?" I said, exasperated by her complaints.

Because, because . . . she had a clientele, she had an admirer and because she yearned for the respectability of a stable, rooted life. It embarrassed her to be a wandering Jew.

Up on the roof, where we did the washing and strung out our clothes to dry, I met Mrs. Linz, a sturdy, dark, curly-haired woman with short legs and powerful calves who was in her thirties and always knew best. She didn't pay much attention to how she looked, habitually wearing khaki shorts and a khaki shirt with old black plimsolls in summer, but I found her grumpily helpful.

"Not like that, like this," she said. "Not this place on the washing line, here is a better place. You bought from that store? You are mad. Go to this one, it's cheaper and better quality. I will write down the address. You want to know this? Why ask me? How should I know? My former husband, *he* knows. I will ask him on your behalf."

She lived in the apartment immediately below my own, had lived there since the day Blum first opened its doors, then with her husband and now on her own with her child, a boy of ten who trapped flies and pinned them down by their wings and tried to look at their eyes through a magnifying glass.

"The child is curious," she said. "The eye of a fly is what interests him and I will not interfere. He will be a scientist like his father."

"Where is he?"

"Not far. He waits for a visa to go to America. The child wishes to go to America too and he can if he chooses, but I will not go."

"Why not?"

"All Americans are conformists."

"I see."

"Like the Germans, who are so very, very boring."

"Though not in recent years."

"That is because of obedience. But they will be punished now."

"Yes, at Nuremberg."

"No. The trials are not punishment but revenge. They will see the fate that is in store for them when they find that they are no longer capable of producing great music and literature. I don't speak of art because I have no interest in painting. It makes me sick."

Mrs. Linz's apartment was decorated in the same style as those of all the intellectual or socialist immigrants of the previous decade: the tiled floors sluiced down with water every day, the walls entirely lined with books, the decorative copper bowls, the ugly German furniture and in her case, pinned to one wall, arms akimbo, a curious dress which had been collected from an Arab village by one of the volunteer assistants of Mrs. Violet Barber at the folk museum in Jerusalem.

Like all the Yekkes, she devoured literature. "I have always been a student of your great novelists and poets, Dickens and Thackeray and Tennyson of course, but also the moderns, James Joyce, W. B. Yeats, Oscar Wilde."

"Joyce, Yeats and Wilde are all Irish."

"Isn't it the same thing?"

"No, not really."

"I'm sure you will find, Miss Sert, that it is."

"I think I know the literature of my own country."

She waved her hand. "Ireland should be glad to be part of a nation which has produced such culture. They are writing in the English language, after all, instead of their own original barbaric tongue."

I told her about my six weeks on the kibbutz. "If ever Palestine will be remembered," she said, "it will be for the kibbutz, its greatest achievement, the only socialist experiment which had really worked. If the British go, there will be war with the Arabs, you can be quite sure of that, and I will take the child to the kibbutz, and leave him there for the duration."

"You won't stay with him?"

"No. I will return to Tel Aviv. Don't look shocked. The English evacuated their children to the countryside, to the farms during the war. It was reported in the papers. The kibbutz ideal doesn't appeal to me at all. I'm too much of an individualist."

"That was my problem," I told her.

"Listen," she said, after we had got to know each other better. "You and I are of a type. We are the kind who break the walls with our bare hands."

On curfew nights, we used to sit on her balcony fanning ourselves, while the child crawled around our feet inspecting ants, and she sewed and mended, and we wiped away the sweat. Down the street you could catch a glimpse of the sea in the fluorescence of moonlight.

"You have come too late," she advised me. "Oh, you should have been here in the beginning, in 1933, when *I* arrived, one month exactly after I saw the window of a Jewish shop smashed and I told my mother that I was leaving and would never set foot in Germany again while Hitler was alive and my uncle said that I may be a Jew but I should consider myself a German first. Because of the end he met I wish I had been proved wrong and he right but I *was* right. Only nineteen and already I knew better than the man who was supposed to be the head of my family, but you see my mind had been trained by political theory.

"The shock of my arrival! Nothing like Berlin but the atmosphere was absolutely *marvelous* for a young person, it was brotherly, everyone knew everyone, no one had any money. I had been in Berlin already an ardent feminist and socialist so to come here was like arriving in a great social experiment where we would begin all over again to make a new Berlin, a city for the masses and for the intellectuals, where we would build a modern life for ourselves. It was not just me, all of us who arrived, leaving behind a homeland somewhere else and finding this new, unfamiliar homeland, were making history in our way."

So young a city, and already it had a legend.

"Twice a week you went down to the harbor at Jaffa when the ships came in from Europe and looked to see if there were any acquaintances. We all expected it to be not a big city but at least a little Berlin. My God, it was more like a town in the Wild West that I had seen at the cinema. There was no anchorage and you had to be taken to land in this little boat. I remember I stood high on the railing and a huge Arab in a red tarboosh and strange trousers yelled at me in German, 'Jump, *meine Liebe.*' Then the Jewish Agency took me in a *diligence*—do you know what that is? No? It's a funny taxi for six people and one horse and this one stank to high heaven. We arrived at a new immigrants' home in Allenby Road which was a large hall with iron bedsteads and army blankets and there were a few people sitting at the end with contraptions made of fire and talking in a language I thought was not human. They were my first Yemenites.

"The conditions were terrible in those days, *terrible*, but I wrote home to my sister: 'Believe me, this place has a fabulous potential for becoming a truly socialist state because here there are no class distinctions—how can there be when there are no classes? So the only thing that must happen now is to stop the immigration so things can develop naturally.' Ha! What an idiot.

"But you know I couldn't find a job. I had no training for this country, I didn't even know the language. German, I knew. English I knew, *of course,* for the literature, the *marvelous* literature. But Hebrew was beyond everybody except the religious boys from the *yeshivot.*" She wrinkled her nose. "Those *Ostjuden.*"

"I have heard this expression before, Mrs. Linz," I said, "and I feel I must inform you that I am of those *Ostjuden.*"

"Then," she said, "we shall have to advance you to a higher level in life but it should not be too difficult. You are quite cultured already." I tried to interrupt her with an expression of outrage, but she pressed on.

"Anyway, I arrived in May 1933 and the first job you could

call a job was in 1937. Four years. Four years of hard labor, supporting myself by hook or by crook. I was a waitress, I was a maid, factory worker. And on Fridays I put on the one good thing I had to wear and went into Mina's where dinner cost the horrendous price of three piastres but there were four courses and at least I was in a pioneer city full of young workers, all in our teens and twenties. The streets belonged to us.

"At first my boyfriends were German. It was inevitable. They were the only people I could communicate with in my own language but I grew to dislike them intensely. They hated the light and they were always taking the bus to Jerusalem at every opportunity they could get to hide in its shadowy alleys and cool their blood amongst its cold and ancient stones. Some years it even snows in Jerusalem but it never snows in Tel Aviv. Have you been in Jerusalem?"

"No. Not yet." I had thought about it since arriving in Palestine. I thought of its golden dome and its fabulous past, the royal city of King David, and the extraordinary sights in a place so old and romantic. I pined too to see the desert, the River Jordan and the Judean hills and the extraordinary phenomenon of the salty wastes of the Dead Sea.

"Horrible town, Jerusalem," Mrs. Linz said. "Absolutely mired in the past. The German colony—not *our* Germans but the Christians who came here in the last century and were absolutely pro-Nazi and were expelled by the British—their neighborhood is planted with northern pine trees. Why? A monument to homesickness, of course. It is impossible to introduce anything modern for there is a law that every building must be constructed from Jerusalem stone, every one, without exception. So of course anyone interested in building with modern materials must come here. Anyway, Jerusalem is a British city, it is the headquarters of government and everything to do with government will always be stifling and conventional though do not mistake me for an anarchist.

"So one day, when I had learned a little Hebrew, I found myself a Yemenite boyfriend and he loved going to Jaffa to the cafés of the Arabs where he felt at home. He was very homesick for the Arab way of life and the European manner in which we were building Palestine was quite strange to him. Anyway, he took me with him. The music, the decorations, it was all so very alien to *me*. I was interested, but unlike him, I didn't want to get involved. We went to see a film at the Alhambra cinema, very posh it was. I sat for three hours and watched *The White Rose,* a very famous Egyptian film in which nothing happens except a man sings in—to my ears—a very terrible fashion. I thought, why can't they have modern houses and modern furniture? Tel Aviv was the absolute avant-garde of modernism. All our architects came from the Bauhaus, as you must know. We were building a European city and the Arabs were stuck in the Orient. But still, it was fascinating—the big palm trees, the smell of spices and flowers, beautiful, though not my sense of beauty. And in the middle of it all the Winter Gardens, a café which was a mixture of the Orient and Germany which my Yemenite boyfriend thought was very confusing. We were both Jews but what did we have in common? *Only* that we were Jews and what, I want to know, does that mean?

"I remember this street when there were only ten houses, and the water only came twice a week. You couldn't wash the dishes or take a shower. People used to come on excursions with picnics to see the new houses being built because it was so exciting to see Tel Aviv develop along the shoreline and everyone marveled at how our European architects worked so hard to bring Europe to the barbaric East. We didn't wait for the Zionist executive to draw up a plan. We just started. We *couldn't* wait. People came, they had nowhere to live, they built houses for themselves. We're the city of formerly homeless people. Oh, life was very hard then but it was *marvelous* for a young girl like me who wished to practice free love. Whatever you do, Evelyn, do not make my mistake and marry. I don't know why people think that happiness lies in sharing a bathroom.

"Now things are not nice. Not very nice at all. Do you know the ideas of Judah Magnes? He is for a bi-national state but the bloody Irgun and the Lehi are doing their best to spread hatred, *abominable* hatred. I have utter contempt for those people. A question, for you. If you knew of anyone who is a terrorist would you inform the British? I'm very divided. On the one hand, terrorism is anathema so you must do it. When it comes to killing people you have to stop and think first and that Etzel shower are anything but thinkers. On the other, how can you give up a Jew to those policemen who on the day of embarking for Palestine were indoctrinated by Mosley? Or to one of our civil servants who form part of the adoring public of Mr. T. E. Lawrence and believe anything connected with Arabs is absolutely *fabulous* and who are secretly disappointed when the people here who are so much superior to them in intellect are in fact the Jews? For you know we established from the very beginning a very high standard of intellectual life. I myself arrived here with a gramophone and records.

"Undoubtedly the terrorists will get what they want and when the British go we will see the frantic joy of the population and then we will be in constant fear of being attacked. There will be a terrible war and we may be defeated and if we are not, on the day that Palestine becomes an independent Jewish state, I will weep. I will have the national identity of a country I do not think should exist. But what is the alternative? Take the man who sells watermelons on the corner of our street. You have noticed him?"

"Yes. Of course."

"You have bought his watermelon?"

"Yes."

"Delicious cool things. He brings them every day from one of the Arab villages a few miles away. No more than three or four miles. He brings them on a camel. Did you know that?"

"No."

"He leaves the camel in Jaffa and he transfers the watermelons on a cart. Now the problem for us is this: we, the residents of Tel Aviv, are spearheading the twentieth century. We are the cream of pre-war Berlin society, we are what remains of the Wiemar Republic, in exile. We have here in our Jewish city some of the best-educated men and women in the world. We have scientists and historians and musicians and lawyers and doctors, everything. The Arab on the street is simply an illiterate man who knows how to sell watermelons. Can an industrious, well-organized minority who are the receptacle of all the most advanced ideas of the modern age be governed and dominated by a majority so patently inferior to us in energy and education and administrative experience? Can we be governed by feudalism and blind devotion to religion and tribes and sects and blood feuds? No. Impossible. Such an arrangement could never work. Our misfortune is that *we* must rule *them* because we are modern."

"Perhaps," I said, "we can send Gropius to see if he can redesign their tents." We both laughed.

"But no," she continued. "It is not comic. It's a tragedy."

"Where is the rest of your family?" I asked her.

"Gassed," she told me. "My mother and my redheaded uncle and my redheaded cousins."

"Why didn't they come here?"

"They did come, for a visit in 1937, but they abhorred the socialism and the disorder. They preferred England and it is true the English are civilized, come what may. They went back to Berlin to arrange their affairs and they never got out."

Mrs. Linz was employed as a stenographer in a large office. Sometimes we took the bus to work together and sometimes we went afterward for a coffee at the Noga café where the intellectuals met and there was dancing at weekends. I saw all the art I could find in Palestine. It was curious stuff, the painters influenced by a Paris training and they depicted the white city in murky colors with stark leafless trees, as if it were an overcast November day in the Bois de Boulogne.

But there was an abstract painter who sometimes came to the Noga and spoke of the vibrancy of the sky and the air in motion, of the local light and the essence of the expanse. It was the soul of matter, form and content that he was trying to express, he said. "The atmosphere is the substance," he told me. "The posture is sometimes the soul." And I nodded and sipped my coffee, not understanding.

In the evenings, the child would crawl around in the garden getting his clothes dirty. He was a solitary presence in our building where everyone had come from somewhere else. The palm trees and orange trees and bougainvillea and the torrid, steamy summer heat and the British shouting at us through megaphones were what was real for him. He reminded me of myself at that age. He was a child without grandparents or other relations and the little society on Mapu, full of immigrants and strangers, was all the world he knew.

ONE lunchtime a few British officers were abducted by the Irgun from their club at the Yarkon Hotel. The streets were flooded with security forces, sweating troops tearing up the pavements and barricading them with sandbags. On my way to the salon, I passed Bren gun nests at Mogen David Square and there were constant cordon and search operations. The kidnappings accelerated. The city was out of bounds to all ranks, and the soldiers in their red berets whom we mockingly called the anemones were armed and went around in pairs like nervous couples. The railway tracks were blown up, trains were dynamited. One drama followed another. There was no relaxation. The policemen's wives whose hair I shampooed and set complained that they hardly saw their husbands anymore, they were busy till all hours rounding people up and interrogating them.

In the apartment building, everyone grew hot and quarrelsome as the curfew dragged on. Mrs. Linz missed her concerts. Mrs. Kulp missed the cinema. Blum missed sitting with his cronies, eating cake. I missed having the life of a normal young person, free to go to parties and other entertainments where I could meet young men.

But our country continued its march of progress. They laid

the cornerstone for a new scientific institute in Rehovot. The scientists were planning to plant castor trees in the Negev because they grew anywhere and from their fruit you could extract products which could be turned into nylon. And if you had nylon you could make anything, from women's stockings to mosquito nets. They were going to try out machines that would turn salt water into fresh and invent devices which would make electricity for blocks of flats by exploiting the difference in temperature between the basement and the attic. They were going to grow grapefruit and oranges as big as footballs and pipless giant tangerines. They were going to build an electronic brain.

"If the child stays in Palestine he will definitely work there one day," said Mrs. Linz who had taken him to watch the inauguration of the institute. "This is our future, you know, pioneer industries, plastics, everything up to date."

"Like magic."

"Yes, magic but on an industrial scale."

The child was learning to take his own pulse with his mother's wristwatch. We looked at him, admiringly. "The new Jew," I said.

A couple of weeks after their abduction, at the beginning of July, the three captains kidnapped from the officers' club were dumped in the middle of the street, groggy with chloroform. Each had been given a pound note to cover the wear and tear to his uniform.

One afternoon, I passed Johnny sitting in a café on Ben Yehuda Street, looking terrible. It was the first time I had seen him since he dropped me off at the hotel and wished me luck. He barely looked up when I approached his table.

"Do you remember me?" I asked.

"Yes, yes, of course. Even with the blond hair. It suits you. Very glamorous." He mashed the remains of his cake with his fork. "How are you getting on?"

"Very well. I have an apartment and a job. I thought I'd have run into you before now." I was wearing a blue dress and white high heels and I had no need to worry if my seams were straight for my legs were brown and I didn't need stockings.

"Yes. Well, I've been a bit busy."

"With what?"

"Oh, this and that." He pushed the plate away.

"Were you arrested at all?"

"Me? No. I've got some fake British papers."

"How did you get them?"

"Ask me no questions and I'll tell you no lies." He grimaced at his coffee. His hair was not sleeked back with palm oil and his shirt was soiled and creased.

"What's up?" I asked him.

"What's up? Don't you know? No, I suppose you wouldn't. How could you?" He stared miserably out of the window. "I still can't believe it. It's just . . ." He began to speak in Hebrew, a long, low, angry mutter. He lit a cigarette without offering me one. I took one from my own packet, on the table. He looked at it. "Sorry," he said, dully. "I have no manners today."

"Something has happened. Can you tell me?"

"If the words don't turn to ash in my mouth."

I considered that he might be in fear of being arrested for black-market offenses. I looked around to see if there were any policemen in the café and saw one.

"There's a cop here," I said, whispering. "Should you go?"

He looked up. "Why do you think that?"

"I don't know. I thought you might be in trouble with the police."

"Well, I'm not, though there has been a catastrophe. An absolute disaster."

I was trying to think of what might have happened. "Has an immigrant ship sunk? Someone you know been killed?"

"No, no, nothing like that. That would . . . Well, never mind.

It's this: my team, Tel Aviv Betar, has been eliminated in the first round of the tournament. And at home, too. And we, *we* are supposed to be the cup specialists. We won in '40 and '42. Now we're out for the count and to Ness Ziona. If Yalovsky gets back from the Jewish Brigade in time, my God, they're going to win the whole thing. It's a tragedy."

After a bit, the penny dropped. I said, "Is this football you're talking about?"

"Of course it's football. I've supported Betar since I was old enough to go to matches. They're my brothers. In fact my brother Yasaf plays for them, in defense. Now, nothing. Nothing to look forward to. We're out, finished. I can't believe it." He shook his head.

I stared at him. "I don't understand why this is important. It's only a game."

"No it isn't."

"Why does football matter to you?"

"It's our national sport. I love all sports. I like boxing—Joe Louis, what a contender! I like tennis and golf, everything. If I ever went to London do you know what I'd do? I'd go and see Arsenal play. That's the other team I support. I read in the paper that they'll be going back to their stadium this season. It was requisitioned for something during the war, I can't remember what. Arsenal at home. That would be something."

"But *why?* Why should you care about people who live a thousand miles away?"

"Because," he said, "a man must have a cause to follow."

"What about the creation of the Zionist state?"

"That's different. Football is about dreams. The Zionist homeland is gong to happen. It's inevitable. The British *will* go. We can get them out, it's only a matter of time, but whether Betar or Arsenal will win the cup this season—that's not a certain outcome and it's not dependent on my own actions."

"I see," I said, but I didn't and I never would.

After a long silence, he looked up. "Well, enough of my miseries. Are you free? Would you like to do something?"

"I don't know," I said, sullenly. He had asked me nothing about myself.

"Listen, let's hop on the bike and go for a spin."

"All right," I said, but only because despite his disheveled appearance, or perhaps because of it, he seemed very handsome and women are affected by that kind of thing, such superficialities.

I had noticed, by now, that something was missing. "Where's your mustache?"

"Gone, for the moment. It comes and goes."

"Why?"

"According to whether I need it or not."

"I don't understand."

"Never mind. You don't need to."

His mood had lightened, a little. We walked down into the street and I got on the bike and we rode through the city, my hair streaming. We drove along the shore past Jaffa through sand dunes and Johnny pointed out the spots where new towns would one day be built on the site of Philistine ones: Ashdod, Ashkelon, their names were. Further on was Gaza and then the border with Egypt but we did not go that far. We turned back and flew through Palestine under starry skies and came home to my flat.

"Hey, nice place," he said, looking around. "How did you find it?"

"I met the landlord in a café."

"Good landlord?"

"Not really."

"Someone should sort him out for you."

"Oh, I don't know, he has his own troubles."

"Doesn't everyone?"

"I have no real worries of my own."

"You're lucky then."

He wanted a cold drink and I poured some lemonade. We sat

on the balcony and listened to the interminable sounds of gramophones and dance bands rising from the cafés on the seashore, coiling their way up my street. Polkas, foxtrots, waltzes, grinding out through the cheap instruments of second-rate orchestras.

"Things sound as if they're getting rowdy at the Scopus Club," Johnny said. "So, Evelyn, what have you been up to since I last saw you?"

I told him about Mrs. Kulp and the salon and why I had dyed my hair. I introduced him to my imaginary husband in Tiberias and explained about my false name. I described Susan and our picnics on the beach and her friends, the inspectors from the various police stations.

"They sound like a right shower," Johnny said, puffing on a Player's.

"You're used to Englishmen."

"True. But we never talked politics. You realize the police are anti-Semitic?"

"I don't much like them but it's nice to feel at home from time to time."

"Home?"

"What did I say?"

"Home. This is your home, now."

"It is. But I suppose if you've lived somewhere all your life, it's bound to rub off. The Germans here, you'd think that Germany would be the last place they think of as home . . ."

"But they can't stop going on about how bloody wonderful Berlin was. Don't I know it."

"Meier on the kibbutz said that people can't live without the past."

"Bollocks. The future, Evelyn. Keep your eyes fixed on the future and you won't go far wrong. If you're walking down the street which direction do you look in? Where you're going, of course. And if you walk backwards? You get run over."

"That's true. But do you never think about the war?"

"No. Why should I? It's over. Finished. That part of my life is done."

"By the way, what do you do for a living, Johnny?"

"Me? I'm a tailor."

Before he left he kissed me tenderly on the cheek and asked if he could come again to see me the following day. Perhaps we'd go to a film, now the picture houses were open again.

He's a very simple man, I thought. He's like a Bauhaus building, straightforward.

I MET him at eight in a café at the junction of Allenby Road and Rehov Ben Yehuda, just before Allenby took a sharp turn down to the beach. Outside, a small chamber orchestra sat on folding chairs on the pavement playing Mozart and Strauss waltzes. It was composed of four men in suits and ties and a woman in an antique black cocktail dress from before the war, cut on the bias. Their faces, bent over their instruments, dripped with sweat. One of the violinists stroked the wood of his instrument between pieces, as if he was afraid it would buckle beneath his fingers in the heat. Johnny was inside, under a noisy electric fan, eating apple strudel.

"Who are they?"

"From Budapest. They were with the symphony orchestra. You know what they used to say ten years ago? Anyone who arrived off the boat without a violin case was presumed to be a pianist. Here, I've got something for you." He passed an envelope to me under the table. "Don't look now."

"What is it?"

"A passport."

"I've got a passport."

"Yes. In your own name. This one is made out to Priscilla Jones. You might need it."

"Where the hell did you get that?"

"Connections. Get a photograph taken and stick it in. What film do you want to see? I prefer action pictures. Is there anything on like that?"

He didn't want me to ask too many questions. Okay. In England I might have dismissed him as a spiv but here, in Palestine, under British occupation, as far as I was concerned he was a hero. A *Jewish* hero and how many do we have of those? How many tough guys have there ever been to look up to? A few fish with sharp teeth swimming in an ocean of vegetable life—old men with beards, bent over their books.

I looked at the films listed in the paper, as the quintet entered, for the third time, the Vienna Woods. It was all just sentimental love stories so we settled for *The Picture of Dorian Gray* with Hurd Hatfield, Donna Reed and Peter Lawford. I liked Hatfield, he was darkly handsome and I'd seen him in *Dragon Seed* the year before. We left the café and I put some piastres into the tweed cap on the pavement next to the woman in the cocktail dress. She smiled at me, sweat dripping down her bosom.

In the cinema, Johnny didn't understand the film at all and shifted uncomfortably in his seat.

"What was that about?" he asked me as the curtains closed.

"Double identity," I said. "But really it's about the unconscious, the idea that we have a self, one part of which we are conscious of and keep control over, and another interior life which is wayward and even dark."

"Do you believe that stuff?"

"Yoohoo," an English voice cried out from a couple of rows behind as we got up to leave. It was Mrs. Mackintosh and her husband.

We were jostled by crowds out on to the street and nearly lost them but they appeared again, at my shoulder.

"Lovely to see you, Priscilla. And you must be Sergeant Jones," she said to Johnny.

"That's me," he replied, with what I thought was a faint trace of a Welsh accent. Everyone shook hands. Mackintosh's was dry, like old parchment.

"So you obtained your leave, at long last," Mrs. Mackintosh said. "I'm *so* glad."

"Yes, and it couldn't have come too soon for both of us. I've missed the old girl, I can tell you." He gave my hand a squeeze.

"Did you enjoy the film?" asked Inspector Mackintosh.

"Couldn't make head nor tail of it. Double Dutch to me, sir."

"Tony was just saying he doesn't believe in double identity," I said, trying not to giggle.

"Not unless we're talking spies. You must have to deal a lot with aliases and that sort of thing when you're fighting crime. Up in Tiberias I'm arresting people for riding their camels on the wrong side of the road and the odd kibbutz boy who's got too handy with a rifle." I looked at Johnny, he was smiling slightly.

"Yes. We do. And we're not helped by the fact the locals speak so many languages," Mackintosh replied. "You can't get the nationalities straight at all. Where they come from, I mean. Some of them can switch between Russian and Polish and Yiddish. And German, too, if the poor devils have been unfortunate enough to have been in German hands. They're the worst, I'm afraid. Absolutely unscrupulous."

"You see in their religion they don't have our idea of forgiveness, of turning the other cheek," his wife told us. "It's utterly foreign to them."

"English is all I know," Johnny said. "My grandma spoke Welsh but all that mumbo jumbo's finished with now. English is the language of the empire."

"For as long as it lasts," Mackintosh said sadly and put his hands in his pockets.

"Well, nice seeing you again," I said. "Let's meet up again soon."

"Yes, a beach picnic would be lovely," Mrs. Mackintosh

replied. "And one day you must come to us, for tea. You should see my garden. I'm having quite a success with my roses this year."

"He's a sad type, that Mackintosh," Johnny said, as we walked off.

"In what way?"

"He's reached the end of the line and he knows it. A lot of them here have no idea—*no idea* what's coming. They don't know what's going to hit them. They're going to lose that empire of theirs. India's going independent. Africa will too, eventually. Britain's going to be on its own, just a little insignificant speck on the map. And chaps like him, loyal servants and all that, men with a sense of duty, there'll be no place for them. They're finished."

"But we won the war."

"Come off it. The Americans did. And the Russians. The game's theirs now. They'll divide the whole shooting match up between them. No. Face it, Britain's had it. People like us are the future, people who are quick-witted and know how to reinvent ourselves in a flash. You'll see." He whistled a Glenn Miller tune as we walked along the street.

That night we became lovers. Who seduced whom? We seduced each other. He reached his hand up to touch my face and I took it and kissed it. His hand, shaking, lay on my breast and I unfastened the buttons of his shirt. He said, "You're so very beautiful and so all alone. I want to look after you." He unhooked my brassiere and my breasts were under his fingers. They were new breasts then. His body was brown and perfect except for a scar on his upper arm where he had been injured by flying debris when the Canadians had bombed their own side by mistake during the Palermo landings. I kissed the scar.

Is there anything sweeter in the world than to lie with your head on the chest of your lover, smoking cigarettes after you have made love and for the first time understood why people do this, all over the world? And there is no greater aphrodisiac: sex with someone you love, which annihilates all the potions of powdered horn and root which by sympathetic magic are supposed to imitate the phallic shapes they resemble. Was I in love with him already? Perhaps. I loved the way that he could deceive the British and play with them but inside he knew exactly who he was.

I loved also the way he accepted people at their own estimation of themselves, whatever that may be and didn't try to guess their motives. "Life is too short to analyze the psyche," he would say. "All I need to do is to know myself, and him I know very well indeed. I have no curiosity about other people. They will tell you soon enough what you want to know. You know who's a friend and who's an enemy without examining their subconscious. The signs are all there, on the surface."

I didn't agree, but as he pointed out, he had got by long enough on this simple philosophy and unlike others perhaps better and wiser than himself had survived five years of war and another year resisting the colonial presence of the British. Who was I to tell him that he was wrong? Perhaps we do not need to know each other after all. Perhaps our compulsion to tell each other our stories is no more than talkativeness and we would be better left in our silences, each with our own essential mystery. Though God knows how you're going to sell that one to the Jews.

W HAT did I *really* want to know about Johnny? Well, he stayed in my apartment two or three nights a week and sometimes I wondered what he did with the rest of his time, but not all that hard. All I was really interested in was whether or not there was another girlfriend somewhere. That he worked in a back room in the Florentin district making suits I knew because he told me. He would get on the Norton every morning after spending the night with me and disappear off down the street, blowing sand around his wheels. He never *wore* a suit, but then not many Palestinians did. It was a casual country. Who did he make them for?

"People."

"What people?"

"The British. They come out here with tweed and worsted and they have to have something lightweight for the climate."

"Who else?"

"Evelyn, this is boring. My work doesn't interest me. It's what I do to earn money. My father got me into it before the war when he realized I was never going to make a civil servant. He found jobs for all of us."

"How many are there of you?"

"Nine."

"Nine? That's a *huge* family."

"I suppose so."

"Where do you come in? Are you one of the youngest or one of the oldest?"

"Second youngest. I have a younger sister. But I was always the baby because there was a big gap between me and the next one up."

"What's it like to grow up with so many relatives?"

"Like being a member of an army. I have eleven uncles and aunts by blood and more cousins than I can count. For my brothers' and sisters' birthdays I make them a shirt. I put darts in the chest if it's a sister. That's it. I use whatever color material comes to hand."

"Will you make me a shirt?"

"Yes, if you want. But it will be like a kibbutz shirt, not fashionable."

"I'd like it if it was made by you."

"Give me a week."

"Okay."

"I'll need your measurements."

"I don't know what they are anymore. I'm bigger since I came to Palestine. Not fat, more muscle, I think."

He looked at me and sized me up. "Like a girl should be, sturdy. I don't like these thin little English girls with no chests and skinny little arms. They don't know how to eat. I want something I can grab hold of in bed."

And all this time I carried on cutting and setting hair at the salon and listening to the shallow chatter of my customers. I tried to explain to Johnny that I could only retain an interest in hairdressing by regarding it as an extension of what I had picked up in the office where I started to learn commercial art: as the arrangement of forms and masses within a given canvas. Or was it a kind of sculpting of a portion of the human form with hair as the plastic material? Dyeing became for me a means of working with color. Instead of mixing oils on a palette, I would painstakingly form an amalgamation of different chemicals which in the bottle would look like no more than a muddy brown but, if the manufacturers had got the formula right, would produce the desired effect—blond, brunette, auburn. With paint, what you saw on your palette and dipped your brush into would be much the same color on the surface to which you applied it. Not so with hair dye, for hair is a living substance (emerging from the part of ourselves which is closest to the brain) so the principles of hairdressing were those of uncertainty and experimentation based, if one had it, on a sound chemical knowledge of the structure of the hair and what affected its disposition—to be straight or curly, pale or dark, thick or thin.

As well as being a minor art form, hairdressing was a far more dangerous and exact science than painting. I was regularly daubing the heads of my ladies with chemicals like hydrogen peroxide which has a tendency to decompose and suddenly explode if not stored under the correct conditions. In fact, if you thought about it in a certain way, the storeroom of a hairdressing salon more closely resembles in its potential for the damage it can inflict a small, backroom bomb factory.

"Good," Johnny said. "If I need to make a bomb in a hurry I know where to come. To Mrs. Kulp's ladies' hairdressing salon on Shenkin Street. Now I've heard everything."

I tried to convince him that there was *something* serious in hairdressing. During my schoolgirl visits to the National Gallery, as well as decoding the symbols contained in a lily lying on the floor and representing trampled purity, or a skull reminding us of our mortality, I would look at the changing hairstyles in the pictures. But the understanding of what the profession really was came to me not in a museum, nor in the Regent Street salon itself, but during the journey to Palestine when I sat on the deck turning the pages of the book that Uncle

Joe had given me, in which I learned for the first time to think like a modernist, to look for the fault lines between the present and the past, the place where ruptures took place.

My mother, when she had cut herself off from her family and rendered invisible those old people in their beards with their nostalgic yearning for the previous century and its certainties, had considered hairdressing to be a very *modern* job. But as her own mother had, according to ritual observance, shaved her head and worn a wig, it occurred to me that once, in every town of a reasonable size in the Jewish world of eastern Europe, there must have been wig-makers. And those men, or even women, perhaps, had gathered the hair in great bags and then styled it into headpieces which their wearers would never remove, for the whole of their lives. Presumably they must have had to have their own hair regularly shorn, though my mother thought that hers had done the job herself, alone in the bedroom in the afternoons, hacking it off with kitchen scissors.

"Yeah," said Johnny. "I remember my grandmother did the same."

"Did you know that it was only after the exile that Orthodox women began to crop their hair and wear wigs when they got married, which makes me wonder if, now that we're on the brink of achieving a national home, the practice can be discontinued? It's just a Diaspora thing."

"Good point," Johnny said.

I told him that there had never been a time in human history when people didn't pay the greatest attention to their hair and its adornment, that it had always been how people marked their rank, trade or sex. For reasons I could not fathom, the religious authorities had, through the ages, imagined that the sight of what was sometimes known as a woman's "crowning glory" was likely to inflame men's passions. I did not say that it had once occurred to me that this might be because the hair of the head made a silent reference to another growth of hair about

which men were not supposed to think and which, to this day—
when bosoms and legs and bottoms have all been accentuated
by prevailing fashions—has never been allowed to be exposed.
Though my mother combed hers and applied a light oil to make
it glossy which I knew because I saw her doing it, just once,
when she came from the bath, her legs spread apart as she sat
on the closed lid of the WC, her skin pink and wrapped in an
emerald green Chinese robe with red-tongued dragons.

"It's interesting how a bottle of dye can turn you from one
thing into another," Johnny was saying. "Just that little bottle
and you fool them."

"I wonder if I sometimes fool myself, too."

"What do you mean?"

"When I'm with the British and they treat me as if I'm British
I *feel* British, not a Jew at all. If I have a passport in the name
of this Priscilla Jones, who's to say I'm someone else, apart from
myself? I mean if I suffered from some form of amnesia and forgot completely that I was Evelyn Sert who would I be then?"

These questions puzzled me but they did not interest Johnny.
He shrugged. "I know who I am," he said. "It's not a problem."

Looking at him, I was reminded of those pages in the book
that discussed the cubist portraits of Picasso. By showing the
human face as a series of disjointed planes and angles, Picasso
had demonstrated that who or what a person was depended entirely on your point of view. The new way of looking at things,
apparently, reflected the relativity of the Einsteinian science and
of the age we lived in which lacked a single, unifying truth or
belief but saw life as fragmented and discontinuous. And this,
perhaps, was the difference between Johnny and me, for he
merely wore a mask which deliberately set out to deceive, behind which he clearly knew who he was, while I seemed to con-
tain several selves and each of these seemed to me as valid as the
next.

But I couldn't talk to Johnny about any of it. It was impossi-

ble to get him interested in ideas and perhaps that was part of
his attraction. He simplified everything so that the way in front
of us was clear, undivided and without mystery. To live, one
needed nothing but common sense and native wit. "There is a
natural way of doing things," he would tell me. "Only follow
the natural way and you will never get into trouble. Don't think
too much. Just do it."

Drinking lemonade on the balcony, I told Johnny all about
Mrs. Paget-Knight and we marveled at the mentality of people
who could send their children away from them at the age of six,
though I wondered if the communally owned babies of the kibbutz did not grow up with the same air of detachment. If their
matter-of-fact attitude to sex was based on some inability to
conceive of intimacy with another and if they would ever be capable of falling in love, which is after all a form of possession. I
had talked to Johnny before about life on the kibbutz and of
free love and of the ideas of Bertrand Russell but he thought
that they were rubbish.

"A man wants a woman for himself and vice versa. Anything
else is like borrowing a library book. Look at you, alone in the
world. Why should you be a library book? No. You want a
home. If you didn't, you wouldn't have come to Eretz Israel.
You *are* home, Evelyn."

So with Johnny all the complicated ideas were made easy and
living in the present tense was reduced to a few energetic neces-
sities—making love and making war. I leaned across and kissed
him and pushed my tongue into his mouth and bit his lip. He
unbuckled the belt on his khaki trousers while I undid the buttons on his khaki shirt. I took my own blouse off and he unfastened my brassiere and held the weight of my breasts in his
hands. Soon we were down on the floor of the square white box
that was my living room, writhing, making the beast with two
backs and our lovemaking tousled my platinum blond hair.

*   *   *

One morning I woke out of a pleasant dream. Johnny and I were walking through an orange grove together. He reached up and picked a fruit for me, straight from the tree and peeled it and put the segments into my mouth. My tongue broke their outer skins and the juice ran down my throat. I looked at my hands and I saw my veins run orange. The sun shone mildly and we walked on, to the sea. The sand was white and abundant. We walked into the waves, fully clothed and stood on tiptoe, submerged beneath the surface and when we got out we were dry at once. It was odd and funny and inconsequential. A good dream and I reached across and touched Johnny awake to tell him about it.

He looked at me blankly, his eyes still sticky with sleep. "Does this have a point, this story?"

"No. It was just a nice dream. What do you dream about?"

"I don't."

"Don't what?"

"I don't dream."

"Of course you do."

"No. I don't."

"Never?"

"Never. I have never had a dream in the whole of my life. I have my dream when I'm awake. The dream of Betar winning the cup."

"That's not the same thing."

"It is to me."

"What happens when you go to sleep?"

"Nothing. I'm asleep."

"Didn't you have dreams when you were a child?"

"No, never. Listen, I exhaust myself during the day. I go to bed, I'm unconscious until I get up. That's the way it's supposed to be. This dream you tell me you just had, why should I envy you for that? I'm glad I don't have to deal with such chaos every night."

"But dreams are messages from our subconscious."

"I don't believe in the subconscious. I've heard of it, but I don't believe in it. It's neurotic, the product of a mind that is confused and conflicted and doesn't see things as they should be. You give me a problem and I can solve it. I don't think there is any problem so big that I'm not capable of finding a solution if I apply my brain to it. I don't worry about it, I don't have anxiety, I don't brood. It's like repairing the Norton. Everything is straightforward if you know how the machine was built. Everything has an internal structure which is visible to the naked eye and logical. In Eretz Israel, so help me God, there will be no head doctors."

"God?"

"A figure of speech. My father uses it a lot."

"But you're speaking as if the most important development in twentieth-century thought never existed."

"What development is that?"

"The ideas of Freud. His understanding of the human mind. Look at its influence. Look at surrealism."

"What's that?"

"You've never heard of Salvador Dalí?"

"No. He sounds like Freud, another neurotic old-world type. What I know about Freud is this. He lived in Vienna at the turn of the century. The place was a nest of anti-Semites. No wonder people felt crazy. They had no fresh air to breathe. They were claustrophobic, frightened. It was the time of the Dreyfus case. There was hysteria against the Jews. The anti-Semites were the hysterics, not us, but they drove us to the same state as them. Head cases. Crackpots. Women with other women. Men with men. All unnatural. And Freud tells me I want to marry my mother. You haven't seen my mother. She gave birth to nine children and her bosom is hanging down by her waist. My father can keep her. Now see what you've made me say. I insulted my own mother. That's what Freud brings out in you."

I did not know what to reply. I had as my boyfriend a man

with no inner life. I could only assume later, when I read more about psychoanalysis, that if he did not dream he must have had some powerful mechanisms of repression, perhaps because he had something even more powerful that he needed to repress. Though looking at him, now, it was impossible to imagine what this might be. Where were the hidden depths? Everything was on the surface. He was an open book.

Johnny never asked me about my dreams and I don't know whether I would have told him or not. At night when I got into bed I would compose myself for sleep in the knowledge that I was about to enter my other life where things were as real as when I was awake. In later years, those long years of exile from myself, I came to love sleep and dreams, but now, in Tel Aviv, in 1946, what I dreamed about was my mother: of her well and young, brushing her hair in front of her dressing table, or shopping for vegetables in Berwick Street market, or showing me how to divide the hair of the head into its "ply"—the strands we would wind around rollers or twist about our fingers into pin curls.

I dreamed of the smells of foreign food from the Italian cafés and of dappled spring skies over Hyde Park, the air smelling of rain, the breeze fresh on my face. I dreamed of buying new sheets and towels at John Lewis on Oxford Street before the war, before the shortages, of my mother and me unfolding each one and holding the ends between us to examine the linen for flaws or stains. I dreamed of the smell of cigars on Uncle Joe's suits and the eau de cologne he splashed on his skin before he came to see us. I dreamed of jam tarts and my mother's laughter and of her bending forward to straighten a stocking seam so I could see the lace of her slip. I dreamed of the two of us listening to the wireless for the war news and of myself trying to tell that frightened pair that everything would be all right—that the war would last for six years and that we would win it—but nothing came from my mouth and I stared at them, wishing for some way to give them comfort.

AFTER a while, Johnny began to ask me more about the women who came to the salon. "The British women I mean."

"Why do you want to know?"

"Because the information is useful."

"To whom?"

"To those of us interested in furthering the cause of the Zionist state. Which includes you, Evelyn."

"What will you do with the information?"

"It's intelligence. Think of yourself as a spy. The more we know about the enemy the better. There were such women during the war."

"My God, you're not expecting me to make love to Mackintosh, like Mata Hari, are you?"

"Of course not. It's just harmless information we're after. Names, addresses. That sort of thing. You could easily copy them from the appointments book, surely?"

"Yes. I could." He smiled at me. The stink of palm oil was gone. I had bought him a new American hair cream which smelled pleasantly of lighter and more masculine perfumes. He ran a nail brush across the tips of his fingers before he came to me. He wanted now to shower before we went to bed, afraid that the sweat on his body would offend me but I told him not to, I wanted to smell him when we made love. I didn't want him to be a ghost, without odor.

"Come here, darling," he said to me, stretching out his hand. "Never forget that I was a soldier and you know what soldiers do, don't you?"

"What?"

"We occupy territory."

So I copied out the names, addresses and telephone numbers of all our clients and gave them to Johnny.

Mrs. Linz stood watching me as I washed one of his shirts in the laundry room on the roof.

"So now you reduce yourself to a laundress," she said.

"I'm just washing."

"Washing for a *man*."

"Oh, why not? Really!"

"Can't he wash his own, your terrorist boyfriend?"

"Don't be silly, Johnny isn't a terrorist, he's a tailor. He may have connections but they're with the Haganah who are hardly terrorists."

"Is that what he tells you?" She stretched a short arm behind her back and scratched. A fly settled on her face and she slapped it away. The child was examining strands of fiber through his magnifying glass.

"What do you mean?"

"Try to use your head," she advised me, folding up sheets. "Think. Not enough thinking goes on in the world."

So I thought. It's true, I said to myself, he has never told me who is getting this information I pass on. I resolved that the very next time I saw him, when he promised he would have my shirt for me, I would ask him who his associates were.

"Anyway, there's an easy way to tell," Mrs. Linz was saying, smoothing the child's little shirts and socks.

"And what would that be?"

"Does he like football?"

"Yes, very much as it happens."

"And which team does he support?"

"Tel Aviv Betar."

"Well, then obviously he is Irgun."

"And why is that?" Really I was exasperated with Mrs. Linz who was *always* right and who *always* knew best.

"Because if he supports Betar he was in the Betar youth movement, that lot of crypto-fascists Jabotinsky started. He will have spent his boyhood marching around with guns shouting death to the Arabs, death to the British, dreaming of a Zionist state that covers the whole Middle East and furthermore he . . ."

That was all I heard. I ran down the steps to my own apartment. But I did not have time to ask Johnny if he was a terrorist because before I saw him again the Irgun blew up the King David Hotel in Jerusalem killing nearly a hundred people, many of them Jews. Everyone knew they were hiding out somewhere in the white city. All hell broke loose.

Now Tel Aviv was cut off from the rest of the world and we, its residents, were cut off from each other. An absolute curfew prevailed. The official communiqués said that anyone seen on the streets would be shot on sight. The phones were dead. Everything was silent and in the stillness of the air, from my balcony, I could hear the roar of the sea on the beach as it might have sounded long ago, before the men and women gathered on the dunes to possess the sand and build on it and to dream their town into existence out of nothing.

Someone from the building pushed a note through my letterbox in Hebrew.

"What does this say?" I asked Mrs. Linz, for I could hardly read the language.

"Oh that, we've all got one. It's a biblical quotation," she said.

"Read it to me."

"It says, *Come, my people, enter thou into thy chambers, and shut thy doors about thee, hide thyself, as if it were for a little moment, until the indignation be overpast.* Very comforting, I'm sure."

Blum looked at his. "It's taken from the prophet Isaiah," he told us.

"I had no idea you were religious, Blum," Mrs. Linz said.

"I am not. But I read Isaiah from time to time. He is full of gloom and despair and baleful warnings to the Jewish people. He suits our age. I prefer him to Tolstoy."

"Barbarian," said Mrs. Linz. "Read Thomas Mann and Musil. Dare to be modern, Blum."

The troops came in their red berets, those anemones, and set up barbed-wire pens on each street corner. Every able-bodied man between fifteen and fifty was rounded up to be searched and every woman or girl between fifteen and thirty-five also. We gathered at the front door of the building. I saw an ill-assorted group from the apartment opposite being marched along in a line—men in shorts and shirts, Yekkes in pressed suits, women in housecoats, a lady in a dressing gown carrying a parasol to protect her skin from the sun. I saw the stragglers prodded with clubs and a man who dropped his hat did not stop to pick it up.

"This is familiar," Blum said.

Two girls in summer frocks with chiffon scarves covering their hair were held for a long time and eventually forced at gunpoint into a truck and driven away in handcuffs. An energetic, pushy press photographer from an American newspaper tried to take their picture but they covered their faces. "Shit," he said, turning to a soldier. "You mean to tell me those girls are gun-girls? Bombers?" He shook his head. "Pretty, too."

Then the soldiers came to us. A woman on the ground floor complained to an officer that she had not been able to take her terrier for his walk. "To do what is natural for all of us, sir," she explained, delicately.

The officer was sympathetic. "I have a Yorkshire terrier myself, as it happens. Lovely breed. Well, a call of nature is a call of nature. Can't let the animals suffer. No, not at all." He called over a private and gave him instructions.

"Simchah is to be walked twice a day," she told me. "How civilized the British are."

Mrs. Kulp, once she had established that her son, the trainee manager at the King David, was unharmed, was offended by her own situation. She had not been removed from the building for questioning. "Don't worry, madam," a lance corporal had told her. "It's just the young ones we're after."

Mrs. Kulp went red. "But how old do you think I am?" she asked, thrusting her bosom at him. I could hear by his voice that he was from somewhere in the Black Country. There was a rash of pimples on his forehead and his white, sweating skin had been badly damaged by the sun.

"Fifty?"

"How dare you."

"Let's see your papers, then. We'll find out how old you are." He walked off, muttering under his breath, "Bloody Jews. Mutton dressed as lamb, the lot of them."

A group of us were assembled on the pavement and marched down to the interrogation cage. Of the women, there was myself, Mrs. Linz and a girl actress from the Habimah Theater who swore at the troops in three languages. "What have we done now?" asked a young lieutenant, smiling. The girl said she'd heard that they had set up their HQ at the theater and damaged some of the props for a future production of *Hamlet*.

"*Chazzers!*" she cried.

"What's a *chazzer?* Anything nice?" the lieutenant asked us. No one spoke. "Somehow, I suspect not. I'd look it up in the dictionary but I don't know what language it is. Best forgotten, perhaps." He winked at me. "Can anyone else offer any light relief?" He turned to Mrs. Linz. "Know any good jokes?"

"None that I would care to tell from inside a barbed-wire fence."

"Suits me," the lieutenant said and turned away to light a cigarette. He looked down at his clipboard and ticked off our names. Someone behind me started whistling "God Save the King." It did not seem to be a patriotic gesture.

"Put a sock in it," the lieutenant said. "Or I'll put one on you."

"These are not very cultured expressions," said Mrs. Linz.

A squad of soldiers entered our building. I was holding the fake passport Johnny had given me and I was frightened. Frightened that they would find, in the kitchen drawer, the passport of Evelyn Sert who had been granted a visa several months ago to enter the Holy Land as a tourist of sites of Christian interest and who should not be residing in a Jewish block of flats in a Jewish city with nothing of any historical or archaeological significance.

In the cage, the lieutenant walked off and a sergeant came up to me and looked at the Priscilla Jones passport. He was a sturdy youngster with short legs and a mottled face. "Funny place to find yourself, Mrs. Jones," he said, looking at the others from the building.

"I know," I said, lowering my voice. "Pretty frightful, really. Bloody Jews, but I try to rub along."

"Where's Mr. Jones?"

"Tiberias."

"Why aren't you with him?"

"We're saving to start a family and I have a job here in Tel Aviv which pays quite well and after all Tony *is* trying to get a transfer."

"If you ask me, you'd be happier in Jerusalem. Not so infested if you take my meaning."

"Yes, so I've been told."

"Beautiful place. Very historic. The stones breathe history."

"Really?"

"I'd move there if I were you. The policy regarding Tel Aviv seems to be to leave them to it, the Jews I mean. And they can have it as far as I'm concerned. This place is a dump. The Christians are all pulling out. There won't be a Gentile copper here before the year's end."

"Then I'll certainly look into jobs in Jerusalem."

He stared at the others in the interrogation cage. Looked at Blum arguing with Mrs. Linz about something and the girl from the theater with her arms crossed and an unhelpful expression on her face.

"Personally, I don't know how you can stand them. Talk, talk, talk, the whole time, I don't know how they can hear themselves think. Silence is golden, is my motto. If I had a long enough leave I'd go back home and hire one of those boats on the Broads for a week. You glide through the water, everything's still, if you close your eyes you think you're . . . Anyway, where was I?"

"Homesick, I'd say." And I smiled at him.

"Too true." He handed my passport back "All in order. Good luck, miss. I mean madam. Sorry for the inconvenience." And I was released.

It took considerably longer for Blum, Mrs. Linz and the actress to return and when they did, Blum was grumbling, Mrs. Linz was smiling contemptuously and the actress was loudly threatening to offer her services to the Lehi.

Stories were circulating now from other detainees in the cage. Someone said he'd heard about a man who had been caught out on the street during the curfew. Asked if he was a Jew and replying that he was, he had been bludgeoned with a truncheon.

Blum said it was a shame that the British sent out to rule Palestine were not "of the very best type."

The actress said there was a single type. "Colonialists, with a colonial mentality."

The argument rumbled on for a few more hours. We were running out of food and getting hungry. The army only allowed us out for a short period each day to go shopping and often you could not reach the front of the queue in time. To solve the problem the troops started to drive around in trucks with bread and water, demanding payment but they were mobbed in minutes and the soldiers too frightened to collect the money.

Mrs. Kulp wanted to open the salon during the two hours when the curfew was lifted. "Women will still be women," she said, "whether or not we live under martial law."

"This isn't martial law, is it?" I asked her.

"It soon will be," the actress shouted.

"Are you frightened?" Mrs. Linz asked me.

"No," I said. But I was.

"This is nothing," she said, "during the Arab riots . . ."

"The Arab riots? You call that something to worry about?" said Blum. "I remember in Berlin when the SS . . ."

I remembered the air raids in London, when we were buried alive in the tube station, listening to the ground shaking above us, the theaters and shops shuddering on their foundations and wondering if we would survive the night. These memories were not held in common with the inhabitants of the apartment building on Mapu but with the soldiers who had moved past our street and were setting up their barbed-wire interrogation cages on Frishman.

ON the fourth of August the siege was lifted and the dead city came to life once more. The news vendors' kiosks were mobbed, people flocked to the zoo to see the baby monkeys, Finkel was playing Hamlet at the theater, the watermelon man was back on the corner and the ice-cream parlors were open again, where I went at once to sit on a high revolving stool, lick at a strawberry sundae and wonder what flavor pistachio might be. Mrs. Kulp's salon reopened and the ladies of Tel Aviv had their hair shampooed and set, permed and restyled because whatever else is true you will never in a million years overcome a woman's concern about her appearance.

Johnny stayed away for at least a week after the siege was over. "You okay?" he asked as he swung through my door, grabbing my face and thrusting his tongue into my mouth. "Hey, let me look at you. What a doll. What's this, a new dress?"

"Where have you been?"

"Here and there, darling, here and there."

"Let me ask you something," I said, as I sat on his knee with my arms around his neck on one of my uncomfortable chairs. "This information I'm giving you. Who is getting it?"

"Those who serve the interests of Eretz Israel, of course." He stroked my hair.

"And who are they, exactly?"

"Oh. It's *that* kind of conversation." He lifted me off his lap and reached into his packet for a cigarette. He lit two and gave one to me. I sat down opposite him. The evening sun cast long shadows on the tiled floor. "Does it matter?" he asked me.

"I don't want to be a dupe. Or a dope."

"Don't you think that the less you know, the safer you are?"

"But I'm implicated."

"Not much."

"But what if that passport you got me hadn't passed muster, or they'd found the other one, what would I have said then?"

He shrugged. "There are always risks."

"Yes, but *what* am I risking this for? What am I involved in? Don't I have the right to know that much?"

A pianist had just moved in next door. He was practicing the "Goldberg" Variations. The notes slithered about the building sounding as if they might have been composed yesterday instead of three hundred years ago.

"Doesn't that guy ever shut up?" Johnny said. "What is that stuff?"

"Bach. He's putting on a concert next month."

"Count me out if he offers you tickets. I like something more lively. You heard Frank Sinatra?"

"Yes. Let's get back to the subject."

"God, this place is bloody hot. Got any lemonade? You know, in the house where I grew up in Jerusalem, we had a fan on the ceiling. It was a very old house, from the time of the Turks. I don't know why those Yekkes who came from Berlin or wherever didn't think to put something like that in when they built these places. Madness. Everything up to date and modern but they don't spare a thought for the climate. The Arabs, *they* know how to build houses for the heat. Maybe one day I'll take you to one of the villages, you'll like it, they're very colorful people. You could . . ."

"I'm losing patience, Johnny," I said, and stamped my foot.

He looked at it, my foot in a red leather sandal. I loved red shoes in those days, and matching red handbags. "Okay, okay," he said. "But understand that whatever I tell you will mean *more* danger, not less. You know what you're asking? I've tried to protect you, to keep you marginal. I didn't want you to be too involved. Listen, I could have had a very different kind of girlfriend, a type I've known all my life, we would have absolutely no secrets from each other. We would be fighting at each other's side. One day, when the real war comes, we would be on the roof together, we would both have guns in our hands and we would be firing them. But that's not what I want, I chose you because you are a very, very pretty girl, because you are all alone here, because you have guts and . . ."

"Because I'm your way in to the British."

"Yes, but that wasn't the first thing I thought. It only occurred to me after I saw you with the blond hair and the new name talking to that policeman." It was the night we became lovers.

"You used me!"

"Darling, isn't it better to be used than to be of no use to anyone?"

I could make no answer to this. I wanted to be loved purely, for who I was alone. But I didn't know if such love existed. I still don't. So I said nothing.

"Who are you? You owe me that."

"Well, my name is not exactly Levi Aharoni as it is not exactly Johnny but a name means nothing. A name is just something on a document. It *tells* you nothing. To you I'm Johnny and that's as it should be. You don't need to know my real name as long as you know *me*. What else?"

"You support Tel Aviv Betar. Does that mean you were in the Betar youth group?"

"Yes, naturally. I was a very tough kid."

"And does that mean you are in the Irgun?"

"Yes."

"Not the Stern Gang?"

"We call it the Lehi, but no, I'm not in the Stern Gang. Between us and Lehi there's a big difference. The Irgun and the Haganah are not allowed to be armed except during an operation. The Lehi have orders to be armed twenty-four hours a day and to shoot soldiers and kill them whenever they have an opportunity. Their idea is that the mothers in England will be shocked and say, 'Bring our boys home.' It's a good plan on one level, but I'm not going to kill someone on sight, just because of where they were born. It would be barbaric. If they hang my comrade Dov Gruner, then I might change my mind, but for the moment, no."

"Did you blow up the King David Hotel?"

"Not me, personally."

"Did you kidnap the British officers?"

"Yes."

"The names and addresses I've been giving you, are they for future kidnaps?"

"Yes."

"And you don't think you are putting me in danger?"

He shrugged again. "To only a small degree. Listen, there are people *clamoring* to help us, to get themselves killed if necessary, all kinds, students, craftsmen. They all want to go on operations and they give me a headache saying, 'If you don't take me I'll go join the Lehi.' I have to find a way of giving a piece of cake to everybody. We have people inside the police, we have girls who disguise themselves as prostitutes. Did I ask you to do that? No. There's a girl from Rehovot, she meets British officers, she takes them to her room, then our guys are waiting outside. What I ask you to do is harmless by comparison. And remember, Evelyn, it was not me who gave you an alter ego. You had that already, two in fact. You'd made your own cover."

"And you assumed that I would support the aims of the Irgun, the violence, the bombs. I'm telling you, I don't."

"Then you're a fool."

"I don't support terrorism."

"Terrorist? I'm not a terrorist, I'm a freedom fighter. Were the fighters in the Warsaw Ghetto terrorists?"

"They were up against evil."

"So am I."

"Oh for God's sake, the British aren't evil. You've lived amongst them, you know that."

"As individuals, no, many of them are not. In fact some have collaborated, they bring us arms if we pay them. How do we always know when there's going to be a search? Because our intelligence is very strong. One of them said he wouldn't take any money for information but he wanted my watch, he wanted a souvenir from a terrorist. It was my bar mitzvah watch. I told him to go to hell.

"But they're anti-Semites, you know. They don't think they are but their distaste for Tel Aviv tells you everything. Find me a goy who loves Tel Aviv. Yerushalayim, easy. That's the Holy Land, but here, there's nothing distracting them from Jewishness. We've got no sites of antiquity to offer them, no beautiful landscapes, no places of pilgrimage. Nothing but Jews. Jewish everyday life. They can manage the Jews when we're something special, Yehudi Menuhin, perhaps. The world is big enough for a few special Jews. It's the ordinariness of the Jews they can't stand. The millions of ordinary Jews with nothing particular to contribute, the Jews from Yemen, from the Polish ghettos, the Jewish riff-raff going about their business being Jews. The Jew-haters think Tel Aviv is just a city with too many Jews making a mess in their precious desert. They don't want anything here but picturesque Arabs in their robes to take photographs of so they can go home and stick them in an album and say to their good chums, 'Look what I saw when I went abroad.' "

"Yes, but there are other means to . . ."

"No. There aren't."

"Ben-Gurion thinks so. So did my Uncle Joe."

"Yeah? I wonder what your Uncle Joe really thought. Where do you think we get our money? We have a man who goes to London every few months, goes round all the rich guys. You want me to check with him whether he has your Uncle Joe on his list? As for Ben-Gurion, he's another fool. Listen, until the King David we had a pact with the Haganah and now the pact is finished because Ben-Gurion doesn't want to be associated with us. He doesn't want his hands to be seen to be dirty. So technically, you can tell yourself with good conscience that you were supplying information to the Haganah but through the intermediary of the Irgun.

"As for myself, the Haganah say we mustn't fight the British by force, only by demonstrations and bringing in illegal immigrants. Bring in illegals? Who did that? Us. Before the war we brought twenty-two thousand Jews to Eretz Israel. That's twenty-two thousand Jews we saved from Hitler, *we* saved, not them. And those who we tragically could not save? Evelyn, ask yourself, how can we be sure it won't happen again? By having an army. And how will we have an army? By having our own country. And how do we get our own country? By having an underground army to drive out the people who are preventing us from having our country. This is simple. This is logic. There's nothing complicated about it. What I am doing now, I will be doing after the state is created."

"You're a tailor."

"For the time being, but soon I'll be in the army again, our army, this time. Maybe I'll even be a general, who knows? I'll be respectable. But until then I pick up my gun with or without permission and I fight."

"So when you're not seeing me, you're killing people."

"No, wrong. You see because I'm good at impersonating the British, what I do is assume the disguise of different ranks. Then when, say, we want to find some rifles, I go to the gate at the barracks at Sarafand while the troops are in the mess hall and I tell whichever soldier is on duty that I have come to relieve him. There is an urgent message, he must go and find his sergeant. I take his place, I let my friends into the weapons store. And people say afterward, 'Oh, I walked past and there was a private on duty. He gave me a light for my cigarette. He had a Yorkshire accent.' Then they go looking for this Yorkshire private and they can't find him. Next time I'm a lance corporal from Manchester, or a captain from Norwich. Sometimes I do altogether different things, but those we'll pass over."

"Like kidnapping the officers?"

"Correct."

"Why did you release them?"

"We didn't have anywhere safe to keep them."

"What about the bombing in Jerusalem. Most of the people who died were Jews."

"Yes. It's a tragedy. But it's war."

"Is that all you have to say?"

"Yes. What do you want to do now?"

"You mean do I want to get on the bike and go to the Galina café to eat ice cream?"

"No, no. I'm not that callous. I mean do you want to chuck me?"

"I don't know."

"Maybe you need to think about it."

"I suppose so."

"Suppose I come back in a few days. I'll bring your shirt, definitely."

"Okay."

"And you'll have an answer for me, I hope." He looked at me and I saw that he was far from certain what it would be. The thought of rejection would be in his mind until he saw me again.

"Do you think I'm being naïve?"

"Listen, these questions aren't easy." His voice was very tender. "They're easy for me because I grew up in the middle of it all and I don't have choices. You're feeling your way in this situation. You need time. I just thought that you wanted to help and that you could do your little bit without knowing too much and getting into too much trouble. I was trying to make things easy for you, to help you make your contribution without a lot of risk. That was all. I like you too much to want any harm to come to you." He paused and went red. I'd never seen this color on his face before. "In fact I like you a lot."

He stood up and we walked toward the door. Before I opened it he held me tightly and kissed me on both cheeks and I wanted more than anything to stay inside the strong circle of his arms. My tears were wet on his skin.

"Don't cry, baby," he said. "Listen, one thing's for sure. It won't be me who chucks *you*."

"You'll be back at the end of the week?"

"Yes. I said so."

I let him go and I closed the door. I heard his feet thundering down the stairs, a bass note to the "Goldberg" Variations, and I walked to the balcony where I saw him climb on the Norton and I watched him until he turned left on Ben Yehuda and disappeared. The night was thrumming. I heard power lines make music from their own vibrations in the heat.

A few minutes later Mrs. Linz came and knocked on my door. She was going out for a short time and wanted to know if I could watch out for the child.

"So. Did the boyfriend turn out to be a terrorist?"

I didn't answer.

She smiled triumphantly. "See?" she said. "I am always right. You silly girl. You *Ostjude* who doesn't know how to think."

AFTER I had got rid of Mrs. Linz and the pianist had finally given up on the "Goldberg" Variations and gone out to some assignation at one of the cafés on the seashore, I looked in on the child. He seemed content, lying on his stomach on his bed, dressed in his little underpants and singlet, reading an encyclopedia. I took a shower but a few minutes after I had dried myself my skin was sticky once again. One evening of terrible humidity an earring had slipped off the lobe of my ear as I was walking along Dizengoff Street. My God! I hadn't even known that the ears possessed sweat glands.

I left the bedroom and went out to sit on the balcony.

I began to consider my customers, the people whose names I had been delivering to the Irgun, how I would watch their reflections in the mirror and try to figure out who exactly they were. For I understood that in the eyes of the Jews of Palestine they were one-dimensional types, as thin as the silver veneer on the salon looking glasses: the *British*, with their pale skins that reacted so badly to the sun and their crazy religion which forced them to pretend to eat the flesh and drink the blood of their second-rate god, and their weakness for dogs and gardens.

I thought of a morning, the previous week, when I was in the salon and listening to me with a half-smile as I said that I thought larger, softer waves might be the next new trend in coiffure, was Mrs. Bolton, my literary friend from the beach. Looking at her in the mirror, I saw once again that she was not a pretty woman, but I had noticed how regularly she came in for her shampoo and set and how she took care of her appearance and cultivated a style of dress which was smart even though it wasn't up-to-the-minute. She had managed to concoct a look for herself that required little thought or maintenance but suited her.

"Appearances are awfully important aren't they?" she said, taking a cigarette from her navy leather handbag. Next came a small silver lighter. Her scarlet thumbnail clicked a little flame into life.

"Oh yes. You can't go out looking any old how."

"My husband and I are both very interested in how things appear." Her hair was a fawn color. She liked it arranged in a style which she could simply run a comb through between appointments.

I remembered that I had had a conversation with her on the beach about novels and that I could not remember who had been discussed. Evelyn Waugh? Elizabeth Bowen? Ronald Firbank? I was not so very clever at managing my different disguises and remembering that it was perfectly possible for them to be checked against each other. So not knowing whether I was supposed to be a hairdresser or an intellectual I thought that as I was now actually playing the hairdresser's role I should stick to that and hope that Mrs. Bolton had forgotten our literary discussions.

"For example, I expect you're an expert in the ways one can completely transform one's identity through hairdressing and cosmetics. Dark roots are always a giveaway. You know all about that sort of thing, don't you, Priscilla?"

"Er, yes," I replied.

She looked at my reflection in the mirror and I looked back at hers.

"My husband is encouraging me to write a detective novel, like Miss Christie and Miss Sayers. Think up a plot, scatter the clues about, how hard could it be?"

"Pretty hard, I'd have thought."

"Oh, I don't know. You just need an understanding of human nature. It all comes down to psychology in the end, that's what George says. He's a lot brighter than people give him credit for. He's always telling me I'd make a good spy. Or perhaps it might not be a detective novel at all but a spy novel. You'd make an excellent spy yourself, Priscilla. What do you think?"

"Me? Why?"

"Because you're a good listener and you're in an occupation where people tell you their secrets. Don't you hear all sorts of gossip—love affairs gone wrong, operations, adultery?"

"What use would that be to anyone?"

"It's a lever, Priscilla, a little lever into people's lives."

"What do you mean? To blackmail people with?"

"Oddly enough, blackmail has never interested me. The financial gain seems pointless. I'm in agreement with Machiavelli, who said, as I'm sure you know already, that knowledge is power."

Mrs. Bolton said she had studied classics at Durham University and having passed the civil-service exams had gone to work at the Home Office in London, sharing a flat with two other girls, in Pimlico. One of them was Bolton's sister. He was a grammar-school boy. She didn't care about marrying beneath her. It was a meeting of the minds, really, she said. The wedding took place the year before the war broke out. They had no children. Despite this solid information, I began to feel that I had no idea who exactly Mrs. Bolton was.

The day before that, as it happened, I had met a young American couple from Brooklyn, delighted to speak my own language with other native speakers who were not British, but Jews like me. They were both wearing blue jeans, turned up into cuffs above shoes they called sneakers, and I remember it so clearly because that was the very first time I ever saw those kind of trousers, on legs crossed on a pavement near Dizengoff Circle in a café where the actors from the Habimah Theater used to come after their performances. They told me that they had not sailed the Mediterranean Sea to get here but had jumped on a plane at a place called Idlewild in New York and flown to Lydda. They took this new form of transport for granted though it sounded a long and grueling journey.

They were Roosevelt New Dealers, full of energy and intelligence, and now that the husband was out of the Marines he had returned to Europe to find survivors and help them embark on the illegal immigrant ships for the Promised Land. When the current work was finished he was going to get a teaching job in one of Palestine's Jewish universities. The wife, who was pregnant with their first child, made jewelry from silver and her necklaces and bracelets were unlike any I had ever seen before. Like the buildings we lived in, they were quite plain and without decoration or adornment, thick curves of metal around the wrist or simple silver drops hanging from the ears. I admired the earrings she was wearing herself so much that she took them off and gave them to me. I offered her money but, smiling, she refused and it was one of the pair that had dripped from my earlobe onto the pavement on Dizengoff Street and nearly got lost.

I expressed amazement at their optimism when everything to me seemed so fraught with danger. "We don't think about the past, Eve," the woman said.

"Why not?"

"We're Americans." And they both began to laugh.

"Listen," the husband told me, "we were brought up in the American way, each generation doing better than the one that went before. My grandfather came to Ellis Island with nothing. All the Jews who came, it was like a match hitting the touchpaper on a rocket, the rocket of American immigration. My father started a business, he made a lot of money, he put me through college. I have my Master's in chemistry. We've wound up with more than the wildest visionary of Lublin had ever dreamed of and all of this we did honestly. We didn't have to pay bribes or beg favors from some tsar or assimilate to Christianity or use our muscle to threaten anyone. Every penny we earned was through hard work—the American work ethic—and our God-given Jewish brains. It's the same for my wife, her family too, the same story. What do we learn from this? That anything is possible."

I knew too, because they had told me, that they were utterly contemptuous of the Irgun. They were bright, sunny idealists without any shadow in their souls. They believed with all their hearts that we were going to build the new Jerusalem. We didn't have a name for our new country in those days. They called it Zion. It would have a political system that would be the envy of everyone else. It would have Nobel Prize winners in literature and science. It would be the accretion of three thousand years of Jewish wisdom. And all this could be achieved by patient diplomacy and negotiation for if you began with violence you would end in violence and no Jew should lower himself to have blood on his hands.

They loved the sun, the heat and the date palms and talked about how the Jews of America would one day come here for their summer vacations instead of Florida or California. Here there was everything you could wish for, and everything was Jewish too. The whole waterfront could be developed as a playground with well-priced hotels offering all kinds of leisure facilities. So they smiled into the future, holding hands, drinking strong coffee and eating almond pastries as the new child grew inside her. I enjoyed the hour I spent in their company, before they gathered up their things and walked off down the street, insisting on paying my bill too.

To which camp did I belong? Not to theirs, though God

knows I wanted to badly enough—the people-with-big-souls party who thought with their hearts and their morals. I did not believe that the laws of Moses brought down from Mount Sinai were going to win us a country and even if they did I somehow doubted that we would be a light unto the nations. Not with Blum and Mrs. Kulp and Mrs. Linz in it, people who were there because they had no choice and if you asked them would rather be somewhere else. Nor was I enamored with Mrs. Bolton's lot, who were all shadow and no soul, who believed in nothing and for whom nothing was at stake, certainly not their own future and their children's future, if they ever had any.

This left the Johnny scheme of things, those who had never entered as a diver into the unconscious world, the pragmatists who said, "Listen, darling. What's the problem? Everything is simple. We *drive* them out. We make it impossible for them to stay."

With hindsight it always seems easy to do the right thing, but we were trying to decide something in those days that people don't often get a chance to have a say in and it was this: would we be a free nation after two thousand years of wandering or would we always be a subject race? Would we be ghetto Jews or new Jews? You know, when you face a decision like that, you have to think very, very carefully. The chance might not come again for another two thousand years. You have to be very sure. But you do have to decide, you can't avoid that.

I chose Johnny's way in the end, the way of the bombs, the kidnapping and murder because I decided to throw in my lot with the tough Jews. We had had our thinkers and now what we needed were fighters, Jews who scared the living daylights out of people. The other choices had their merit, but Johnny's seemed to promise the most certain outcome. Now, of course, knowing what we know, perhaps I would have decided differently but the future is a door into a darkened room and however much you fumble for the light switch you will never find it. People are always telling me that they knew what was going to happen, how it would end up here, but that's not how I remember it.

We were all idealists in our own fashion and we did what we did from a good heart. As I sat on my balcony at dusk, watching the soldiers move along the streets, shouting orders at us through megaphones, the date palms heavy with fruit and the air heavy with heat and sweat, I thought: "We'll force them out. We'll make them see that they have no choice. The terror won't last long, and then we'll have a country and there'll be peace. Some of these men will come back one day as tourists. They'll lie on our beaches and we'll sell them ice cream."

Time was rushing, it was streaming through me like fast beams of light. I could hear a radio in the apartment below me playing the music of one of the swing orchestras, on the next street the sound of hammers and saws and drills and concrete mixers, a new building under construction, and further away still traffic along Ha Yarkon. There was no peace here, no tranquility, just an ardent sense of life going on. The two-thousand-year-old exile had its beloved child, our city, Tel Aviv, and I was going to stay here to watch it grow up.

I DID not have my own gramophone when I lived on Mapu Street but I was always surrounded by music. There was the pianist next door who practiced, practiced, practiced. His apartment was filled with musicians from the Palestine Philharmonic who, on announcing their formation a decade ago, had received a telegram from Toscanini declaring that he would conduct their inaugural concert to demonstrate to the world his opposition to fascism. Consumed with terror, these émigrés from Germany and Austria had held thirty-seven rehearsals in three weeks.

I had been taught music at school, learning the system of notation and practicing scales on wooden recorders whose mouthpieces were wiped with a disinfectant-soaked rag between lessons. But from my neighbor and others in the building I learned for the first time to appreciate the great masters, and the little lessons which filled an important gap in my cultural education took place while bombs blew up the railway lines, banks were raided in Tel Aviv and Jaffa, there were paper shortages, bread rationing, and eleven new kibbutzim were established in a single day in the Negev Desert and were welcomed by the Bedouins they found there, according to the newspapers.

One afternoon, Blum knocked on my door and invited me to come and listen to a brand-new record which he had won in a raffle, having reluctantly parted with a few mils for the ticket, the proceeds going to raise money to feed war orphans who were living in makeshift arrangements somewhere in the countryside.

I was suffering from menstrual cramps which had not been improved by the consumption of some unidentifiable fried meats from a street vendor. The stomach of a sheep? It didn't bear thinking about. Johnny never came when he knew that the curse was due. The smell of women's blood offended him. "I had a lot of sisters when I was growing up," he said, "and they all used to bleed at the same time. You couldn't get into the bathroom. I found one of their bloody rags in the rubbish once when I was a boy. It made me feel sick."

"Didn't you see blood on the battlefield?"

"Certainly. But that kind of blood is clean."

So I had only my own company and I told Blum that I would join him in a few minutes.

I walked down the stairs, my back aching, and knocked on his door. He called out that it wasn't locked. At his table, he was threading new hair into the holes on a doll's linen scalp where too vigorous yanking by childish fists had pulled it out and made the toy partly bald. He put the doll down and poured me a glass of lemonade. Even indoors he wore his jacket.

"Now this composer, Miss Sert, in his later work became very difficult. Very difficult." Blum blew on the shining surface of the record and polished it with a soft cloth. "He sought to rob music of everything that is worth anything. But the piece that I am going to play you now is from his early period when he was a young man living in Vienna and it is called *Verklärte Nacht* which means, of course, 'transfigured night.' "

"What's his name?"

"Arnold Schoenberg."

I settled into one of Blum's well-upholstered chairs. I felt the menstrual blood trickling inside me and I remembered, as Blum crossed the room and placed the needle on the disk, that I had only one pad left and as soon as the shops reopened I must go out and buy more. I took all precautions against pregnancy. Mrs. Linz had bossily sent me to a sympathetic doctor on Ben Yehuda Street who had fitted me with a rubber contraceptive device like the one my mother had had.

The needle touched the first groove and a sound of utter melancholy and foreboding filled the room. I shuddered. Blum sat with his fingers gripping the chair arms, a small wooden packing case of dolls' spare parts by his side: waxy limbs and heads and torsos.

Listening to the music I thought of the saplings that had sprung up on the first bomb sites of the war and the weeds that scrambled over the rubble. I thought of the overgrown gardens that became like the forest, places of secrets and hidden things, grass growing in the cracks of disused air-raid shelters. I felt my temperature drop and there was a sudden hemorrhaging of blood from my body.

Blum got up and turned over the disk. The mood changed, there was a moment of lyric sweetness and I cried out at the beauty of it and this tenderness expanded until it overthrew the darkness. I thought my heart would break with a certain kind of sad happiness and when the record finally stopped my face was wet with tears for I had found something that no one could ever take away from me again: the past. My mother's face was in that sweetness, smiling at me as she looked up from her movie magazines when darkness had fallen over London, the lamps were lit and the raid had come and gone and spared us.

"Miss Sert," Blum said, in the long silence that followed the last notes. "Do you know the story of this music?"

"The story?"

"Yes, of course, there is a story. The music is a setting of a poem by a great German poet of the last century, Richard Dehmel, who was one of the foremost representatives of the

Zeitgeist movement, which means the spirit of the times. A shocking individual who chose subjects for his work which are quite unsuitable for poetry such as the alleged miseries of the working classes. He also held dubious ideas about the mystical powers of intimate relations between men and women which he believed to be the only basis for a full development of the personality and even for a spiritual life, though what *that* might be I cannot say. Personally, I find him a sensationalist."

"Tell me the story of the poem," I said, feeling a strong affinity with this German precursor of all the ideas of free love I held dear.

"Its sentiments are repulsive though the music almost allows one to forget it."

"Oh for God's sake, Herr Blum," I cried, "*do* go on."

He glowered at me. "For a young lady brought up in the capital of the most civilized country in the world, you lapse into terrible manners, Miss Sert." I thought this rich coming from him, one of Tel Aviv's shark landlords. However, I apologized. I could not say that my sanitary pad was filling with blood and I wanted him to get on with it so I could slip back to my own apartment and find the last unused one.

Blum cleared his throat and began. "A man and a woman are parading through a park on a clear, cold moonlight night. 'The bare cold grove' Dehmel describes it as, the moon coursing above the high oaks and not a cloud to obscure the light of heaven. *Very* atmospheric, yes?"

"Yes," I agreed.

"Then there is an outburst, the woman confesses to a terrible tragedy. Now we find that this pair are not husband and wife, not at all, they are lovers! 'I walk in sin beside you,' she tells him. It seems that she had met a man she did not love, and yearning for a purposeful life, for motherhood and the respectability of a wife's station, she married him. Soon after, she realizes she has made a dreadful mistake for now not only has she met the man she is telling all this to, but she also finds she is carrying a child by her legally married husband. You might think she would be filled with shame that she had betrayed her husband but it turns out that the man she believes she has betrayed is in fact the lover! And why? Because our poet believes in the authenticity of true love and rejects the bourgeois conventions of marriage.

"Now the lover has an astonishing reaction to what he has heard. A decent man would order her to return to her husband, he might even find in himself the arousal of a great abhorrence for this lady, but far from it. He instructs her that the child waiting to be born should not be a burden on her soul (and this is where we hear the duet between violin and cello that I observed you liked so much), that he forgives her transgression against him, though one wonders about the poor husband in all this. He tells her that this miracle of nature has transfigured what might have been a night of tragedy. 'This will transfigure the other's child,' he tells her. 'You will bear it for me, from me / You have brought radiance on me / You have made me a child myself.' And the whole wretched business ends with them clutching each other as they walk off, no doubt to a life of living in sinful relations, such as I observe all around me in the so-called Jewish city."

"Gosh," I said.

"Gosh? What word is this?"

I giggled. The story seemed to me to be both highly wrought and silly, typical of what Meier and the ideological free-thinkers on the kibbutz would have described as the diseased, melodramatic social relations of the last century. No doubt my mother might have found this story very beautiful but I regarded it as only a staging post en route to the free, open, liberated ideas of my own times.

Later that evening I asked Mrs. Linz if she knew the piece and the poem.

"Of course," she said. "This young woman's big mistake is to believe that her future lies with a man. Look, she has rushed into marriage merely to fulfill some bourgeois conventions. Then she finds a lover and what does she do? She tries to recreate the exact same conditions with him. This is not a new woman, this is the oldest kind of woman that there is, who believes that fulfillment only lies in doing a man's laundry. You know what I think of that?" She made a fastidious little spitting motion with her mouth.

"Why did you have a child?" I asked her, passing over my fruit bowl. She helped herself to a peach and then waited with it in her hand. "A plate?" she said. "A napkin and a knife? You don't expect me to bite into it do you?" Oh, there were always formalities with the Yekkes.

I went into the kitchen and got her what she wanted. She sat there in her shorts, operating on the peach like a surgeon with a scalpel, separating the hairy skin from the damp interior. "If you don't enjoy cleaning for others surely motherhood is exactly the course you should have avoided like the plague," I said.

"It was not intentional," she replied. "Linz raped me."

"My God!"

"Yes. It is true. I married him out of caprice. The following day I woke up and saw he had shed some hairs on the pillow and I thought, 'This is going to make me sick, seeing this every morning.' I knew at once that I had made a terrible mistake and that there should have been no marriage. So I shrugged and got out of bed to go home and he caught me by the hips and began to make love to me. I told him, 'You cannot do this without my consent.' But he did not need it. Of course when I discovered that I was pregnant I considered having a termination because there were plenty of unemployed doctors who would have performed it for me. But I had two reasons for rejecting that course. The first was that I was too poor and I certainly had no intention of asking Linz for the money. The second was that this child was something I had made out of my own flesh and blood and why would I want to destroy something I had created? It seemed perverse."

"So you stayed with Mr. Linz?"

"For a few months. He's a very boring man. The hair that came off his head on to the pillow is all gone now. He is very bald. And he is fat. Once I thought he had the body of a Greek god. Now he merely has the body of a middle-aged Greek, which is precisely what he is, one of the Jews from Salonika."

"I didn't know there were Jews in Greece."

"There are very few now. In 1939 there were Jews there but they were largely exterminated. They eliminated the ones from Salonika and Rhodes and Crete and Corfu. The Salonikans were a terrible crowd. They all came from Spain originally, after the expulsion, the same year, incidentally, that Columbus discovered America. Did you know that?" I shook my head. "It's ironic, I think. Anyway these Salonikans, having lived under a very benign and intellectual Moorish rule, were then left to their own devices in Greece and fell into a trough of mysticism which in turn degenerated into oriental sorcery and they became obsessed with all kinds of nonsense such as magicians and miracle-workers and fortune-tellers and amulet-makers, let alone being plagued by disasters such as piracy from the sea and epidemics of typhus and leprosy. Which shows, I think, that we People of the Book are no better than anyone else and must be dragged kicking and screaming toward reason as our Arab friends must also be.

"It was only when the Ottoman empire was falling apart that the Salonikans entered into modern life and developed a European intelligentsia. And so it is here. With the defeat of the Turks in the Middle East, it is possible for existence to assume its true pace which is its trajectory into the future. My husband arrived with his mother and father as a baby in 1910 and coming to mature years just as the first crush of Berliners arrived was exposed to some mental fresh air. Hence he is now a physicist and has the offer of a post at Stanford University in California which he is anxious to take up."

"What an interesting story," I said, thinking that I must have seen these Greek Jews on the streets of Tel Aviv, but how to recognize them? "Do they maintain any habits or customs that they brought from Greece?"

"Well, I can only speak of the poor Salonikans. All they have left, now, the few that survived, is one little legacy which reminds them of the past and you know what it is?" She laughed. "Not great works of literature, not music or painting or philosophy but their food. Yes. Linz made me make little meat pies which he called *pasteles de carne* from beef and eggs. He said his mother would prepare them for him when he was a child but mine were vastly inferior to hers. As he *so frequently* told me. Of course even the name of this dish tells you that it came originally from Spain."

"Is Linz a Greek name?"

"Not at all. It is *my* name. *I* am Linz."

"You didn't take his name when you married?"

"Of course not. Why should I?"

"But how is that possible?"

"Anything is possible, Miss Sert, you simply have to make your feelings known, very, very firmly. In the office where the marriage took place, they said I could not be legally called Mrs. Linz so I insisted that if on the documents I was Mrs. Carasso in real life *he* would be Mr. Linz!"

"Perhaps you should call me Evelyn," I said.

But she stared at me as if I were mad, for Mrs. Linz was a Yekke through and through and some formalities were sacrosanct.

It was a little cooler now. Even I noticed it. The air in the evenings was balmy rather than sweltering and I looked forward to the winter with feelings of delight. I went to the kitchen and made coffee for us both and cut slices of a cake I had bought from the café on the corner of the street in this city in which it was possible, when the British did not try to stop you with their megaphones, to live almost entirely out of doors. I was thinking, while I waited for the grounds to percolate, of what a strange thing a Jew was, how many forms we took. As I did so, a Jew with a beard and a long black coat and curious twisted curls hanging from in front of his ears passed on the other side of the road.

"Look at this," I called out to Mrs. Linz.

She walked into the kitchen and I pointed at him, retreating along the street toward Rehov Ben Yehuda.

"Oh, those curiosities. They exist in the eleventh century. They have no dynamism at all. They live the lives of vegetables. It is a pity you don't have a camera to record his image, for people of that type will be extinct within the decade."

I DID not look to Johnny for intellectual company—I had enough jaw-jaw with Blum and Mrs. Linz and her friends. To tell the truth, I was consumed with lust for him. Perhaps he was a kind of physical addiction of the kind that only comes upon you once or twice in your life. I thought about his body all the time, its hardness, the way he felt inside me, his skin with a rash of freckles across the top of his chest, the scar I licked, the hard lips, the roughness of the khaki trousers he wore and his hands unbuttoning them and my own trembling as I pulled my dress over my head. I wanted to give him all the satisfaction he wanted, to watch his face while he reached his climax and cried out in Hebrew things I did not yet understand. I had the shirt he had made for me now. It was blue. I never wore it outside, for as he said, it was just a kibbutz shirt, but as soon as it turned cool enough I slept in it.

When he didn't turn up at the apartment, and it was impossible because of the curfews to go out with Mrs. Linz to a café to listen to her intellectual friends discussing the latest ideas from Europe beneath a pall of brownish smoke, I would sit on my small balcony drinking coffee, wishing I had a sketchbook and pencils or even a camera so I could try to record the sights of Tel Aviv in such a way as to make sense of my world. Or even a school exercise book in which I could keep a journal.

But most of all I wanted to draw Johnny, and so I went and bought paper, together with some good pencils, and I persuaded him to lie on the floor by the balcony and pose for me. I was planning in my mind a painting I would execute one day which would show him with the white city and the roaring waves and the wide sky in the background: the new Jew and the new Jewish city. I wanted to paint the shadows that the bones of his pelvis cast on his stomach and the long toes and the lines that were beginning to appear round his eyes and the precise shade of reddish-purple that his balls were.

When I first asked him to pose for me he agreed, but reluctantly, because he believed that this was something only women did. He said he felt a fool, lying there immobile being looked at. He said he was worried that the finished picture might fall into the wrong hands and he would be a laughing stock. I asked him, point blank, whether he had had many lovers before me and he blushed and told me that the girls he had grown up with were very strait-laced. The Irgun girls, in particular, had no time for romance.

"But I couldn't have been the first," I said, puzzled, for he knew what to do exactly.

Now he went an even deeper red. "During the war . . ." he trailed off. So I suppose he meant prostitutes. "And a kibbutz girl from time to time." He did not like this kind of talk, it embarrassed him. I wondered if I embarrassed him too. I had never met anyone attached to him. I did not know a single friend. "But that's to protect you, darling," he told me.

I made my pencil study and he looked at it. "Is that how I appear to you?" he asked, coldly.

"Yes. How do you see yourself?"

He shrugged and changed the subject. I tried to explain the history of representation to him but he knew almost nothing about painting. I took him to the art museum on Rothschild Boulevard in the house that had once belonged to Tel Aviv's first mayor, Meir Dizengoff. The street was broad and shady, a sandy promenade ran down the center lined with tall trees, the name of which I didn't know and Johnny knew only in Hebrew. People strolled up and down as if they were in Vienna or Berlin. Newspaper kiosks stood at each intersection and we looked at the mansions that the city's first citizens had built for themselves before the first war.

Inside the museum we examined dim old brown pictures of rabbis which seemed to form the bulk of the collection.

"Is this it?" Johnny asked, frowning. "This is art?"

"No, no. I thought there might be something more modern."

"Let's get out of here."

That afternoon he showed me the teeming life of the white city, the garment district where he worked and where the earliest examples of Bauhaus buildings could be found, before the architects had figured out a way of adapting them to the climate, when they did not understand how important it was to make sure that each room had enough windows so they could create a cross-wind and before they had thought of the *brise-soleil*, the little ledge that cast a shadow into the interior. I saw shops stocking everything, run by people who came from everywhere, and though they spoke to each other in Hebrew *everyone,* I noticed, counted out money in their own language. We passed a store selling nothing but brushes—"If it has bristles, I stock it," the owner proudly told us. And indeed he had yard brushes, toothbrushes, bottle brushes, scrubbing brushes and something that wasn't a brush but had bristles: a selection of doormats. "They brush the underside of the shoes."

Walking beside Johnny I noticed how gradually the architecture changed and stopped being quite so modern and the style and idioms of the construction became completely unrecognizable to someone like me who had only ever seen the Georgian terraces of London, or the red-brick rows of Victorian villas at Hammersmith or, at the outer limits of my childhood world, the pre-war red-roofed semi-detached houses that frayed the edges of London, each with its own garden, front and back.

Because I was English and not American, came from a place with a continuous past, I did not understand then that when immigrants settle, they try to rebuild the land of their origins. These buildings, some of the earliest in the city, before the big population explosion of the 1930s, grew out of a yearning to construct Odessa and Moscow and Warsaw, and once inside them to try to forget the perpetual blue skies and the yellow, implacable sun.

I was surprised that we stopped long before the city gave out, where the streets grew very narrow and seemed to belong in a different town altogether. "What's that?" I asked, pointing with my bare arm.

"The slums."

"Who lives there?"

"Not Yekkes, that's for sure."

"But who?"

"The usual mixture. Arabs. Poor Jews, *really* poor. It's dangerous and dirty. You don't want to go there. Listen, during the war they had cases of bubonic plague. It's a cesspit. One day we will raze it to the ground."

It was called Manshieh and it frightened me. It was full of disease and squalor and it was like a small cancerous sore on the free and healthy body of the Jewish city.

That night Johnny stayed with me and slept by my side. After we had drifted into sleep in each other's arms I was woken by sounds and when I opened my eyes I realized they were coming from him. He was asleep but mumbling, fragments of Hebrew and even of English, and a long shudder ran through his body. Suddenly he screamed and I cried out, "What is it Johnny?" but I saw that his eyes were shut and that he was still sleeping.

Next morning I said, "Johnny, darling, you had a nightmare last night."

But he only looked at me and said, "You know, Evelyn, that's impossible, because I told you that I do not dream."

So then I knew that what Johnny had told me, that it was possible to have no interior life, was incorrect. Everyone has. He just didn't recognize its existence.

Later that day I talked to Mrs. Linz about the slum district and she asked me if I ever heard the muezzin, the man who called the people to prayer at the mosque, and I said I hadn't, for I had not known there was such a place in Tel Aviv. From then on I listened for it and sometimes I caught a trace of that alien sound though it was a long distance for it to travel, up the long boulevards to the white city where nothing was old and everything had an explanation.

AUTUMN came. One night, Mrs. Kulp's salon was raided and nothing was taken but some jars of chemicals from the back room: hydrogen peroxide and other inflammable and unstable materials.

Then Mackintosh was kidnapped. He was taken from his house in the morning, when he had finished his breakfast and was walking past his roses, his newspaper folded in his hand. His wife, who had waved him good-bye from the door, turned away, and when she stepped back seconds later to cry out that he had forgotten his sandwiches he had vanished. She looked along the street but could not see him. A Rover which had been parked there overnight was gone. The air was limpid and she stood in her floral wrapper on the doorstep, gazing at the space he had just occupied, puzzled but not yet apprehensive. Lupins and hollyhocks and Michaelmas daisies bloomed in her flowerbeds and the beds upstairs, still warm from their sleeping bodies, were not yet made. The houses glittered in the morning sun and the brightness of them as usual hurt her eyes which were weak and sensitive to sudden changes in the light. I know all this because she told me when, tearstained and desperate, having run to the police station to find out if he had arrived and having been informed that he had not been seen, she bumped into me on the Allenby Road on my own way to work and she sobbed against my chest, beating her fists against me.

"Why did we come to this bloody awful place?" she shouted at the passers-by. "Bloody Jews. I hate the lot of you." I knew it was not real anti-Semitism, just fright, and that if Johnny had vanished in the same way I would have raged against the Mackintoshes and the Boltons of this world myself.

There was a terrible mood in the salon that morning. Women hung their heads on frail necks as if in submission to their own execution. Hair refused to curl. Mrs. Kulp and I smiled and smiled, our smiles pasted onto our faces with the strong glue of our own convictions, but everyone who was in that morning knew Mrs. Mackintosh. "What harm did they do to anyone?" the women asked each other, helplessly.

The Jewish customers felt nervous and outnumbered. They drank coffee and buried their heads in magazines or loudly proclaimed the shame of it all. Only one, Mrs. Held, began to discuss quietly but emphatically her pleasure in the news of the hanging of the Nazis at Nuremberg the previous month. "I recite their names," she said. "Frank, Frick, Streicher, Rosenberg, Kaltenbrunner, von Ribbentrop, Sauckel, Jodl, Keitel and Seyss-Inquart. Not in this world anymore, none of them. So we have justice, we have finished one piece of business at least." She took out her compact and reapplied her lipstick and blotted her cheeks with powder, looking defiantly about her when her face was done.

She had once been a miller's daughter and lived in a wooden house by a river on a flat agrarian plain in eastern Poland. She remembered the threshing machines and the stones that crushed the wheat and the clouds of flour that rose like downy heaven. She remembered her father's *tallis,* hanging on the back of his chair and he and her brothers walking to the wooden *shul.* She remembered the exiles coming from Russia, the Red Jews who had escaped after the failure of the 1905 revolution and who took refuge in their town, and the pogroms that followed soon after. She remembered the journey to Palestine when she was ten years old and the gangs of Jewish and Arab laborers digging foundations into the sand dunes. She recalled watching Mayor Dizengoff's house being built, the same one which was now the art gallery, and a town so small that he would ride out on a white horse every morning to inspect it in his light, high-buttoned coat and a black bowler hat. "He was the first mayor of Tel Aviv but it felt like he was the first prime minister of Palestine." And that, she said, was only twenty-five years ago.

"I was there at the birth of a city," she said, turning to the other customers, the frightened and outraged British women. "And who among you can say that?"

She told me all this as the women of the colonial regime must have retreated that morning into their own memories: child-hoods under the Raj and the smells and sounds of India; the de-nuded landscapes of the Pennines and the cold winds blowing through slate-roofed towns; hills spread like butter with yellow broom in springtime; a bus up the Brompton Road on a Sep-tember morning when the windows of the shops were filled with the autumn styles and children's names were being embroidered onto tapes and sewn into school uniforms, and pens and pencils and compasses were purchased and put tidily into satchels with a square of sandwiches in greaseproof paper and a twist of sweets.

So we were all homesick in our own way, for each of us has a past and carries it inside us and you can never put it away. It always returns at moments when you least expect it, such as a November day in a brash violent city when a decent man had been kidnapped and his wife tried to shut from her mind the various fates that might await him, knowing that there were ter-rorists who were always armed wherever they went and would shoot on sight and perhaps even, one or two of them, for the pleasure of it.

"Who's got Mackintosh?" I asked Johnny when he came that night.

"We have."

"As a result of my information?"

"Of course."

"What's going to happen to him?"

"That depends."

"Are you going to kill him?"

"Not if they don't hang Dov Gruner. We might flog him though, in retaliation for flogging one of our boys."

"That will be a humiliation."

"Yes. It's a humiliating punishment."

Three days later Mackintosh had not reappeared but the news of his abduction was eclipsed by something else and passed out of sight altogether, as if it had never happened. In Haifa the British Army were tear-gassing and clubbing illegal immigrants whom they were herding on to deportee ships bound for Cyprus, the new prison island that was the fate of the DPs in the aftermath of the King David bombing. They killed a sixteen-year-old called Isaak Klausenbaum who was the leader of a defiant band of concentration-camp survivors. The immigrants were screaming and running from the ship with blood on their faces and the tear gas rose from the decks in a dense cloud. Women were holding babies whose eyes had disappeared into their swollen flesh from the gas. The reports of this event made me feel sick. When I ran my comb through the hair of the wives of the men who had carried out these atrocities, I wanted to stab its tail into their skulls.

People were being shot almost every day. Some nights I was woken by machine-gun fire. The gangsters and the terrorists were vying with each other to see who could claim the highest death toll. Another man went to an unmarked grave, killed when the car he was driving which was full of explosives blew up. Posters appeared on the walls and at first I couldn't read them but gradually, as I learned more Hebrew, the messages swam into my consciousness and another dimension of the city revealed itself, one which promised us that very shortly we would be free.

A plainclothes policeman was found shot dead in broad daylight standing at a bus stop near his house. His name was not released for some time but when it was I saw that his wife came in every fortnight for a shampoo and set.

"Did you do that, Johnny?" I said.

"No. Not us. It was the Lehi. Just coincidence. Don't you know that's not our style?"

The soldiers who were disembarking in Palestine, and the officials back from their leave, were talking about a strange upheaval in the world beyond this little part of the Mediterranean's rim. They were talking about the terrible, terrible cold that was across Europe. They spoke of gales sweeping the coast of Britain, trees uprooted, ships run upon the rocks and the Straits of Dover the coldest place on the continent. A Siberian wind was crossing Italy, that peninsula of sunshine and plenty, with Bologna under snow and two men frozen to death in Milan.

But the worst fate awaited Germany where the shadow of death stalked through its houses, the temperature fell to minus 23 degrees and there was almost complete industrial paralysis.

"In Germany," Blum said, "they are freezing to death while here in the *Jewish* city of Tel Aviv, I observe that it is 15 degrees in the metric system of measuring temperature. What does this tell us? And when you add to this the tidal wave in Japan and then the earthquake in that unfortunate country, one understands that our enemies, the Germans and the Italians and the Japanese, as well as the current foe, the British, are being punished for their crimes against the Jewish people. I do not speak of God. I don't believe in that, let's just call it fate."

I watched the cold on the newsreels. I watched them foraging for fuel and food and aiming pickaxes at the frozen ground to bury their dead. "Let them read the Book of Lamentations," Blum said. "They want to know how to survive everything life can throw at them? Come and learn from the Jews. We have a whole book about it."

Mackintosh was dumped on the street near Dizengoff Circle one morning, a week after his kidnapping. They had flogged him. Not long after that, the Mackintoshes went home to England for good. A picture postcard arrived at the salon from Newquay where they were taking a rest cure, going for long walks along the shut-up winter promenade. It was very peaceful, Mrs. Mackintosh said, but bitterly cold and the rationing seemed worse than ever.

I TOOK the number 13 bus to the zoo, to see the elephant named Bungo. It was on the edge of the white city and beyond it were orchards and orange groves and the villages of the Arabs, people who had nothing to do with us nor we with them. I hardly knew the country I was in, nor did I want to. I had no curiosity. I tasted the East in the foods I sometimes ate, the bean pastes and flat breads which were the legacy of Turkish rule and the salads with mint which came from the people we grudgingly shared the land with. The white city was enough for me as the kibbutz had been enough for the pioneers of Hashomer Hatzair.

I had seen an elephant before, in the zoo in London in Regent's Park. Its skin was gray and wrinkled and I disliked its smell. I went to the zoo in Tel Aviv not from a love of wild creatures but because it was something to do when I had exhausted the private galleries. There was plenty of theater in Palestine but little of it was in a language I could fully understand, apart from the plays put on by enthusiastic amateurs among the British colonialists who mounted productions of *The Pirates of Penzance* and J. B. Priestley's *An Inspector Calls*.

The zoo was full of animals which had come from somewhere else. There was nothing indigenous to the country, whatever it was that naturally inhabited the place. It was a menagerie of foreigners like the giraffes from the Sudan, exotic and out of place. Many years later I was told that that child's pet, the hamster, could be said to be a native for it had been discovered by a Jewish scientist in the 1920s on the border with Syria from where it was introduced to the rest of the world.

I bought an ice cream and sat on a wall eating it. It was cool enough now for a cardigan. In the sky mottled clouds had started to gather. It felt as if it might rain. The previous week I had stood on my balcony and heard the wind howling on the beach, stirring sand storms. People huddled in the cafés and ordered bowls of pea soup. Rain lashed the walls of our sparkling white building and stained patches began to appear on the concrete. Already discoloration was noticeable. Mrs. Kulp said the foundations were cracking.

The weather changed back again and I thought that that was it for the winter, it had finished, a little disturbance. But then an inspector called.

He stood with his hat on and his mac belted tightly round his waist, his face pockmarked and lightly sweating. An ugly man, I thought. Who would want to wrap her legs around *him* and call out his name or go to sleep thinking about his body?

"Mrs. Jones," he said.

"Inspector Bolton. How nice to see you again. You must be off duty." I looked around for Mrs. Bolton.

"No. Not me. I'm always on the prowl."

"Who are you trying to arrest now?"

"Not sure. It's the worst bloody place for getting people's identities straight."

"What's the crime?"

"That's what I want to know."

"How cleverly evasive you are, Inspector Bolton."

"Evasive. Big word for a hairdresser. I tend not to use those jaw-crunchers myself. But I'm just a grammar-school boy. Nothing posh about me. I didn't go to the university."

"I don't know where I picked it up. Probably from one of the customers."

"Would you care to join me for a cup of tea, Mrs. Jones?" He smiled and held out a hand. The hand was small and encased in a brown leather glove; it emerged from the sleeves of his coat in a dainty manner.

We left the zoo and walked along the street until we came to a café. He ordered a pot of tea for two but dismissed the display of cakes, "Unless you'd like one, Mrs. Jones. I don't have a sweet tooth myself."

"Not me. I'm dieting." A diet sheet had been handed round at the salon. It was all the rage. Johnny strenuously disapproved and kept trying to force-feed me forkfuls of meat from his own plate.

"Odd thing the amount of cake that gets eaten in this country. And almost no beer. Completely upside down if you ask me. How's your husband, Mrs. Jones?"

"Tony? Oh, awfully well. I went up to Tiberias last week to see him."

"Call me old-fashioned but I'd have thought a wife belonged with her husband."

"I'm sure I'm just as old fashioned as you are but I do think that during the war we girls got used to knocking about a bit on our own. Tony and I will be together again, just you wait and see." I smiled at him, as sweet as the cake he had turned down.

To my horror, he opened his mouth and began to sing in a tuneless voice. "There'll be bluebirds over the white cliffs of Dover tomorrow just you wait and see." I looked around at the other people in the café, the Jewish mothers and their children. They smirked beneath the napkins they used to dab against their mouths. "Lovely voice, Vera Lynn, the voice of England," he said.

"Yes."

"Are you fond of her yourself?"

"Quite. But"—and here I found myself repeating Johnny—"I prefer some of the American crooners like Frank Sinatra. More up to date."

"Ah yes, America. Funny place. Nobody's from there, if you take my meaning. Immigrants, the lot of them. I don't know how they get on at all. Odd business."

"Well," I said, "how do *you* get on *here?*"

"I just do my job, that's it. I shouldn't have thought Marjorie and I will be around much longer, anyway. They're phasing out the British in the Tel Aviv force. We're overrun by Jewish policemen already. They're a rum lot. Hard to tell whose side they're on."

"I thought you said you didn't take sides."

"No. I don't. As I say, I've never seen a side worth taking. But I've got a job to do and you can't have personal loyalties when it comes to arresting people."

"I suppose not."

"Personally, I'll be pleased to leave. My mother-in-law came out on a visit last year and observed that it would be a lovely country if there were completely different people in it, which is one point of view, but if you ask me it's always going to be a land of troublemakers. In the meantime, it's getting so we can't really operate properly anymore as any kind of effective ruling power. We're pretty well living behind barbed wire, as it is. In fact, we've rounded ourselves up." He began to laugh at this. "Yes, that's what we've done. We're so frightened of the terrorists we've put ourselves in protective custody. More tea?" I shook my head.

"I'll tell you what though, when I leave Palestine I hope I never speak to another Jew again. They've murdered too many of my friends. Martin, for example, excellent detective, expert in counter-terrorism. Gunned down on a tennis court in Haifa in cold blood. Another thing I saw, after they bombed the King David, half a human corpse impaled on a tree. Horrible. But that's terrorism for you, Mrs. Jones. That's the sort of people they are. What goes on in their minds, do you think?"

"I haven't the faintest idea."

"Really? Is that so? I would have thought you were quite close to that point of view."

"What on earth do you mean?" He offered me a cigarette from a silver-plate case and I did not take it because I did not want him to see that my hands were shaking. He looked at me sharply and withdrew the box.

"At the beauty parlor you must hear all sorts of things."

"Inspector Bolton, I give perms to respectable ladies. I don't do a short back and sides for gunmen."

"Those Jewish women are all sympathetic, though, aren't they?"

"I have absolutely no idea. We don't discuss politics." Now I wished I had taken the cigarette because I needed one.

"Really? Not interested yourself?"

"No."

"Me neither, but it's a bit difficult to avoid around here. Personally, I think we *should* pull out. Leave the Jews and the Arabs to fight it out on their own. It will be a mouse war. Two mice struggling over the same bit of cheese. Absolutely insignificant. You know how I describe Palestine?"

"How do you describe it, Inspector Bolton?"

"Half the size of a cemetery and twice as dead." He began to laugh again. "I've heard some of the public-school types in Jerusalem say that they wish the bloody Jews could just go away so we can govern the Arabs in peace. I think they find the Yids dangerously intellectual for their taste and mine too, come to that. Of course the Jews aren't going anywhere. They'll stay here and have their own little civil war between themselves which the intellectuals will lose because they always do. It will be those thrusting businessmen who come out on top. That's the way of the world."

"Have you applied to leave Palestine?"

"No. I'll see it out. I have a bit of unfinished business to attend to, tie up some loose ends. I want to get the people who kidnapped Mackintosh for starters. Have you any idea who they are, Mrs. Jones?"

"Inspector Bolton, you ask the most extraordinary questions. How on *earth* should I know a thing like that?" I thought of Johnny and how he had this sort of conversation all the time, where you had to keep your wits about you.

"I don't know, Mrs. Jones, I really don't. I just find that people often know quite unlikely things, the sort you wouldn't consider in your wildest dreams when you first look at them. Appearances can be deceptive, that's a first law in detective work. But your husband probably knows that."

"Tony isn't your rank, he's concerned with far more mundane matters, I'm afraid."

"What rank is he, Mrs. Jones?"

"He's a sergeant."

"Very nice. Perhaps he'll get a promotion. He could start with building up a little nest of informers, they're always a good way for an energetic man to get his career going. People who play for both sides always come in handy."

"Well, Inspector Bolton," I said, putting on my gloves, "this has been absolutely fascinating but I must be on my way."

"Very nice seeing you again, Mrs. Jones. You'll have to come to us one day for a meal."

"That would be delightful, thank you."

"I'm sure we've got lots more to talk about."

"I'm sure."

"My wife says you hide your light under a bushel. She thinks you're much brighter than you let on, but Marjorie says that's women's problem, having to hide their brains. She's very modern, in her own way."

"Oh, I'm not modern, Inspector Bolton."

"Aren't you? Then I'm deceived. Or not. We'll have to see."

He stood up, belted up his mac, put his gloves back on and tipped his hat and walked off. I sat and watched him go. I realized that he had left a pound note on the table to pay for our refreshments, enough to buy a pair of good shoes, let alone a pot of tea.

I heard the lions and tigers and other wild beasts roaring in the distance from their cages and the air was full of the smell of their excrement. It was four o'clock. The sun had gone below the horizon and I was cold. I caught the bus back to Mapu and thought for the first time that I hadn't a clue how to get hold of Johnny in an emergency.

I WAS so glad to see him, when he came two nights later, turning the key I had had made for him in the lock, walking into the room with his patent-leather hair and the reappearance at long last of the pencil mustache. I was so glad to have a conversation without artifice or double meanings. I ran over to him and held him tightly and kissed his face. "What's up?" he asked me.

I told him about the meeting with Bolton at the zoo. I hoped he would throw his head back and laugh and tell me I was worrying over nothing, but he didn't. He stared at me and lit a cigarette.

"Bad," he said. "Well, not good. I'm going to have to look into this. Maybe we'll stay here tonight. No, I don't think we'll go out."

I made us a rudimentary dinner of eggs and salad, chopping the tomatoes and the cucumbers as finely as I could as Mrs. Linz had shown me but my dice were larger and clumsier than hers and my eggs were not right. The yolks and the whites were not sufficiently bound together. My dressing for the salad was too vinegary. I did not use a good enough quality of oil.

Johnny looked down at his plate and smiled. "You never learned how to cook? Your mother never taught you?"

"My mother didn't cook much. She refused to learn when she was a girl because her mother was trying to marry her off and when the matchmaker came she cooked him such a terrible meal he told her she would never find a husband, or at least not the kind her family wanted for her. We used to get food from the Italian restaurants, they would bring the leftovers from lunchtime to us."

"One day I'll introduce you to my mother. She's a cook. And how."

"I'd like to meet your family."

"Now isn't the best time but one day, sure enough."

And by that, I felt assured he meant that in due course we would get married.

"Do you still want to be a soldier after independence?"

"Yes." His fork moving like lightning round the plate, which he protected with his arm.

"You eat very fast."

"You learn to do that in a big family. Kids are like wolves. They'll steal anything from your plate if you don't watch it. Also in the army you got your food down you as quick as you could in case they changed their minds about it being mealtime and told you to go polish your boots or dismantle your rifle or some other fun they had up their sleeves."

"And yet you want to go back to soldiering when we have our independence," I said, forking a piece of tomato into my mouth. The vinegar burned my tongue. "Haven't you had enough of war? I have."

"What do you know about war?"

"I lived through the Blitz."

"Oh yes, that. I forgot. Civilian war."

"It's all war."

"No. It isn't. You know what? I always wanted to be a soldier, when I was growing up a tough, cocky kid in Jerusalem and Betar put a rifle in my hand and told me I was going to be a fighter one day. All my childhood heroes were Jewish warriors—King David, Spartacus, Ben-Hur. I never loved the guys like Moses, the wise guys, the sages, the prophets. No, I read my Bible to see who in those olden days went to war for us Jews. I couldn't stand the Hasidim—you seen them? The guys with the beards who pray all day and all night? What for? If there is a God, he had nothing to do with us getting kicked out of Eretz Israel during the time of the Romans, it was lousy soldiering. When I first heard about bombs I thought they were the greatest thing in the world. Yeah, the greatest.

"I'll tell you what war is. It's a man's business and if women get hurt that's a tragedy because they've managed to stumble into something that has nothing to do with them. War is noise and blood and feeling you're going to vomit the contents of your stomach. It's obeying orders, because if you don't they'll shoot you. It's stumbling around in the dark because you don't know why you're on this beach or going up this hill because they're not going to give slime like you any idea of the bigger picture. It's trying not to shit your trousers and telling yourself, 'If I shit my trousers now no girl will ever sleep with me,' at a time when no girl has yet and that's the best way you can think of to stop yourself from total humiliation. But all these things you take for granted because that is what being a soldier is, and what being a man is.

"And I'll tell you what war isn't, and that is talking, having a conversation, like we're having now. When a battle is going on people are silent, withdrawn, locked inside their own heads thinking whatever it is they want to think about but what they're not doing is sharing their thoughts with anyone. I spent three days—three days and three nights—cowering in a foxhole with my mate Jim Pritchard and beyond tossing a coin to see who would crawl out into the whizzing shrapnel to refill our canteens with water we didn't say anything to each other the whole time. Not because we didn't have anything to say. But because we were paralyzed with fear."

He reached into his shirt pocket and threw an empty box of Player's on to the table. "You got a cigarette?" I passed one over to him. He looked at me. "I can tell by your face you don't like what I'm saying. Come on, spit it out, what's your problem?"

"I can't," I replied, "help thinking of the bomb at the King David. I heard that there were corpses hanging from trees. Do you condone that?"

"How long is it going to take us to live that operation down? My guess is a year. In a year people will have forgotten about it." He then did something I had never seen him do before. He blew a smoke ring. "Good trick, eh?" He smiled and reached across the table, across my unfinished plate of food, his arm knocking over the salt cellar which poured a glittering white hill on the red checked cloth. "Listen, Evelyn, there is nothing so transforming as a bomb. If you want to reinvent a city you put a bomb in it. Everything will be flattened and you can start again from scratch. You can impose any dream you like on a bomb site. And you know who was the greatest bomb-maker of them all?"

"Who?"

"A Jew. A Jew invented the world's best bomb. Albert Einstein who made the atom bomb and ended the war."

"I think it's a bomb that will end the world, never mind the war," I said, lighting a cigarette for myself and attempting to carry out the same trick of the smoke ring. He opened his mouth and showed me how to put my tongue to make it work. Still I failed.

"Keep out of it, Evelyn, forget smoke rings and forget war. You don't know what you're talking about. I tell you again, war is men's business not women's. Have I ever asked you to plant bombs, to carry a gun? Never and I never will, though there are girls in the Irgun who do exactly that and would love me to be their boyfriend, but I don't like that kind of girl. It isn't natural. It isn't normal. Girls like things to be nice and war is not nice,

no, not nice at all. But it's how the human race has always resolved its problems and how it always will."

He went and stood by the window and looked out into the
dark city where the British lived, huddled behind barbed wire.

"You know, when I was in the army, a British soldier said to
me, 'We gave you a railway and schools and hospitals. We gave
you a water supply. We gave you telephones. Why aren't you
grateful?' The British aren't so bad as colonialists go but they
will never understand our ingratitude. The Empire is coming to
an end, it's collapsing in slow motion before their own eyes and
it's going to finish in looting and humiliation. They're finished.
Instead of asking me why I plant bombs, why don't you ask the
British what they're going to do next? That's a big question. Do
you think they have thought about it?"

"I don't know."

"Me neither. It's not my problem. I don't care one way or the
other. Listen, we aren't going to need the British when we have
our own state because America will be on our side, the American Jews will make sure of that. Everything British will fade
away and the only thing of interest which the papers here will
report from London is the football results."

I began to laugh because Johnny reminded me of a child. A
great child, a wonderful one, the kind any parent would love to
have. He was loyal and devoted to the things he attached himself to. He didn't ask inconvenient questions and ignored the
ways in which life turned awkward. I looked in the mirror of his
mind, a confused and conflicted being, and he reflected me
back, simplified.

"How are Arsenal getting on?"

His face brightened. "Pretty good. After a terrible season
there's been a major revival. I've got hopes for the match against
Sunderland. Anyway, the English will always have their football
which they taught the world to play, including us. Now for *that*
I'm grateful."

We went to bed and he began to reminisce about his child-hood in Jerusalem and told me about the golden-domed mosque and the shadowy alleys of the old city. He described the burning desert in the south of the country and the sea at the Gulf of Aqaba. He told me about the archaeologists who were still searching in the Judean mountains for the legendary fortress of Masada where the Jews had been besieged by the Romans and slit their own throats rather than surrender. He talked briefly about the man he called his "captain," the leader of the Irgun forces, and of his love and respect for him: Menachem Begin, "who will also go down in history like those guys of olden times."

There are many different ways to make love. Some are charged by eroticism and others by the deepest affection and on this night it was the first way that we took. We did things then which are not unusual to read about in a newspaper and which even a child can see today. But in the small and insignificant British colony of Palestine, amongst a crude and ill-mannered people with no memory of the exquisite world of the courtesan, they were voyages into the dark. We did things I thought then that no one had ever done before. We were slippery with sweat. My orgasm was ferocious and took a long time to arrive and it drew me into a few moments' sleep. When I opened my eyes again, he was watching my face.

"Evelyn," he whispered. "Don't worry, I won't let any harm come to you."

"Yes, but who's going to protect *you?*"

"Don't worry about me. I'm a man. I protect myself. That's the order of things."

Just before I fell asleep again, I thought of Mrs. Linz and pitied her, the new woman who had no need of any of this.

Next morning he stayed as long as he could. I made him breakfast, salad and eggs again and white cheese and bread. In the shirt he had made me, I walked down to the street with him and watched him get on his bike and take off down to the sea front. Then I climbed the stairs to my apartment and got dressed, straightening the seams of the stockings it was cool enough to wear, painting a Cupid's bow on my lips, and filing the rough surface of a fingernail. I parted my hair and examined the roots to see if any dark growth was showing.

Johnny had said that there was a natural way to be a man and a natural way to be a woman. He made me want to be a natural girl, as Mrs. Linz was not. Was it surprising, I thought contemptuously, that her husband had raped her, trying to turn her back into a woman instead of the weird hybrid thing she had become?

B UT the next day, someone else came. He waited for me after work. Night was falling on Tel Aviv. He took my arm and walked me down to the beach. We sat on the cold sand under the cold stars and the sea sucked in its breath.

"You have to clear out," he said. "It isn't safe, anymore."

"Are you sure?"

"Of course. We know because the police are entirely infiltrated. There's a file on you at the station."

"Where shall I go?"

"Everything is taken care of. Go home, pack your suitcase. We'll see you later. Make sure you're ready."

"When will I see Johnny?"

"I don't know. I only take care of this end of things. You speak Yiddish?"

"No."

"Okay, we'll take that into account. Don't worry, everything is under control."

"What's your name?"

"Too many questions." He put his hand lightly over my lips. He was in his thirties, stocky, tough, a little bruiser. He spoke to me in English but I think his accent was Polish or Russian. The skin on his palm was callused.

"Can't I even ask where I'm going?"

"Stumm." His hand pressed harder against my mouth.

It was just before Christmas and the salon was full of British wives having their hair done for the festivities and after that would come the new year, 1947, which we hoped would be the date when we got our freedom. I felt bad letting Mrs. Kulp down.

What else did I feel? Fear, naturally. Perhaps Mrs. Linz was right. I should have refused to collude with him.

But I could not disguise the urge I felt toward what was about to happen to me, that I was to enter the dark center of our struggle against the colonial masters. I was going to the place where Johnny was, where a bomb was a cleansing, transforming instrument. I was beginning to perceive the shadowy force of the organization as it moved from the periphery of my life to encompass me. Like it or not, Johnny and I were both part of an army, illicit but powerful. It wasn't the kind of army that took part in great set-piece battles to acquire territory and which had rules of engagement and you had a rank and a number and there were laws about what you could or couldn't do, but it was an army nonetheless. A people's army which operated inside what we took to be everyday life and for such a war weren't women ideally placed to play our role?

I was moving through history, I was in it. I was no longer the hairdresser's daughter, or the dilettante would-be artist, or the useless immigrant, or the squirreled-away girlfriend. I was important enough for orders to be issued and arrangements made and messengers sent to meet me. I was no longer adorning the surfaces of reality but altering its internal structure as the chemicals I used on the heads of my clients did.

I went back to the apartment on Mapu and packed as much as I could into my Selfridges suitcase. I didn't tell anyone I was going. My rent was paid up. I had nothing to feel guilty about, but I was sorry not to see the child before I left. I didn't know when I would be back.

They hadn't said when they were coming for me. At two in the morning I fell asleep on the bed fully dressed. At seven I was woken by the key turning in the lock, the key I had had cut for Johnny. A girl came into the bedroom and told me to get up. She was dressed like a man, in khaki shirt and trousers.

"You ready?" she asked me in Hebrew.

"Yes," I said. I told her my Hebrew wasn't that good.

"Fine," she said. "I speak six languages. Pick one."

"English is all I know fluently."

"Then you're a fool."

I turned back at the door to look at the interiors of my modern apartment. The white walls were various shades of gray in the early light and the wooden chairs and picnic tables were also gray. We walked down the steps. Outside the sun cast mild shadows. Red flowers were struggling over a crack by the door. Another crack, higher up, had been clumsily pasted over with brown, gravelly cement which was ugly against the white plaster. The building looked as if it were catching bubonic plague or maybe smallpox, some kind of disease at any rate.

The girl led me to a pre-war Humber and slung my suitcase onto the back seat. We drove to King George Street, turned left across from the park, and passed through a pair of obelisks into a blind alley. There was a house at the end guarded by a stone lion with hollow eye sockets on a pedestal. The house was a perfect semicircle and it was strange to eyes used to ultra-modernity, to geometry and right angles, to see a building decorated with wrought-iron balconies festooned with laundry and ornamental stone pots and on the façade a Medusa-like head beneath a stone bow.

She led me up the stairs into a room with a Victorian bed, like the one my mother slept in all my childhood, made of metal shaped into flowers and leaves but this one had only an army blanket on it. Other than that there was a chair. I stayed in the room for several days and fairly regularly she brought me food but no information. I had nothing to read. The window looked out on to the back of other buildings but the blinds were lowered. I missed the sea. The room had a strange smell that was familiar but I couldn't pin it down. Then I remembered. It was the smell of the rooms of my mother's flat when the furniture had gone to the sale room and it stood, almost empty, on my last night in England before I embarked on the journey that would take me to Palestine. A smell that said that other people had been here before me.

Boredom made me lose count of time. The girl brought me some books, eventually. One volume was the poems of Jabotinsky, the philosopher of the Irgun. I read this:

> From the pit of decay and dust
> Through blood and sweat
> A generation will arise to us.
> Proud, generous and fierce.

It sounded like blackshirt stuff to me. The American couple and Mrs. Linz had been right about that. But Johnny would never have read it. He only read newspapers.

I began to paint pictures in my mind. I painted a picture of the view from my balcony on Mapu, the sea at the end of the street across Ha Yarkon. I painted the cars parked outside the buildings and the new Jews hurrying or strolling along toward their jobs or with bathing costumes and towels toward the beach. I wanted to paint a picture where you could smell the fragrant air and feel the sun on your bare shoulders and because all this was taking place in my imagination and not the difficult world of pigments I was able to accomplish my ambition.

Then I painted Johnny standing naked on the balcony and the pictures grew more and more pornographic and had less and less to do with art until they stopped being paintings and became something else.

I think Christmas came and went.

The girl came back with a box and handed it to me.

"What's this?"

"It's a wig."

"Why do I need a wig?"

"Because where we're going they're not used to seeing blond girls."

"Where are we going?"

"You'll see."

I opened the box.

"This is the kind of wig the religious women wear," I said. "What the hell's it made of? Horsehair?" I put my nose to it and it smelled of horse and someone else's scalp-sweat.

"Maybe. It was the only kind I could get." She laughed. "My grandmother who came from Bialystock wore a wig like that."

"I can't wear this."

"Miss, you have to."

I put it on. There wasn't a mirror. She looked at me. "The wig is okay but now the clothes aren't. You need more modest ones."

"Well, I haven't got anything like that."

"Fine. I'll go and buy some."

She came back in fifteen minutes with the kind of garments I had sometimes seen for sale and wondered who would ever buy them.

"Put them on."

"You're rude," I said.

"Who cares?" she replied.

I got dressed. She began to laugh. "If Efraim could see you now."

"Who's Efraim?"

But she only laughed at me again and I thought, "So now I know Johnny's real name."

"I think," she said, "we call you Gittel from now on. A nice Yiddish name."

"I don't speak Yiddish."

"Okay, Miriam. Miriam Levin. A dutiful wife. You speak any French?"

"Yes. A little."

"Good. You are an orthodox French lady from Paris. Your Hebrew isn't too hot because you haven't been here long, maybe just since before the war. The only Hebrew you know is the kind you pray in." She was laughing so much she had to wipe the tears from her eyes.

"You're a hard girl," I said.

"Yes," she said proudly. "I am."

"Men don't like that. Johnny—I mean Efraim—doesn't."

"Don't make me turn nasty. Efraim will marry an Irgun girl one day. You're nothing. A little diversion. He's already been formally censured."

"Over me?"

"Yes. I don't know what's got into him. To run these risks for something like you."

"What do you think I am?"

"Irrelevant. Come on, let's go."

It was late morning. We went down the dim stairway into the bright sunlight of Tel Aviv, blinking, shielding our eyes. We got into a different car from the one I had been brought in and drove down the Allenby Road south toward Jaffa. My face beneath my wig stared out behind the windshield at the women whose heels clicked on the pavement, their silk or nylon stockings swishing together. I wanted to jump out and run my comb through their hair.

THERE are slums in every city but why should there be slums in the newest, most modern city in the world? How can human life degenerate so fast? Why can't we *live* our idealism? The unpleasant girl was taking me to Manshieh. I didn't want to go. The car pushed through the peddlers and hawkers and pimps and prostitutes and people with the scars of diseases I didn't want to think about. It was raining again and the air smelled of rotting vegetables and shit.

"Why here?"

"Because it's a no-go area for the British. It's out of bounds to troops and the people will murder the police if they show their faces. There are lots of stabbings. Watch your back." She smiled, joyously. She'd have liked it if I died a sudden and violent death. "The ones you have to watch out for are the Arabs. Ramadan is coming, it's on its way. They want everyone to close their cafés, like them. Not a chance. Why should we put up with their religious craziness? Haven't we got enough of our own?"

What *was* that place? It was chaos. It was dirt and disorder, squalid and stinking. The white city didn't touch it. Perhaps it had its own charms but I couldn't see them.

We pulled up outside a two-story house. The façade had crumbled off in patches. We went inside. The girl went away for

a while and left me. There was a blue cloth on the table and on
it a folded Hebrew newspaper with an oil stain across its front
page. On the wall hung a sentimental painting of a saucer-eyed
child standing in an orange grove. On a shelf was a brass meno-
rah and a pair of brass candlesticks. Fat and spices thickened
the air. A cat came up and rubbed itself against my leg. I hate
cats. I reached out to pet one when I was a little girl and it
scratched my hand. It was a shop cat. It was trained to feed off
rats. It knew nothing of fur-stroking and meowing. I sat and listened to a clock ticking in a cheap tin case. The wig was giving
me a headache. I didn't know whether or not I could take it off.

The girl came back with a middle-aged man and a younger
one. "I recognize you," I said to the boy who was a year or two
older than me.

"Who are you?"

"Remember the kibbutz?"

"No."

"You must do. We learned Hebrew together."

"I don't know where I learned Hebrew. It was a long time
ago. Maybe a year. I have enough to do in life without remembering things."

But I knew it was him and that he recognized me. I saw the
tattoo on his wrist. I remembered the number, even. It had a 2
and a 7 in it. I think his name was Moishe, but names changed
here, no one stuck to the same one for very long.

"They'll take you," the girl said.

"Where are we going?"

"To the safe house. Where you stay for a while until things
calm down."

"How long will that be?"

"Who knows?" Perhaps she meant, who cares? She turned
her back and went away. I was left with the two men.

We walked along the alley, which was slippery with the rain.
"When will I see Efraim?" I asked them.

"Who?" they said.

How can you know someone if you don't know their name? How can you love them if you cannot even fix them long enough to say, with any certainty, who they are? If everything is fluid and in the process of self-invention how can you make a home for yourself in our own life?

"Johnny," I whispered and two tears coursed down my cheek.

"What's the matter?" the middle-aged man inquired. "Is it personal or political?"

"I don't know," I said. "I don't know anything."

"Good."

I looked at him. How many of these tough, stocky little Jews could a country hold? Men with thinning hair and big forearms, who smoked cigarette after cigarette and whose sentences always threatened to run through many languages, whose home was in themselves and their own simple ideas of what was right and wrong and what they wanted.

The house they took me to was no different from the one we had just left. They showed me to a bedroom with an army cot in one corner. I put my suitcase on the floor, sat down on the one upright wooden chair and began to cry. I cried in silence. Outside, beyond the peeling green paint of the wooden shutters the rain had stopped. The world stank of bruised tomatoes and rancid fat and very faint on the air an indescribable smell, except that all smells come from something specific and this one derived from a man who lived two houses away, who had been wounded in a gunfight and whose leg was turning gangrenous.

I vomited on the floor. Moishe came in. "What's this? Sick?"

"I can't stay here," I told him.

He wandered out again and came back with a tin bucket and a floorcloth. He kneeled down and wiped up my mess, then he left and shut the door behind him.

After a while I heard the two of them settle down to what sounded like a game of cards.

A couple of hours later, the middle-aged man knocked on the door. "You hungry?" I shook my head.

"Fine," he said and went away again.

Then, after more time had passed I had a rage for water. I went into the main room and they were still there, smoking and gambling. "I'm thirsty," I said.

Moishe went out of the house and came back in a moment with a jug. He poured some water into a glass. "Here," he said. "Anything else you need?"

"No."

"You will soon." He went to a cupboard and gave me a piss pot. It was from the previous century and decorated with flowers. Someone must have brought it from Russia.

I went to sleep. Night came. It was cold.

They were still up talking.

Then I was sick for a few days. I don't know what I had. I slept a lot and when I woke up I saw the wig sitting on the chair. I was still dressed in the religious clothes the girl had given me. My flesh stank of sweat and dirt.

Moishe wasn't around anymore. The middle-aged man, whose name was Yitzaak, came and asked me if I was better. I said I supposed I was. There was no point in telling him of my fear and loneliness. "So what?" he would say. I could hear it.

It was a country of so-what people. So-what you are cold and hungry? You want to know about cold and hunger? Let me tell you where *I* have been. *I* know cold and hunger. So-what you miss your mother? *My* mother was gassed. And my father and my grandparents and my sisters and brothers. So-what you want your boyfriend? *My* boyfriend was murdered by British soldiers. I was never going to outdo them. They had skins like elephant hides and they brandished their suffering at you like heavy clubs. They'd bash your brains out with those clubs if they could.

Suffering rarely ennobles. I know that now. At least with

Moishe his scar was visible, anyone could see it. You looked at him and you had your explanation. The suffering that was to come would not make *me* any better than I might have been, either. It didn't give me a big soul. It hardened my heart. A callous grows around a damaged place.

Forgive us. The evil we were making was in our circumstances.

Yitzaak sat down at the table. "Want to eat?"

"Yes. Something."

He unwrapped some vegetables from a newspaper and began to chop them up for a salad. When he'd finished he put what he'd made into a cracked blue dish. He wiped the blade of his knife along his shirt and then kissed it before putting it back in a drawer.

Then he went out. I waited for a few minutes. He came back with some slices of meat and a loaf of white, east European bread. He put some meat on a plate for me and tore off a piece of bread and lifted a handful of salad onto it. I looked down at it.

"Eat," he said. "Eat or die."

"I have no knife and fork."

"Fine. Here's a knife and fork." They clattered on to the table. "You want salt? You want oil?"

"I don't want anything."

"Eat or die."

I ate. I finished most of what he had given me.

"So," he said. "Your mother was a prostitute?"

"What!" I cried.

"That's what I heard."

"My mother was *not* a prostitute."

"Fine. So she wasn't. I don't care either way. There's plenty of prostitutes here. If you wanted to be a prostitute you could make a good living. The religious boys from the *yeshivot* would like you dressed like that. It would give them a thrill when you took your wig off. You want to meet a prostitute?"

"No."

"They're interesting people. I like talking to them. We have girls who pretend to be prostitutes to lure the British but that's a high-ranking job. They don't go to bed with them. They wouldn't be so great at that. They're very pure, the Irgun girls."

"And I am not pure?"

He shrugged. "I don't judge. Maybe you should meet some of our prostitutes, the Jewish girls, not the Arab sluts. You want to do something now? With me? He smiled and played with the knife that was lying on the table.

"Efraim would kill you," I shouted at him.

"Names, names, names. I don't know anyone called Efraim."

"You know who I mean."

"Yes. He talks about you a lot. He's crazy about you. You're right. I don't think he wants to share. Very selfish. The Kibbutzniks, they don't mind sharing. Moishe says you were very popular on the kibbutz." He looked at me, a short, hard man who knew nothing of the new woman but only the old one, of which there were two kinds.

I could have taken the knife and stabbed him because when you are trying to overthrow the old systems violence is the only way, as he knew himself.

"Everything is changing," I replied. *"Everything."*

He looked at me. "So what?"

FINALLY Johnny came. He looked glossy and well-washed. Only football miseries could make him disheveled. "Shit, Evelyn, what the hell has happened to you?" he said, holding me in his arms. He looked around. "Have they been taking good care of you?"

"No."

"No?"

"How could you let them do this to me?"

"What have they done?" He looked at me. "Are you angry?"

"Yes."

"Oh. I know that anger. I've seen it. Tell me everything, angry girl."

I told him. He smiled when I spoke of the rude girl. He was expressionless when I told him about the middle-aged man who thought I was a slut.

"Fine," he said. "Get your things. We're going."

"Do I have to wear this wig? I hate it."

"You're safest in the wig, but it's up to you. You're not stupid. Make your own judgments. It seems I can't be around to protect you all the time. I wish I could, with all my heart I do. But it's impossible. I have to recognize that."

As we were walking out, he turned his head and said something in Hebrew to the middle-aged man. He spoke very fast. The man shrugged. Johnny put down my Selfridges suitcase, walked over and punched him in the face. The man was howling, blood was running from his nose. This gave me a warm feeling inside. A fatherless child, I had a man who was prepared to commit an act of violence in my defense. I looked at Johnny and was sexually aroused. If I had told him what I felt, I know what he would have said: "This is normal, it's natural."

For a few minutes I no longer wanted to be a free woman. I wanted to be Johnny's little hausfrau. I wanted to be a soldier's wife who cooked for her husband and tended his battle wounds. I wanted his children. Is it not nice to have someone to take care of you, not to have to think for yourself? Isn't it a rest from the tumult of living?

"Where are we going, Johnny?" I asked him as he strapped my suitcase to the back of the Norton.

"Not far. Not far at all."

"I don't like Manshieh. I don't want to stay here."

"Not Manshieh. Somewhere else."

He took me to a place I had never been, called Neve Tzedek, hadn't even noticed it in my wanderings around the city. It was a lost world, far to the south, almost in Jaffa.

"What is this place?"

"It's old. Older than Tel Aviv."

"How can that be?"

"Sometime in the last century Jaffa was getting overcrowded and the Jews built a suburb for themselves. Now it's part of Tel Aviv. We've swallowed it up."

We drove into a maze of sun-bleached houses built in a different style. Neve Tzedek was quietly crumbling into dust. The narrow streets were broken. Weeds and flowers grew everywhere and date palms pitched themselves up wherever there was space for them to grow. Everything was small in Neve Tzedek, including the people: the women who trudged along with their shopping, the men carrying bits of machines rendered down far below any obvious function. Stray dogs shat themselves without disturbance from embarrassed owners. There were no sounds of any traffic. No cars. It was very peaceful. It was cool but above us the sky was very blue. Johnny took me to a school.

"You can stay here," he said. "You can pretend to be a teacher and teach the children something. Art maybe. But if there's a fire, get out fast."

"Why?"

"It's an arms cache."

"Do the teachers know that?"

"Sure."

This was nice. It was very nice. It was pleasant. I was going to be part of a community of intelligent people. I was looking forward to it. Perhaps I really would become a teacher one day, why not?

Johnny was talking to a woman. She was shaking her head.

"No go," he said, when he came back.

"Why?"

"It isn't as safe as I hoped."

"Where to now?"

"Don't worry, darling, we'll find somewhere."

I got back on the bike. I was being ferried around the city like an unwanted parcel.

Next we drove a short distance to a single-story house that was painted the color of ochre. Short palm trees obscured the windows. Dry, broken shutters hung half-open. Johnny opened the door which was not locked.

"Ah. This is okay," he said.

"What's this?" I asked him as we went inside. It was cold and the light was dim and the shadows that it cast had blurred edges. Old chairs and tables stood, covered in dust.

"It's deserted, abandoned. I don't know how long, people don't want to live in places like this anymore and who can blame them? It must be sixty years old. I like new things, new places, don't you, Evelyn?"

"Yes," I said, thinking of my apartment on Mapu with its revolutionary kitchen.

"But this is good. It's okay for now. You'll have to get water but I can fix that. Look, the stove works." He craned his neck upward. "Hey, the roof's good. No holes, no leaks." He turned to me. "Darling, I'm going to get you food and blankets, everything you need. You're going to be fine here. It won't be long. How can it be long?"

"Can I go out?"

"Yes. Go out as long as you're careful. It's a good neighborhood. No one will betray you. The British don't come here. Watch out for the Arabs but they won't bother you if you keep your head. You'll be fine."

He went away and left me alone. I sat down on a chair and felt very, very tired. I felt like Mrs. Linz when she arrived in Palestine and they took her to that place where she saw the Yemenites for the first time and she had sat on her suitcase and cried. I was in a foreign country, too, in exile from the white city.

He came back an hour later with blankets, sheets, a paraffin lamp, enough food to feed an army. "I took this from my parents' house. I don't know what the hell my mother will say when she finds out." He giggled. "Hey, go and make up the bed."

We lay down together and said nothing for a while. He began to make little soothing noises to me. He started to sing me a lullaby and I cried again, for it was the lullaby my mother had sung to me when I was a child, a Yiddish song: *"Schlof, mein maydele schlof,"* he sang.

"How do you know that?" I asked him through my tears.

"Everyone knows it," he told me.

We made love very quietly. Peace came down on the world.

We slept for a while. Then the muezzin sounded, slipping from Manshieh into the alleys of Neve Tzedek, and Johnny said, "I suppose it's dusk. I suppose I have to go now. I hate to leave you on your own."

"I'll be okay," I said.

"You sure?"

"Yes."

He got up and dressed. He leaned forward to lace his boots. I kissed him again. "Yes, yes. I'll be back. I'll bring you books and newspapers. Just tell me what you need. I'll get you a radio, no problem. Oh. Shit, that isn't possible. No electricity." He touched my face. "Darling, Bolton's never going to find you. Forget him. Just use your head and you'll be safe."

So I was alone with silence. It was so quiet in the house and in the alleys outside. For years I have tried to figure out the difference between loneliness and solitude. In Manshieh, guarded by those two terrible men, I was lonely. Here I felt at rest. Time stopped. It just gave up and stopped dead in its tracks. Nothing happened. It was as if someone had pulled its plug out from the mains. There was nothing to power it forward.

Every day a child would knock on my door and give me a newspaper, which I never read. Johnny had arranged that. Soon, the child arrived with a sketch pad and pencils and a cheap tin box of watercolors. I imagined Johnny on his bike weaving through the violent noise of the insistent city thinking of me, trying to guess what I wanted.

The days drifted but I wasn't bored. Sometimes I went out and had short, rudimentary conversations in Hebrew with my neighbors who did not bother me, just as Johnny said. It was a place where people minded their own business. We talked about nothing, the nothing that is everything if you do not preoccupy your mind with higher things such as ridding yourself of colonialists or the struggle to become a free woman: a baby's tooth coming through; a bad back; a fickle lover; how to get stains out of your best dress.

One day, venturing along the street in my wig and my modest clothes, I came across a man sitting at a wooden table on which there were four typewriters.

"What languages do you speak?" I asked him in Hebrew.

"All of them," he said.

"Not really?"

"Pretty much."

"What are you doing?" I asked him in English.

"I'm the typewriter. I write letters for people. I have four keyboards, Roman, Hebrew, Cyrillic and Arabic."

"What letters do you write?" The fingers that tapped the keys also tapped a long column of ash from his cigarette.

"I type love letters and letters to creditors and letters to doctors and letters to mothers and letters to sons. And sometimes to fathers. I am the author of many fictions, as you can imagine. Last week I wrote a letter to Poland saying that the sender was doing very well and was rich and had married a high-born lady from Warsaw when in fact he's a house burglar and lives with an Arab girl. But that can't be written because it's not a Zionist message you want to send back to over there. Yesterday I wrote a suicide note for an illiterate woman. Another woman, who came from the camps, wanted to dictate her memoirs to me for possible publication but though it was probably a lucrative commission in terms of its length, I said no. No one wants to read about those times. I told her, forget it, no one is interested."

"What did you do before you became a typewriter?"

"I was a doctor. We're overflowing with doctors here. We're like ants in an anthill. I sometimes perform abortions if I can get the work but it's more infrequent than typewriting. Jews want more Jews these days, not less. Anything you want written?"

"No. But thank you."

I left him there in the sunshine, at his table which he rented for a few mils from the woman whose house he sat outside.

I went home and stretched out and waited until it was time to go overground once more. My body felt heavy and round. My breasts seemed enormous in my hands.

After a few days I stopped wearing the wig. The dark roots of my hair were showing through. The children were frightened of me at first, then they laughed and pointed. I laughed too. My eyebrows were growing back but I didn't have any tweezers to pluck them with.

The child brought notes from Johnny. He couldn't come. But he would. If I needed to get a message to him, give it to the child. The child would be there every morning without fail. I could be sure of that. He was being paid.

I began to plan a picture of Tel Aviv in olden times, in the 1920s before they built the white city. From the vantage point of my painting you are standing at a window. A table to the left holds a plate with an oversized orange and a banana and next to these a green pot containing a plant with pink leaves and pink stems. The street is populated by small figures, couples walking together, a woman carrying some kind of burden on her head, a tethered donkey. The houses on each side, framed in the window's view by pink curtains edged heavily in scalloped lace, have wrought-iron balconies and on the right there is a three-story octagonal structure of colonnaded recesses from Turkish times but really it is a mongrel, a mixture of bits of buildings I had seen, jumbled together.

The charm of these arrangements is disturbed by two elements: the first is a series of pylons on the left-hand side of the road with cables stretching above the rooftops; the second is that the street leads down to the sea—not a sun-dappled, azure stretch of water, but a black roiling ocean on which a two-funneled ship vomiting smoke is powered by formidable engines to the shore.

I dreamed about my picture the night I first imagined it and for many years to come. I dreamed that, like Alice, I stepped through the glass into the painting and walked along the street toward the shore. I stopped a strolling couple along my way and asked them, what is this place? Where am I? But they were dumb and could not speak. I stopped the woman with the burden on her head. Where am I? I said. And she looked at me, with surprise, and answered, home.

My painting speaks of the command to return from exile and I had obeyed the injunction. Was home. Whatever happened, I would never leave Palestine, this strange, violent, mixed-up place where things were not always pleasant, indeed rarely so. Where people's manners were bad and they spoke roughly, but to the point. Where everyone came from somewhere else and everyone had a story to tell and these stories were not always inspiring or lovely. Where life was chaotic, because that is what life is. Where the past was murky and tragic and the future had to be grasped by the throat. Where Europe ended and the East began and people tried to live inside that particular, crazy contradiction.

I sat outside the derelict house in the shade of the date palms and I was dreaming, as God in some stories is said to be dreaming the world and all of us in it, going about our business. I was dreaming Tel Aviv, from the towers of Jaffa and its fishing fleet, through Neve Tzedek to the white city and beyond where it ran out into sand and there was nothing but orchards and orange groves and Arab villages which meant nothing to me, nor me to them.

The child stopped coming and I forgot to wonder why. I had everything I needed, I was self-sufficient and every day was more or less the same.

THEN time, which had slowed down, began to speed up again. Mrs. Linz would start shouting at me if I ever saw her again for I had no excuse. I looked at the moon and I knew that I was my mother's daughter, the hairdresser's daughter, not a freedom fighter for Zion against the might of the Empire.

Where was the child? I asked the typewriter but he didn't know who I was talking about. There were lots of children littering the alleys of Neve Tzedek, who could distinguish between them? He looked at me. "Is there anything else I can do for you apart from type a letter?"

"No," I said. "Definitely not."

"Good," he said. "Excellent. Congratulations. A new baby for the new land of Zion. What will we call the baby? What will we call the new land? Some people want to name our child Israel."

What would Johnny say? He would say, "This is normal. This is natural." I just had to find a way of communicating the situation to him. So despite everything I was very, very happy.

Something had entered my bloodstream which stopped me from using my head, the hormones that tell women that childbirth doesn't hurt and babies sleep all the time. Why had the little boy disappeared? No. I couldn't think of a reason. Johnny said he would come because he was being paid, so where was he? It took me two days to understand that the child was no longer in Johnny's employ. He wasn't getting his wages. And the only reason for that was that Johnny wasn't around to give them to him.

In the abandoned house, I went to the pile of newspapers. I looked at the dates. January had come and I hadn't noticed. It was 1947 now.

Incidents were taking place daily. The roads and railways were mined. There were raids on army installations. A district police headquarters had been bombed with a hundred casualties. A British judge had been abducted by the Irgun while in the middle of presiding over a case in a Tel Aviv court. A British businessman had also been kidnapped and the two of them were being held hostage until there was a stay of execution for Dov Gruner, the Irgun boy who was still being held at Acre. In London an MP said in parliament, "The British Empire is being insulted by a bunch of gangsters."

There was a small item about the capture of a middle-ranking Irgun terrorist. Johnny's face looked out at me from the page. He was named as Levi Aharoni and a number of other aliases followed. The trial seemed to have taken place very quickly. There was a short report of some courtroom exchanges. "Yesterday we fought the Jerries together, now do you want to know why I turn my guns against you?" Johnny had said.

"No politics," the judge had ordered.

"Look at British justice, they won't let me talk, even."

His commanding officer gave testimony that he had been a fine soldier and that it was a great blow to find out that he had been a traitor and a terrorist. The judge sentenced Johnny to death for a string of atrocities stretching back to just after the end of the war. About twenty dead were specifically named.

"Count how many telephone poles there are in Palestine," Johnny had shouted as they led him off, "because that's how many coffins you'll have to prepare if you're going to execute me."

The condemned man was held in Acre prison, the report concluded.

I lay on the floor reading this. I was very, very cold. My limbs felt like lead. My hair was full of dust. The baby was shriveling inside me.

I heard Mrs. Linz's voice in my head, sounding in an echo chamber. "It is as I always warned you," she said. "Those who choose the gun will fail and end up in shallow graves or at the end of a noose."

"Oh go away you bloody bitch," I cried. "Leave me alone."

I stood up and walked down the street to find the typewriter. He was sitting at his table reading the paper.

"What's going on?" I asked him. I looked around, the whole world seemed unfamiliar.

"Today I typed a letter for . . ."

"No. In the city."

"We might be near the end," he said. "They're sick of the situation. The government is about to bring in martial law."

"What will that mean?"

"I don't know. I don't know how the British operate. I hear they are bringing a lot of new troops into the country. They're sending the women and children back to England."

"I don't know what to do," I said, to no one in particular.

"Go home," he said, kindly. "Wait. That's what we're all doing, waiting. Waiting for the new state to be born. Just wait. It won't be long."

"Then what?"

"Who knows?"

I walked back to the abandoned house, a pregnant woman whose boyfriend was to be hanged. I wanted to return to the building on Mapu. I wanted to be amongst the intellectuals. *They* would know what to do. But I didn't dare.

I ran out of food. The neighbors fed me. I ran out of paraffin, they gave me some. Every day, I walked along the street to see the typewriter who summarized what was going on in the newspapers. My clothes were too tight round the waist. I found a cracked looking glass in the house and stared at myself. My hair looked terrible. I cut most of the blond part out. I looked as if I had come straight from a camp, but fat, not thin. My whole body was round.

While I was camped out in the derelict house in Neve Tzedek two great armies were crossing Palestine in opposite directions.

"What's news today?" I asked the typewriter.

"The country is bloated with British soldiers disembarking from the ships, it says here they overflow the camp at Sarafand. Poor boys, who thought the war was over and they were going home. But they find there is unfinished business." He laughed. "They have been sent to fight the Jews. Do you think any of them have ever seen any Jews before?"

Only on the Pathé newsreels, lying around dead, in piles.

"Now in the other direction goes another crowd, the evacuation of the women and children. They are running through the streets purchasing trunks full of clothes. This is strange. Why? I don't understand."

"Because at home," I said, "clothes are still on the ration."

The time was over, I guessed, when I would be mistaken on the street for a Christian girl. Priscilla Jones would have to be folded up and put away. As for Evelyn Sert, who had entered the country as a biblical tourist, she was no use to me either. So at the very moment when Palestine became a country of Jewish women (apart from the Arabs, who didn't really matter) I had no identity at all.

"What's worrying you?" asked the typewriter, folding away his newspaper.

"I haven't got any documents. I don't know how to get any more."

"No one will come here. All will be well. No one is going to harm anyone. They won't hang those boys in Acre. They wouldn't dare."

I don't know what he knew or didn't. Probably this was just general conversation but I had to take comfort from what he said. So I thought that if I could just hold on long enough, I would see Johnny again and everything would be all right.

The baby was growing. It was about eight or nine weeks old. It must have had eyes by now. We lay in bed together at night, two pairs of eyes staring into the darkness.

I stopped painting pictures in my mind. I kept being woken by the sound of bombs going off in the white city. The British imperial identity was disintegrating in front of us, the new Jewish one was being born, but I was nameless and invisible and my little ego couldn't bear it. I missed my mother. I missed Mrs. Linz. I missed Uncle Joe who surely would have known how to help me. I sat alone among my pile of old newspapers, examining my cracked and dirty nails.

One morning I had had enough of solitude. I decided to take a risk and I left Neve Tzedek to walk to Allenby Street and watch for myself the collapse of the British Empire. I did this so I would have the memory of it to tell my grandchildren.

T HE streets were choked with cars. Women were crying, children were looking bewildered. The shopkeepers were standing on their doorsteps watching them go. They were wondering what it meant for their takings. A few of them were concluding sales at the wound-down window of a vehicle. A woman was buying food. "Will there be anything to eat on the airplane?" "I don't know. I've never been in one." Another woman was hugging her dog. "What's going to happen to Yorkie?" she was whispering. "Please, will someone help me." A Jewish woman ran over to her. "I'll keep your little dog," she said. "I love all animals. Give me your address in England. I'll write to you and tell you how he's getting on." "I don't have an address. I don't know *where* I'm going. What's going to happen to me?" Her husband appeared, in civilian dress. "Now, old girl," he said to her. "There, there. Best not to cry." He attempted to take the dog from her. "You'll have him put down," she suddenly shouted. "I know you will. You've never liked him. I've heard you. 'Bloody mutt.' You'll hit him over the head with one of your precious golf clubs."

Scenes like these were happening at intervals amidst much dignity and graciousness. Some women were saying a round of good-byes to neighbors and favorite Jewish shopkeepers.

"Palestine is my *home* you know," a woman told a baker. "I've been here since I was a girl. My father was in Kenya before he came out. They're sending me back to England. I hardly know it. I'm going into exile, but you people know all about that."

The baker smiled sympathetically but after she had turned away he burst out laughing.

Others were kinder. I saw genuine affection there on Allenby Street. But let's face it, we were delighted to see the back of them. All the Jews were whispering the same thing. "Can't be long now." "No." "A few months." "Maybe just weeks." "Dr. Weizmann's coming back. He's on his way from London. He's been negotiating with the British. There's going to be partition. We'll have our country, the Arabs will have theirs. It's the best way." "The Arabs will never accept it." "They'll have to. The British will make them." "That's a laugh. The British can't make anyone do anything anymore. They're washed up. Look at them, fleeing for their lives."

I stood on the corner of Allenby Street and Rehov Bailik and thought how that intersection marked the crossroads in our lives. One was the street named for the British general who had marched into Jerusalem in 1917, the other for the Zionist poet who had come from Budapest in the last century. The white city began there.

People had started to look into the sky, watching for planes. One passed overhead. Perhaps it was the first batch of women leaving, people said. They waved. I looked up too. Many of us were smiling. By and large there was a good feeling in the air. It was warm and there was a mild breeze blowing in from the sea a few streets away. The cafés were full. I wished I had some money so I could venture into one for a few minutes to have a piece of cake which I had not eaten for ages. Imagine a Palestinian without his daily pastry! It was inconceivable.

A fist grabbed my arm. I looked around. An arm was extending from the rolled-down window of a car. I got the fright of my life.

"Mrs. Jones, how pleasant. Need a lift to the airport?"

They were in a Rover. Bolton was wearing his belted mac. His wife was dressed in a navy costume, with a coat with a fox-fur collar resting lightly round her shoulders. It was her hand that was on me.

"No, thank you," I said, "I can make my own arrangements."

"I must say, Mrs. Jones, you look quite different. I would hardly have recognized you," Bolton said.

"But *I* did," said Mrs. Bolton. "Easy to fool a man, but another woman is a different matter. Personally I always thought the platinum blond suited you but everyone can do with a change now and again, though I must say you do seem to have let yourself go, rather."

"Jump in," Bolton said.

"As I say, I have my own arrangements." People walked up and down and took no notice. A Yemenite woman was shaking a baby. Two men were consulting their watches. Someone with a mental illness who had probably been in a camp was crying and muttering. A kibbutz girl was running along the street in pursuit of something or other. An Arab led a camel through the traffic. The driver of a bus swore at him.

The two of them got out of the car and stood in front of me.

"We've missed you at the salon," Mrs. Bolton said.

"Oh, I got fed up with waiting for Tony so I joined him in Tiberias." My teeth were chattering.

"Yes, that's what Mrs. Kulp said." I felt a surge of warmth toward poor foolish Mrs. Kulp who nonetheless knew how to tell a lie with the best of us.

"I really think there's no time to lose," Bolton said. "Do get in."

"As you see, I have nothing with me. No suitcase. No passport. And Tony will worry."

"Is he still in Tiberias?"

"Yes, of course."

"Funny," Bolton said. "Because I'd heard on the grapevine that he'd been transferred to Acre and I thought, dear me, Mrs. Jones won't like Acre much. Nothing for her there. Nothing at all."

"I do think you should come with us."

I was trying not to cry.

"Yes. It's for the best."

"I don't think you really belong here."

"Perhaps none of us do." My eyes were filling with tears.

"You're quite right. But you know you're really out of your depth."

"I've managed to conclude some unfinished business," Bolton said. "That makes me quite chuffed. I'm not a vengeful man. I'll be off myself, quite soon, I expect."

"We thought we'd start a nursery growing fuchsias in Kent," Mrs. Bolton added. "We like fuchsias."

"It's a restful occupation. We're looking forward to a rest."

"I'd rather stay if you don't mind," I whispered.

"No," Bolton said. "I think that's pretty much out of the question. I don't know what might happen to Jones. He's a resourceful man. He might just manage to get a transfer out of Acre or there again he might end his days there. The last one's no good for you. The first one is no good for me. And it certainly won't do you any good in the long run, either. So do get in, Mrs. Jones." He was holding the car door open.

"I don't have any things."

"I can lend you something," Mrs. Bolton said.

"I don't have my passport."

"I'll smooth things over when we get there," Bolton said. "Leave it up to me."

They gently began to shove me into the car, like a slow-motion abduction. I turned to the people milling on the streets.

They weren't paying any attention. HELP ME, I mouthed, soundlessly. But no one saw, no one came.

Mrs. Bolton was in the back seat, next to me. Her arm was resting on mine. Bolton started the engine. I turned my head and saw the American couple sitting in a café. She had on a necklace which looked like a string of silver pebbles. They caught sight of me and waved and smiled. HELP ME. The woman put her hand to her ear then smiled and spread her hands in resignation. She put them to her lips to make a megaphone. I could just make out what she was saying. "Catch you later." Her husband took her hand. They sat in the sunshine smiling. They looked very happy together and happy with the general situation of mayhem on the streets and why wouldn't they be? They were watching one of the minor incidents in the collapse of the British Empire. They must have thought much the same as I had: it would be something to tell the grandchildren. Hot tears were coursing down my cheeks. The woman held a finger to her eye and made a sad face, then a gesture with her hands to ask, "Why?"

But Bolton was accelerating down the street. I turned my head and saw the last of them, smiling and perplexed.

"In case you're not quite up to date with the details of the evacuation," Mrs. Bolton was saying, "Mrs. Gutch, the wife of the undersecretary, has already left and Mrs. Wilson-Brown whose husband is director of public works and their three children. Oh, and Lady Astley, of the British Council. *They* had armored cars accompanying *them*."

"Assassination risk," Bolton said. "We're lower down the pecking order. No one's interested in us."

We drove beyond the borders of the white city. We were in those orchards and orange groves that I had always known existed.

"What sort of place is Lydda, George?" Mrs. Bolton asked.

"Lydda?" I asked startled. I was thinking we were going to Haifa, to the docks. I had just that moment thought that I could give them the slip there, maybe make my way north to the kib-butz where they would surely hide me and keep me safe.

"Yes. The RAF is taking us as far as Cairo and then it's BOAC from there to London," Mrs. Bolton said.

"Arab town. Not much Jewish about it. Big trade-union feel-ing. We paid the Yids more than the Arab workers and there was a strike there in the 1930s I believe. We brought in Jewish strike-breakers. Did the trick."

"Isn't that fascinating, Mrs. Jones?"

I said nothing because I was feeling sick. I had never been to an airport. I didn't know how they worked. We drove on in si-lence for a while. Mrs. Bolton reached into a hold-all and took out a week-old edition of *The Times*. She started doing the crossword. "Are you good at puzzles, Mrs. Jones?"

"No."

"I enjoy them. Mental gymnastics, eh? Sure you wouldn't like to try a clue? Here's one . . ."

"Oh, do shut up," I said.

Mrs. Bolton drew in her breath. "I think we'll ignore that, shall we, George? Mrs. Jones is a little upset and anxious which is hardly surprising under these rather trying circumstances. My husband is a great believer in calling a spade a spade but some-times reticence is the best way."

I looked at her beside me. She was imperturbable. What would you have to do to disturb her clever complacency? A bomb might be the only thing that could ever do it. What did they say when they were alone together? I would spend a long time thinking about the Boltons and what sort of creatures they might be. They were a complete cipher, like their crossword puzzles. What did they stand for? I have no idea. Did they think that standing for something was a kind of corruption? They had turned not believing in anything into a high art form. They had developed nuanced exchanges and made irony and double meanings a kind of empty, dazzling dance of the mind. In fact they were a premonition, a precursor of how things were going to turn out. They were the future of the Empire, but that, as they say, is another story and it isn't mine.

On the outskirts of Lydda we ran into an army roadblock. Bolton got out of the car, asked for the most senior officer available and walked off a few yards with him. The soldier stood with his arms clasped behind his back, his head to one side, listening. Finally, he nodded.

Bolton came back to the car. "Everything's hunky-dory," he said.

"Oh good," his wife said. "I am glad."

We drove through various military patrols until we got to a kind of shed. Hundreds of women were milling about. Children were crying or looking excited. Outside, I could see airplanes on the tarmac. I'd never been so close to one before. "That's what you call a runway," a man was explaining to his son.

"We've sent a telegram to our chaps in Cairo," Bolton said to me. "The situation has been explained. You'll have papers waiting for you there."

I nodded. There was a terrible lump in my throat. "What then?"

"Up to you. They'll fly you on to London, of course, or you might want to try your luck somewhere else."

"I'll get back," I said, defiantly.

"Not just yet. The border has been closed to all Britons. If you have a British passport you can't get in at all."

"How ironic," said Mrs. Bolton, turning to me.

Behind me a woman was shouting. "Don't you realize what you've done? You've turned us into bloody DPs."

"Oh do calm down," someone said. "You're making a frightful impression."

"I'm a DP," I said.

"Not at all," said Bolton. "You have a passport. People would kill for that."

"You'll need to attend to certain other irregularities in your situation, though."

"What do you mean?"

Mrs. Bolton turned to me. She had light blue eyes. "I'm a great believer in the view that a woman needs a husband, a steady chap. Choose the right one and you can have all the freedom you want. It's the formalities that count, everything else is a matter of negotiation. Pragmatically speaking, you need to get yourself sorted out. Quite quickly, I'd have thought."

We boarded the airplane. Bolton clasped his wife's hand for a moment then let it go. He winked at her. It was a very lascivious wink. For a second I tried to imagine their sex life. God knows what they got up to.

"Good-bye, Mrs. Jones," he said, extending his hand. I didn't take it. He shrugged and turned away. His shoulders heaved. I think he was laughing.

We sat on the runway for a long time. Behind me, a cross mother was saying to her daughter: "It's all very well being natural when you are twenty-three, but at thirty-three it's more difficult and at forty, impossible. How do you think you came by your femininity? Picked it up in the street? My dear, it's an art, one you must work on all your life, through clothes, through cosmetics, through perfume. All artifice, I agree, but after all, this airplane—what is it but artificial? It's an invention."

The girl made a sulky noise.

Mrs. Bolton smiled. "How true."

The machine we sat in was juddering. It began to move. The pilot drove us forward. We lifted off the ground. Some children began to cry and a woman stifled a little scream. I looked out of the window and saw the land beneath us. In a moment I saw the Mediterranean Sea. I saw the white city, laid out like a grid. I saw cars moving along the roads. It was a very blue day. In the streets of Tel Aviv people would be craning their necks to look at us. Beyond Tel Aviv were brown hills and other countries.

Someone was explaining terminology that was new to me: taxiing, banking.

Beneath the roar of the engines Mrs. Bolton was saying something. "France. A very irregular sort of place. Would suit you down to the ground, I'd have thought."

The Mediterranean was packed with traffic, on it and above it. The captain pointed out the tiny shape of a troop-carrier. We turned south. We flew over the Sinai desert where Moses and the Children of Israel had wandered for forty years. Jesus only wandered for forty days and forty nights. Forty years! Beat that, goyim, Uncle Joe had once said.

"They've been Jews for absolutely centuries," someone was saying, "and most of that has been spent in exile, one way or another. Why do they want to change their tune now?"

I thought of Johnny at the end of a rope, his tongue hanging out.

"You're green, dear. Need the sick bag?"

I nodded. I vomited into a paper envelope.

"Can't be long now." She smiled.

Then I turned my head and was sick on her lap. The sick, a thin porridgy stream tinged with green bile, dripped from her skirt and onto her right leg, down the calf and the ankle and settled on her shoe.

A S I say, scratch a Jew and you have a story. Mine is no
more significant or interesting than anyone else's, but get
us to stop telling it! That you will never do, if the Jews are still
here in another millennium.

One day I returned to the white city, but when I say one day,
I mean many, many years later when my marriage had been the
greater part of my life and my husband was dead and one of my
two children dead.

I flew the length of the Mediterranean Sea, over Rhodes and
Cyprus.

I came out into the airport which was in the same place as the
one I had left fifty years before, though barely recognizable
from that airfield which had been not much more than a collection of sheds. There was a badly executed mural on the wall in
the baggage area depicting the heroic struggle of the Zionist
project, just like one that Leah and I might have painted at the
kibbutz, and it seemed to me that it was not at ease in this neutral, international space before you surrendered your bags to
the eyes of customs control. Under it, dark shadows of men
gathered, bearded, black-hatted, black-clad. They held boxes
from New York stores, containing more black hats. Time had
twitched and drawn them from a forgotten crease in the past.

They made their way to the Eldan desk to rent cars and cell phones. They spoke Hebrew with an American accent. They disappeared into their cars or into the shared taxis that went to Jerusalem. Above us, departing passengers ate pizza and watched planes from many countries zigzag back and forth on the runway. The security people looked at everyone with X-ray eyes, convinced that they could see through our disguises and to who we really were.

I had given my account of myself at the embassy in London. A Jewish widow who wished to rest her bones in the Promised Land stood in her Harrods coat before them and listened, smiling, while they told me that if I wanted to make *aliyah* I would need a *ketuba,* my mother's marriage certificate. But there is no *ketuba,* I said. And my grandmother's? Lost somewhere in Latvia or handed on, maybe, to one of her children whose names I did not even know. These difficulties were still being examined and discussed, and memos written and rabbis consulted and community leaders addressed as I entered Israel on an extended tourist's visa. A private detective I had engaged was searching the burial sites of the East End of London for the graves of my grandparents. We need records, the men from the Jewish agency said. Give us documents. Go and dig up the past.

From the past there is no escape. The past is *everything.* Meier on the kibbutz was right.

I left the terminal and got a cab with a driver with scars on his face who tried to cheat me on the fare. "In the Jewish city?" I thought, in my innocence.

We were on a six-lane highway. The traffic on its own was a nightmare. After a while, when we had turned across a bridge above the freeway and entered a grimy metropolis of some kind, I said, "Where am I? Where have you taken me?"

"Tel Aviv. Where you asked to go."

"This isn't Tel Aviv."

"You been here before?"

"Yes. Before independence. Where are all the white buildings, where is the white city?"

"You're in it."

"That can't be."

"Listen, it may have been white once, but it's not white now. You want nice apartments, go to the suburbs, go to the dormitory towns."

In the distance the skyscrapers rose like white swords from the business district in the south, near the little minaret of Jaffa.

Once, an Arab had sold watermelons on the corner of Mapu and Ben Yehuda streets and I had imagined him waiting for the day when the desert would rise up to engulf us. But he had not reckoned with Jewish ingenuity. The Tel Aviv of the Mandate days was still there, as the ruins of Ancient Rome are still there, fragments of another, underground city, like the bones of the dead sticking up above the ground but it wasn't sand which had buried it. Like Troy or Pompeii, it lay beneath archaeological layers of advertising billboards, peeling plaster, graffiti, forests of electrical wiring, naked neon light, natural gas tanks, Dumpsters, air-conditioning motors, transformers and air grates. Brown air. Brown buildings. Soiled vegetation photosynthesizing brown light in the disheveled gardens. Grubby cats foraging for abandoned meals in the grass, choking on chicken bones. The white city, I have to say, and this is an understatement, was an eyesore. Who knows, perhaps it was the ugliest place in the world?

"What happened to Ha Yarkon?"

"You're on it."

"Where are the cafés?"

"I remember cafés here, when I was a kid. But they got rid of them years ago to build the hotels. Which one do you want? Sheraton, Dan, Holiday Inn? Look. Nice hotels, very modern. All the luxuries you could ask for."

"They're in the way of the sea. They block the view." The hotels rose up like high concrete castles defending the coast where there had once been cafés with noisy gramophones and the British officers' clubs and the clubs of the officers of the Free French and the Free Poles and all the other scraps of armies that found themselves encamped in the Middle East.

"Of course they are. Tourists come here and they want a view. We give it to them."

"Where did you get your injuries?" I asked him.

"Lebanon. Where else? You wanna hear my story?"

Look at it this way, we are the people of the Book. It is the first thousand years of Jewish history and though we have no second volume for the next two thousand years, each story a Jew tells is part of that book. We have no choice but to listen. Our history was in our story, for the Arabs of Palestine, it was the land. Without a story we're not Jews. Without a land they're not just DPs, they're an abstract idea—a cause. That's not a human being. This is the great wrong we did them.

He started to tell me how he had come from a village in the south of Poland with his mother and father when he was five years old, in 1950. "You know how they survived the war? A Polish farmer hid them. Isn't that something? They got right through the war and then the minute it was over, the anti-Semitism started up again, like nothing had happened. *Nothing!* So what should they do but leave? They dumped us in Herzlea, in tents, where from the age of six my mother would send me out into the garden with a stick to kill snakes. What a country! We were terrified! My God, it was so primitive. My parents spent all their time talking about how much they missed Poland but also how much they hated it, how fantastic it was to be in Israel and how terrible the life was. Confused? I was a confused kid, all right.

"Then we got sick of the heat and the dirt and we came to Tel Aviv. Listen, it was *worse.* The old people, the pioneers who came out in the thirties, they sneered at us, they called us *Ostjuden.* You know what that means?"

"Yes."

"Now you want people who are really primitive, you look at the Moroccans and the Yemenites. *Them* they should have put in tents. I mean, where would they have ever seen a house before they came here? And the Ethiopians, my God. That's Africa, isn't it? It's the jungle. But you know who were the worst of all? You know who I hate the worst?"

"Who? Tell me your hatreds. Let's hear the lot."

"The kibbutzniks. They wanted me to be a sabra. They wanted me to forget I was ever a Pole. They said, 'The parents we can do nothing about but the children, we can remake them in our own image.' Like hell they could. They wanted socialism. Listen, we spent five years under socialism after the war, in Poland. What good did it do the Poles? The kibbutzniks. I'll tell you about them, they were rich compared to us. They had swimming pools. Some socialism. I know those guys. I fought next to them in my unit during the war, not just Lebanon. I fought in '67 and '73 and '82 and if I have to I'll fight all over again, but not my sons. *Absolutely not.* If it kills me, I'll make sure they get rich. Stockbroker. That's a job I would like them to have. But if we make a peace with our enemies, do you want to know who will make it? People like me. Not my stockbroker sons, certainly not the religious boys who won't fight and those guys who come over from Brooklyn who think they can tell me I can't drive my cab on Shabbat or eat pork and that we'll never give up this place or that place that is mentioned in the Bible. No. The only people who get to sit at the peace table are the ones who made the war. And another thing . . ."

He took me to the apartment on Mapu. The glittering white surfaces were shit brown. Mercifully, palm trees had grown up in the spaces between the buildings, and overgrown oleander and hibiscus bushes hid some of the dereliction and decay. Inside, the common hallways stank.

Mrs. Linz let me in. She leaned on a stick. "Arthritic hip," she said, curtly. The khaki shorts and shirt were long gone, so were the crumbling rubber sneakers. She had a mass of well-cut, curly white hair but otherwise she was dressed in a skirt and a blouse and a string of pearls like any nice German woman of her age. I walked into the apartment. The same furniture, the same brass bowls, the same Arab dress, arms akimbo. The bookshelves were still packed but now there were paperbacks. The only difference.

"Where is the white city?" I asked her, after I had sat down and she had poured me a glass of Coca-Cola, cold from the fridge.

"It turned brown," she said. "A matter in part of poor maintenance but also corrosion from the salt air. The law that protected the tenants was a disaster for the buildings. Blum was not the only one who had no money to maintain his investment. It was a correct idea, of course, but it had consequences which we did not foresee."

"You were the Weimar Republic in exile," I said, remembering. "How old are you now, Mrs. Linz?"

"I am eighty-five."

I arrived in October when the weather was starting to cool down. I walked the streets of the city. The trees were so much bigger now and mercifully they cast a bigger shade. I still don't know the name of those trees that grow along Rehov Allenby and Rothschild Boulevard where one day in 1948 David Ben-Gurion had gone to the art gallery which had once been the home of Mayor Dizengoff in the days when the town was small enough so that he could ride out each day in his high-buttoned coat on his white horse and inspect it. Among the brown paintings of rabbis Ben-Gurion had declared the state and the Palestine Philharmonic played "Hatikvah," which was now the national anthem, and in doing so became the Israel Philharmonic. Then they went home and the next day the war started.

The religious people had gone, they'd left for Jerusalem or B'nai Brak. They think Tel Aviv is Sodom and Gomorrah. "I used to think the Hasidim were vegetables," Mrs. Linz said. "But now they have woken from their slumber. They still live in the medieval times, but now they are medieval types with guns." Where Mrs. Kulp's salon once stood there is a place where you can have a tattoo or a ring inserted in your nipple. The thought makes me sick and I always turn my head away when I pass. Next door there is a bar where the homosexuals drink coffee for, despite every other change, Tel Aviv does remain the place where you can eat cake at any time of day and night. There were no British in their shorts, shouting at you through megaphones, just boy and girl soldiers with their rifles. "Wanna score?" they asked each other.

I traced the steps of my weeks spent on the run. I turned off from King George Street, a shabby thoroughfare of bargain-basement shops, into the alley and the stone lions still stood but less like statues and more like models of extinct creatures in a science museum. The telegraph lines were covered in some kind of creeper. The city's first buildings, the ones with traces of Odessa and Kiev in their concrete bones, were derelict. I walked through the Carmel Market on my way to Manshieh and *that* was just the same. The same foodstuffs on sale, the same pimps, the same prostitutes doing their shopping, just different nationalities because it's the Russians who control the trade now. It made me smile, this. With vice, nothing changes.

But at the end of the street where Manshieh should have started there was nothing. It had vanished from the earth, only the mosque remained, and where the houses had been a bus terminus and a parking lot in the shadow of the skyscrapers of the bourse. "What happened?" I asked an old man passing by, with his shopping.

"To what?"

"To the houses, the people?"

"What do you mean?"

"There used to be a place here. It was called Manshieh."

"Oh yes, that's true. It was mainly an Arab neighborhood. We chased out the people and then we demolished it. I don't know why they didn't blow up the mosque too. You know what they did? They used the minaret to post their snipers during the war of independence, in which I fought, incidentally."

"What did you do?"

"I drove the Arabs out of Jaffa. What the hell did they think they were doing there? This is the *Jewish* city! Tel Aviv. The Arabs can go find their own place." He spat on the ground. I watched him go off, lugging his shopping. Every few yards, he stopped for a rest and looked at the sea and looked at the towers of Jaffa and sucked from a plastic bottle of a brightly colored orange drink.

I walked toward Neve Tzedek. At least *that* remained. As the white city of Tel Aviv had declined so the old original quarter had found a new lease of life.

"Who lives here?" I asked a girl.

"Yuppies."

The school where I had nearly been a teacher was a performing arts center. I sat in the café and drank a cappuccino. The air was still and fragrant. No need of a typewriter, now, I thought.

I walked along Allenby Street which I last saw when I was abducted by the Boltons. Where were they now? I hadn't thought about them for years. Perhaps, if they were still alive, in an old people's home with ticking clocks and dried flower arrangements and shaking fingers bent over the crossword puzzle and the smell of incontinence. Allenby was in a bad way. The shops were run down and sold things you wouldn't want. The people who shopped there looked poor. Poor and angry, which is a potent mixture. They jostled and shoved each other aside and shouted. Two fat, fair-haired women were having a terrible row in Russian outside a shop that advertised in both Hebrew and

Cyrillic letters that it sold pork. One of the women tore open her bag of meat and threw it in the other's face. In retaliation she reached in her bag and got out a knife. People were ringing the police on their cell phones. I looked up and saw the blue sky between the overhanging branches of the nameless trees.

I went everywhere. The zoo was gone. It had once been on the edge of town but then it was swallowed up by the neighborhood that came to surround it, whose residents complained of the noise and the smells. It was relocated, as a kind of safari park, somewhere. The Galina café where the young mothers of Tel Aviv ate ice cream in the afternoon with their babies and the Yekkes sat on the sand was gone too. Demolished the previous year. "It was in a terrible state," Mrs. Linz said. "Neglect, as usual. It was best to put it out of its misery."

"How strange that the most emphatically optimistic architecture ever built should have had such a short life span."

Mrs. Linz shrugged. "I know. And we were building with an *idea*," she said.

"It will be the end of the century, soon, the Jewish century."

"Oh, I can't stand labels."

"But it *was* the Jewish century—the century when the Jews left eastern Europe and the masses went to America and entered modern life and made their contribution to the creation of the American identity. The century of the Holocaust but also of Einstein and Schoenberg and Hollywood and Saul Bellow and Philip Roth and . . ."

"You don't read those dreadful people, do you?"

"Of course."

"*Ostjuden*. Like Amos Oz and David Grossman. Particularly Oz, one of those weavers of the founding myths of Zionism."

"Well, what do you read?"

"English literature, the greatest in the world. William Trevor, Jennifer Johnston."

"Mrs. Linz, they're Irish."

"It is the same thing. Anyway, I hope to live to see the next century and let's hope it is another kind altogether, one without labels."

Some hope.

One day, in 1947 in the city of Nice, I had walked through a high, wrought-iron gate in a stone wall on a kind of escarpment above the old town which you reached by a lift in a tunnel. It was very calm up there, with the red roofs below me and the birds singing sweetly and the dome of the Negresco Hotel, where the rich people stayed, glittering in the sunlight. For years to come I would wake up from a dream of that cemetery, of the snowcapped mountains and the blue sky and the glimpses of the sea below, the cypresses and the umbrella pines.

I walked on across the hill. The port was below me. I felt the roughness of a wall abrade my skin as I touched it. I came to a gate and on it a sign said that this was *Le Cimetière israelite*. Just inside some men were constructing a mausoleum. The sweat was on their backs.

"What's this?" I asked one of the laborers, in my girls'-school French. It nearly came out as Hebrew. *Mah zeh?*

For the Israelites killed in Poland, they told me. The Society of Israelites had urns ready. They were going to put in ashes from the crematoriums. The laborer lowered his voice. And bars of soap.

A man was walking through the cemetery. He was watching me. He saw me looking at another tombstone, a few feet away from him. He was watching my mouth move silently as I read. He was trying to make out what I was saying to myself and as he read my lips the words formed in his mind as Hebrew. So he walked over to me. I looked up, startled.

"What's your name?" he asked me.

"Evelyn Sert," I said.

"Are you a Jewess?"

"Yes."

He was my future husband. His name was Leopold, but I called him Leo.

The British officials in Cairo had handed me—"under instructions from Jerusalem"—a passport in the name of Evelyn Sert, with a notice pasted inside indicating that the bearer was prohibited from entering Palestine. And a very small amount of cash. Mrs. Bolton had boarded an airplane bound for London. We did not say good-bye. I took a third-class berth on a ship to Marseilles.

The engines were beating the waters but I was oblivious, asleep, inert, shell-shocked.

I was remembering my first home. How, when I was a child, I would come back from school sometimes when my mother was working at the salon and wander through our little rooms piled on top of each other in the higgledy-piggledy eighteenth-century flat. I would watch the weak sunshine that made its way over the roofs opposite to penetrate our sash windows and lie in pools on our carpet with its repeating pattern of thornless roses. The silver-plate coffee set, tarnished from too much polishing; the Russian samovar which Uncle Joe had bought my mother; the china dish of fading rose petals; and in a glass-fronted display cabinet like Blum's her collection of Dresden china figurines which she saved up for, with her tips from the salon. How many? Twenty? I'd never counted. She had shepherdesses, a pierrot, a rustic youth. When I was a child they were my friends. I gave them names and invented stories for them. I paired some of them off as sweethearts. As I grew older they seemed shallow and sentimental, striking fixed poses with their little china arms.

But they were what I thought of on the ship that took me away from Palestine, my mother's face floating into my mind, as it always would in the years to come when the weather was cold or I was lonely and longed to be a child again. I was at the center of the universe in the middle of all the slightly grubby chintz domesticity, where my mother had built one nest of seduction and allure for her lover and another of safety and love for me.

That place of refuge was where I lived for the first part of the voyage. I thought I would stay like that forever and that they would land me on the shore and I would be a vagrant, a derelict person crying in the sunshine. I painted myself thus, in my mind's eye, a grossly pregnant woman who was also one atom of the flotsam and jetsam of postwar Europe.

But Palestine had taught me something, the hardest lesson: that there is no choice but to act, to take charge of your life. You can indulge your inertia only so far and then you have to snap out of it. In the end you *must* do something. From then on, I thought about nothing but my situation, driven into exile on the very eve of the Return. What to do? What to do?

I lived on my wits and on the tough kibbutz survival skills I had been taught plus a large bottle of Guerlain's Shalimar which I slathered myself with every morning. I stole the perfume from a shop in the rue du Suede. I remembered Uncle Joe's maxim: "The only thing worse than being skint is looking as if you are skint." I was reassembling my femininity but it was hard because my hair was so very short. It was almost like Jean Seberg's in *A bout de souffle,* but that was ten years in the future. I looked like I might have just come out of a camp, except I wasn't thin.

After we met, in the cemetery, Leo took me to lunch at an expensive restaurant on the Promenade des Anglais.

I told him a story, then he told me his. He was a great talker, Leo, not in an argumentative way, not like the Jews who, as the old joke has it, if you bring three together you have ten opinions. No, he was a *descriptive* talker, a user of adjectives and other embellishments which I'd forgotten about in Palestine where verbs were the thing, verbs. The doing words.

As I listened I was watching him. I saw the well-pressed suit, the formal knot in his tie and the way he counted his change twice and carefully calculated the percentage of the gratuity, not, I surmised, because he was mean, but because he was precise. I looked at his face. He was a small, slightly built man but with a certain elegance of figure. He was a Jew from Berlin who went to America in the 1930s, a violinist in one of the studio orchestras, playing on the soundtrack of the movies. That's him you hear on "Some Enchanted Evening" if you've ever seen *South Pacific*.

He was lonely and looking for love. He was a reader of the bittersweet fictions of Stefan Zweig. Another Yekke, but one whose backbone was not ideas but romanticism. I thought, "I can handle him."

He asked if we could meet again the next day and I said yes.

I only slipped up once with him during our whirlwind courtship, and that was a few days later when we lunched again at the same restaurant.

As we admired the flames of the crêpe suzette the waiter brought us for dessert, there was a stir. Forks and knives clattered down on to the table. We both looked up.

Entering the salon, carried on two petite limbs, was some sort of a fairy tale: meters and meters of sea-green grosgrain, gathered and tucked and artfully diverted into a frock reminiscent of another time and century when women had nothing to do all day except ornament society.

"You're staring at that dress as if you've never seen anything like it before," he said. And indeed the expression on my face, at that moment, must have been overwhelming bewilderment. Totally unbeknownst to me, while the Jews of Palestine were into the final stages of their life-and-death struggle against the British for their future and I was sitting among old newspapers on the dusty floor of Neve Tzedek, in Paris Christian Dior had turned the clock back fifty years and launched what quite paradoxically came to be known as the New Look and this was the very first example to have reached the Riviera. He had restored to women what they had craved for so long during the bleak years of rationing and aerial combat. Their femininity. And you know, I was as enthralled and enraptured as anyone else.

So something passed into history for me, at lunch in that restaurant in Nice in March 1947—the brief moment in my life when I had been privileged to live in modern times.

It wasn't hard to get Leo into bed, not hard at all. At first I made a mistake by being too forward, by undressing, instead of allowing myself to be undressed. I had to unlearn everything about the hotness of passion and become a kind of courtesan. I had to learn the very thing that my mother had known and that I had dismissed as being old-fashioned, and it was allure, because that is what attracted Leo.

What is that? What is the eternal feminine that men love so much? Silence. Mystery. We are blank canvases onto which they can project their fantasies and women who are successful in love understand this intuitively. The magazines tell you "be yourself" but nothing is further from the truth. Be the self *they* want you to be and yet always let them know you preserve something inside that they can never quite capture, that eludes them, because men are hunters and it is the thrill of the chase that excites them. All you have to do is figure out what the fantasy is, and you have caught them. My mother knew it. I learned it in a single day, watching Leo, listening to him. That's what being a good listener means. They talk, you calculate.

He smoked small cheroots and inspected the gleam on his shoes when the shoeshine boy returned them to him. He fussed over ties and shirts. He took his money out of his trouser pockets and made neat little piles of the change on the dresser. But he was a good man, I could see that at once. *He* would never lose his temper and cry out *Ostjude!*

He said my body puzzled him. He didn't understand the long, brown well-muscled legs and the curvaceous stomach and the heavy breasts. He said I was a paradox. I had a narrow scrape when a vendeuse in a dress shop he took me to, to buy me some frocks, said, "But madame is tanned! Have you come from the colonies?"

He moved me into his hotel. Every morning he read aloud to me from the newspaper. "Listen to this," he said, excitedly. "The British in Palestine have decided to wash their hands of the place. They've said that the Mandate is unworkable. They're handing it over to the United Nations to resolve. They're preparing to pull out." He shook his head, smiling. "All over the world little guys are challenging big guys. It's amazing. Do you know what I should do? I've a good mind to drop everything and just go there and fight."

I smiled to hear this. Leo in Palestine, his exquisite sensibility grappling with the appalling heat and the shortages, the curfews, the searches. Leo in the Irgun! He would be paralyzed by indecision.

"Oh!" I cried. "Do you plan to desert me?"

And he reached across the table and took my hand for a moment and looked at me, meltingly.

All this calculation was going on in my brain but somewhere else I was frozen like the winter that had gripped Europe.

One evening, walking along the Promenade des Anglais under a clear and starry sky, he suddenly turned to me and asked, "Evelyn, are you pregnant?"

I gasped. "Why do you say that?"

"I was just looking at you as you walked beside me, in silhouette, in that white dress. And now your face is very white, under the moon."

"Yes. I am."

"But it's only been three weeks. Surely . . ."

"No. You're right. I was pregnant when I met you, I didn't know, though. I have only known for a few days."

He was silent. And summoning every atom of the Jewish will to survive against all the odds, I said this, which I had been preparing for some days: "The transgression wasn't against you, it was against myself. After my parents were killed I was so lonely. Everyone was affected by the war, I wasn't the only one to lose someone, but it was different for me, I had no one left. I met someone. I had a great yearning— for a purposeful life and for happiness. I had a yearning for motherhood. I wanted a child at my breast, I wanted to watch a child growing up in a family that loved it, as I was loved. I wanted someone to love me but it was a child whose love I craved.

"I chose a father for that child. I allowed my body to be embraced by his, though I shuddered with repulsion when I did so. I realized that he would always be a stranger to me, because I didn't love him and never could. Nonetheless, we married. My baby will not be illegitimate. This is my husband's child. Seven weeks ago he died. His heart gave out at the age of twenty-six. There was a weakness there all along.

"And even when he died, I didn't love him because you don't choose love, it chooses you. I came to France to recover my equilibrium and I met the man I should have met first. *You* are the one I was looking for. You are the one who should have fathered my baby. Even if my husband were still alive, it would be you I was unfaithful to, if I let him kiss or touch me. Life has taken its revenge on me. I shouldn't have been so headstrong, I should have waited. I should have waited for you. And now I'm waiting for the sentence you will pass on me."

He listened to my "confession" in silence. It was agony waiting for him to speak. Finally he said, "The child is mine. This other man will be forgotten. Let him rest in his grave in peace. Our life together will be tender. Come here, come to me."

So I knew that he remembered the poem, for *of course* he would have played the music, *Verklärte Nacht,* which Blum had made me listen to one afternoon in the white city, when I thought I knew everything and how everything would turn out.

Instead of denouncing me, Leo had chosen to take the part assigned to him. "Why should the child you have conceived be a burden on your soul?" he whispered. "Why should I condemn and sentence you? There is only the heart that loves and suffers, this is all that matters."

And as he kissed me, he later said, he felt the radiance fall on himself. Which was just as I'd planned.

It was a new twist on an old trick. Why did he fall for it? Why didn't he smell a rat? Of course the poem was familiar to him but isn't the very power of romance its familiarity, that we tell ourselves the same old stories over and over again? Is there any new way of saying anything that is to do with love? I don't think so. The heart finds its familiar grooves and runs along them and the music emerges, the song of all time.

My daughter Naomi came to visit me in Tel Aviv, though reluctantly. She had grown up to be a girl with no interest in either art or music. She has a hard, analytical mind. She enjoys tricky sums and statistics and became a lecturer in international relations at the London School of Economics. I went to listen to her once, but I couldn't understand a word of it. She hardly remembered anything of our time in America, before her brother died and Leo turned his back on California and brought us to London.

I had thought she and Mrs. Linz might get on, for Mrs. Linz votes for any communist candidate she can find or else for members of the Arab lists. Once a week, with her stick, she takes the bus to Jerusalem and makes her way to the office of the human-rights organization where despite the painful stiffness in her hands she types up Palestinian testimonies of the atrocities committed by our army. Heartrending stuff. She brings them home sometimes for me to read. I can't stomach too much, it makes me sick to think anyone would do these things, especially a Jew. The Palestinians are themselves, of course, capable of equally ghastly deeds such as torture but, as the people I met from the camps had taught me, suffering very rarely ennobles. Primo Levi is the exception, not the rule.

Naomi, however, does not accept Mrs. Linz at her own estimation of herself. For the first time Mrs. Linz met her match.

"Mrs. Linz, do you not understand that you were doing *exactly* the same thing as the British?"

"Explain," said Mrs. Linz, her arms folded across her chest.

"Colonialism assumed that it was bringing enlightenment to benighted peoples. You Zionists took exactly the same attitude to the Arab population, and of course to the Jews from North Africa and the East who followed. Your ideas are inherently colonial."

"So we should have left them as they were, in their primitive darkness?"

"You should have respected their culture."

"This was not a culture. Where was their music, their literature?"

"That is *your* idea of a culture."

"Oh, you are a relativist and a reactionary. People like you make me sick, you post-modernists. You believe in nothing. You have no center. Who are you? You have no idea. You think everything is the same, when it is not. Your generation never lived through evil times. One thing is not as good as another. If you wish to argue with someone, go and see my son the atomic scientist who in 1967 left Stanford University and came back to defend his country. Why? Was he a soldier? Of course not. He went to a kibbutz where the men had been mobilized to their units and he drove a tractor for the summer. The country was swollen with jubilation and *hideous* patriotism and everyone was so triumphant. It was ghastly. You could not get away from the *arrogance*. My son has brought together two ideas as dangerous as each other—nuclear weapons and right-wing Zionism. I could have rid myself of this child, in the womb, you know. There were people who could have performed the operation. I was mad not to have done so. It would have saved me and the rest of the world a lot of trouble."

And so the argument went on as I stood at the balcony and watched the sun setting and thought of the pictures I used to paint of a street of long ago, and a ship sailing along the shore, its red and black funnels belching black smoke.

I wanted to say to Naomi (but knew that I was no match for her intellect), "Listen to me for a change. Don't you understand that we have no choice but to live through the portion of history that is allotted to us?"

No one likes Tel Aviv. The tourists make their way from the airport straight to Jerusalem which has history, it has "soul." I rarely go. I can't stand the place. If Mrs. Linz had her way, she'd evacuate all the inhabitants of the Old City, blow up everything—the Wailing Wall, the churches, the Dome of the Rock—and build something useful, like a hospital. I agree with her.

Tel Aviv is dirty and chaotic but at least it's alive, not a museum. Now that we've destroyed Beirut it is the only city left on this far Mediterranean coast that can really be called the Levant, a mongrel metropolis of aliens among aliens. By the bus station there's a shanty town of illegal immigrants, mainly from Thailand and Romania. They're not Jews. As far as they're concerned, Israel is just another rich country, like any other. Which reminds me of that line from the Book of Jeremiah: *Behold, I will gather them from the North country, and gather them from the uttermost parts of the earth.* Maybe that has been the purpose of this place all along, to be a magnet for strangers.

Yesterday, I went to the Carmel Market to buy our fruit and vegetables and meat. I took the bus back up Ben Yehuda. The streets still smell mysterious to me and the palm trees still rustle above my head. the light seems a little older than it does in the suburbs. I could hear the sound of the "Goldberg" Variations on Mrs. Linz's CD player as I climbed the stairs.

Mrs. Linz unpacked the shopping. She showed me a letter that had come from America, from Blum's grandson, a Seattle millionaire who made his fortune from the computer industry. He wants to do up our building, return it to its former glory. Already a few places have been restored around the top end of Bialik Street, at Idelson and Hess, and they stand out like a sore thumb in the brilliance of their whiteness. They make my heart judder when I see them. The past is always returning to us.

Johnny, for example, isn't dead, he's somewhere in the city right now. Perhaps I'll bump into him one day, though it's a bigger place than it used to be. Only a few weeks after our wedding Leo had looked up from his copy of the *Herald Tribune* which he scanned every morning for news from Palestine.

"Ha! Listen to this. An underground Jewish army has assaulted an apparently impregnable British citadel in the heart of a Jewish city. They have shot their way in and shot their way out taking all the Jewish prisoners with them and gone to ground."

"What do you mean?"

"There has been, Evelyn, a mass breakout at Acre prison. All our freedom fighters are now at liberty, except for that poor boy Dov Gruner. It came too late for him." He shook his head in sorrow and pity, for the British had hanged Dov the previous month.

As marriages go, mine turned out to be a successful one and only those who have never married themselves would ask if it were happy or unhappy. It was an accommodation, a partnership. It was a life not a love affair and there is a difference. Love affairs belong to the young or to those who don't have a life, or not a proper one, at any rate. Leo and I had a life. But all those years, after I had been turned back on the brink of the great homecoming, mine was a heart in exile, a heart that is thwarted.

The only consolation I can draw from this is the thought that perhaps the heart that has loved and suffered is the only one worth having, and Leo told me once of a talmudic saying, that there is nothing so whole as a broken heart.

When your child dies, something in your brain becomes dead flesh, you're never whole again. My son—the son of Johnny and me—died at the age of six. He was killed by a balloon at his own birthday party. He was blowing it up when he stopped and took a breath. The balloon ran screaming down his throat, wrapped itself around his windpipe and in a minute or so he was dead. I was at the end of the garden, in my studio, when this happened, putting in a few more minutes to yet another painting of the white city and a strong wind howling on the sand of the seashore. "What kind of mother is late for her own child's birthday party?" I found that Naomi had written in her teenage diary. *"Mine."*

The death made Leo and me hard but in different ways. Both of us were in mourning for the dead child and we lit a candle in a glass for him, every year on the anniversary. Leo shook his fist at the heavens and cursed God. We looked around for someone to blame but we could find no one to pin it on but the Supreme Creator. There was no one else to bear a grudge against, no one to sue. Leo took on God as his personal adversary. "Look what he's doing to us now," he shouted, but I became the opposite. I was tired of hearing about the never-ending sorrows of the Jews. I watched the world go to war with Israel and time after time Israel always won.

If you think the world is out to get you, how can you *not* fight back?

Mrs. Linz ran into Johnny on an El Al flight from Tel Aviv to Frankfurt in the early 1970s. "I recognized him at once, that terrorist boyfriend of yours. Well, I was wrong on one count. He did not meet an early grave. Instead he was serving tourists with drinks and plastic plates of kosher food with plastic knives and forks, running up and down the aisles, fastening people's seat belts. Of course you know there was no advancement for that Irgun lot in the new Israeli army. Not at all, you had to have a documented record of resistance with the Haganah. Your terrorist boyfriend, I'm afraid, picked the wrong side. Of course, he was not intelligent. I realized this at once when I spoke to him at the back of the plane.

"He was terribly bewildered about his fate, how he had wound up like this. He said, 'Mrs. Linz, you know as well as I do that things were done that weren't pleasant, things that people don't like to talk about now. How is it when they tell the story of the birth of Eretz Israel they tell it like there are only heroes with no blood on their hands? Only innocent people. I wasn't innocent, I was no victim. I did the dirty work. Someone has to and why not me? But in five minutes they forgot about the dirty deeds and pretended they didn't happen.' Oh, he was very perplexed. But I looked him in the eye, standing there in his nice uniform and I said, 'Don't worry, *I* have not forgotten what you did.' One day when he dies his wife will want a military funeral and the amusing thing is he will have to go to the British to get one, for that is who his military record is with."

Tonight, when Mrs. Linz was watching a documentary on television, I went and took a chair out onto the balcony. I stepped out there gingerly. God knows how safe it is. The weather is warming up again. They built the city the wrong way around—the boulevards should have gone *down* to the shore, rather than running parallel to it, to force the air up into the town. You can hardly get any breeze from the sea at all anymore, with the hotels blocking the way.

The bougainvillea was scrambling up over the cracks in the masonry. It's an old plant, now. I don't know what its roots are doing to the foundations of the building or how deep the foundations were dug in the first place. The whole structure feels unstable to me. A gust of heat hit my face, heat from the traffic, exhaust fumes.

What I wanted to do, more than anything in the world, was to see someone once more. Not Johnny, my old love, who has faded out of my recollection, as all passion fades in the end. No, the person I was dying to talk to was the girl who sailed the Mediterranean Sea in search of the Promised Land in all her hope and certainty. I went back into the apartment and found my handbag and took out a packet of cigarettes. I don't smoke much these days, just one or two in the evenings once or twice a week, with my coffee. I love the smell of nicotine, especially when it's mixed with other unpleasant odors like cooking fat and petrol and suntan oil and people's sweat. It is the smell of chaos, of people grabbing life by the throat, a state of mind that has always charmed me.

I lit my cigarette with a lighter Leo gave me for our fifteenth wedding anniversary and I closed my eyes and when I opened them again, she was there, sitting opposite me, looking along the street.

I stared at myself, at the stiff curls and the terrible, thick red lipstick like wallpaper paste, the artless dab of rouge on the un-lined skin with a spot or two round the mouth, the badly made clothes, and I smiled. My God, there have been so many im-provements in hairdressing and cosmetics in the past half-century and of course we have the Jews to thank for that: Estée Lauder, Vidal Sassoon (who, as few people know, was one of the young Jews from the East End of London who made their way to Israel in 1948 to fight for the new country, proving that even hairdressers have their uses).

"Oh *you*," she said.

"Yes. Me."

"What a wasted life you have had," she said, lighting her own cigarette. "I gave you such a good start. There was no reason why you could not have made your way back here *years* ago, but you lost the courage of your convictions." There was an ashtray next to her full of stubs.

"Don't smoke too much," I said, "particularly that brand, they're killers. I don't think my life has been wasted."

"What do you have to show for it?"

"Peace of mind. Intellectual pursuits. What is love? It's nothing."

"No. It's everything. How can you live without passion?"

"Well, when the Change came, I found I was free of all that."

"I mean the passion of dreams, of idealism."

"Adolescent stuff. Now, it's the stories that interest me."

"I don't care about them. I only care about *doing*."

"It's *why*, that I care about. I want to understand you."

"There's nothing to understand."

"Don't you wonder about your father? Don't you want to find out anything about him? Don't you want to know where your mother came from? Naomi is getting a visa to go to Latvia to try to discover how our grandparents lived."

"Why are you so interested in the past? It's the future that counts."

"The past is everything. You'll see."

"You only say that because you haven't got a future."

She shook her head and lit another cigarette. "You don't know this yet, but they really are very harmful."

Her platinum blond hair was a terrible color. The penciled-in eyebrows were just awful. I wish I could be that age again, with all the advantages we have now of subtler shades and a less aggressive use of make-up. My own hair is tinted several different layers of gray and white and silver. I have had to explain, quite sharply, to my hairdresser here how it is done.

"Can I," I said, "at least give you some make-up tips?"

But she turned away and looked up the street. She was waiting for Johnny, waiting for him to ride up on his Norton and take her to a movie and then bring her home and make love to her and whisper to her about how they were both freedom fighters and they were making a brand-new country which would show the world what the Jews could do when left to their own devices.

She was so proud. Proud and frightened and angry. I looked at her again before she faded away and I wanted to take her in my arms. I felt such envy for her, envy and compassion. I was envious of a wholehearted certainty I have never felt since, for a deep-seated knowledge that we were taking the right path to the future. I was so envious of beings who were whole of heart and could act from their hearts instead of the wriggling path of the intellect. But I felt compassion too, the compassion you feel for the pregnant woman who always thinks her child will be the best and brightest kid who ever lived, a child who will always love her and never disappoint her and is bound to grow up to be Einstein, not a thief or a serial killer.

But what can you do? If there is a story, there is going to be an ending and another thing life has taught me is that not many of them are about people who lived happily ever after.

The sun was down. The city was darkening. Mrs. Linz turned off the television. People were walking past our building from the theater where Mrs. Linz and I had been the previous week to see a play about atrocities committed by our soldiers in Gaza. I noticed a greasy smear on the wall from the incident last month when Hamas bombed a café and fragments of cake were hurtled through the neighboring windows. I went into the kitchen and poured us both a cold drink, for whatever else changed, after fifty years it was still hot, even in spring, and being a Latvian I'll never get used to this damned climate.